6|14

HACKNEY LIBRARY SERVICES

B

THIS BOOK MUST BE RETURNED TO THE LIBRARY ON OR
BEFORE THE LAST DATE STAMPED. FINES MAY BE
CHARGED IF IT IS LATE. AVOID FINES BY RENEWING THE
BOOK.
(SUBJECT TO IT NOT BEING RESERVED).

PEOPLE WHO ARE OVER 60, UNDER 17 OR REGISTERED
DISABLED ARE NOT CHARGED FINES.   PS.6578

Five interesting things about Julie Cohen:

1. In high school in the USA, my best friend and I used to spend our chemistry lessons writing novels about us having sex with rock stars.

2. Despite this lack of scholarly application, I graduated summa cum laude from Brown University. While I was there I wrote a daily comic strip about an Elvis impersonator and his pet squid.

3. I came to live in England because of The Beatles, and because I fell in love with a guitar-playing Englishman.

4. I have a postgraduate research degree in fairies in children's literature, which has very few practical applications.

5. The Englishman and I have recently had our first child, who will be English as well, I suppose.

Also by Julie Cohen

Spirit Willing, Flesh Weak
Driving Him Wild
All Work and No Play . . .
Married in a Rush
Delicious
Being a Bad Girl
Featured Attraction

One Night Stand

Julie Cohen

little
black
dress

First published in 2007
by LITTLE BLACK DRESS
An imprint of HEADLINE PUBLISHING GROUP

First published in paperback in 2008
by LITTLE BLACK DRESS
An imprint of HEADLINE PUBLISHING GROUP

A LITTLE BLACK DRESS paperback

2

ISBN 978 0 7553 3483 4

Typeset in Transit511BT by Avon DataSet Ltd,
Bidford-on-Avon, Warwickshire

Printed and bound in Great Britain by
Clays Ltd, St Ives plc

Headline's policy is to use papers that are natural, renewable and recyclable
products and made from wood grown in sustainable forests. The logging and
manufacturing processes are expected to conform to the environmental
regulations of the country of origin.

HEADLINE PUBLISHING GROUP
An Hachette Livre UK Company
338 Euston Road
London NW1 3BH

www.littleblackdressbooks.com
www.headline.co.uk

For Dave and Nathaniel, with thanks for
'Mummy's Mucky Book Hour'.

Acknowledgements

As always, thanks to Anna Lucia, Brigid Coady, and Kathy Love for phone calls, chocolate and spa-going. You're always right, you know. Thanks to my agent, Teresa Chris, and my editor, Catherine Cobain, for being charming while making me work harder. Although some of the features of Reading mentioned in this book do exist, I have taken liberties with geography and detail. All people, ducks and general dinginess are products of my own imagination.

One Night

Another Saturday night down the Mouse and Duck. Jerry, the landlord, was swearing in the kitchen. Paul and Philip were nearing the end of their pints and arguing about football in the preliminary step to arguing about whose turn it was to get the next round. Gets Drunk, Gets Horny, Gets Angry Man was steadily making his way through his fourth pint and was making the lip and eye movements that signified that he was having an imaginary conversation with himself. Maud and Martha were eyeing up the karaoke machine through their haze of smoke. And I'd spilled half a pint of Stella over my shoes when I was serving the group of students who were starting to get loud over in the corner.

I made sure that nobody was watching me, and topped up my orange juice with vodka from the House Special optic.

Jerry exploded from the kitchen, swearing at the top of his lungs about frozen peas. I raised an eyebrow at him, a reminder of the conversation we'd had last week when I'd informed him that if he wanted to start getting a higher class of punter in the pub he should stop coming out with torrents of filth at the least opportunity.

'Did you order any blimmin peas, Eleanor?' He corrected himself, running a tattooed hand over his buzz-cut scalp.

'No,' I said. 'I haven't ordered anything since I got the healthy-option chips and you said you wouldn't trust me any more.'

'But *peas*,' Jerry protested. He caught the glance of the student who had innocently ordered fish and chips. 'Just a minute,' he called across, and disappeared into the kitchen again.

I thought about what my agent had said to me on the phone that afternoon about my latest erotic comedy novel: *It lacks the whiff of reality, darling.*

How would my agent in his London office like this whiff of reality? Stella-soaked shoes, fag smoke, and no blimmin peas?

I took a swig of my drink, grimaced at the taste of vodka, and filled it up to the top from the optic again. It tasted even worse now, but it was starting to make my knees feel unaccustomedly weak.

Hugh stood up from his seat in a secluded corner and I stashed my drink underneath the bar out of sight. He'd put on a designer shirt for a Saturday night, and he'd done something to his hair that made it stick up in a more orderly way than usual. It was much more effort than the Mouse and Duck required; he was probably going on somewhere else.

When he got to the bar Hugh handed me his glass and I put it under the lager tap. 'She'll have cider and black,' he said, jerking his head slightly to indicate the blonde girl taking up a sliver of the bench he'd left behind. I'd never seen her before, but that was hardly surprising.

'I don't believe you're going to sleep with someone who drinks cider and blackcurrant,' I said.

'I like girls with sweet tooths.'

What he meant was that girls with sweet tooths liked him, but I didn't bother to correct him.

'How old is she? Seventeen?'

'Twenty-two. She's got a job somewhere.'

'Somewhere. You're really smooth. Do you know her name?'

'Harriet.' He said it confidently, and then glanced back over his shoulder. 'Yes, definitely Harriet.'

I restrained myself from gulping more of my drink. Hugh had a nose like a bloodhound. It probably came from sniffing out all that firm young female flesh. Instead, I turned away from him and poured blackcurrant into a pint glass.

'Better make sure you get her name right,' I said. 'You don't want to be crying out the wrong name in passion.'

'That happened to me once.'

'I'm surprised it was only the once.' I flipped the lager tap off over Hugh's drink and began to fill the blonde's glass with cider.

'No, not me – I've never done it,' Hugh said. He was leaning on the bar, enjoying the conversation more than I was. 'It happened to me. The woman yelled out "Joe!"'

'You sure she wasn't saying "ho"?'

'It was definitely "Joe".'

'And what did you do?'

'I carried on. It was at a point where it was difficult to stop.'

'That's your problem, Hugh. You're such a damn romantic.'

I put his blonde's purple drink on the bar next to his pint of lager, then thought, *screw it*, and retrieved my drink from under the bar. Hugh's eyes narrowed as I took a sip.

'What are you drinking?'

'Orange juice.'

'No you're not, you're acting weird. What are you really drinking?'

Bloodhound nose. This was probably how he always showed up at my house whenever I cooked a meal or uncorked a bottle of wine.

I shrugged. 'It's a screwdriver.' Which consisted of considerably more screw than driver . . . or was that more driver than screw? I giggled.

He frowned. 'You don't usually drink at work. Are you okay?'

'It's Saturday night, Hugh. Lighten up.'

'Have you had bad news about the book?' he asked in a lower tone, so the rest of the pub couldn't hear.

He knew me too damn well. 'Of course not,' I beamed. 'After sixteen books I should know what I'm doing.'

'What about Horny/Angry? He hasn't been bothering you, has he?' Hugh gazed down the bar at Gets Drunk, Gets Horny, Gets Angry Man. He had a name, I thought it was Norman – at least he responded to Norman when he was drunk. But Horny/Angry fit him much better and it was easier to remember.

'Nothing is wrong, Hugh. Everything is exactly the same as it always is. Nothing ever changes around here. I just fancied a drink, that's all.'

He looked at me, then back at Horny/Angry, who was

still in his own little world, for now. 'I didn't think you liked vodka.'

'I love it.'

Hugh leaned his chin on his fist. 'I'll stick around here if you want me to.'

'I'm just having a drink.'

Hugh has this way of staring at you and assessing you. His brown eyes go all intense. I'd seen him use this technique on many women and for some reason it made them melt.

Not me, though. 'Your blonde is waiting,' I said.

He raised his eyebrows, shrugged in capitulation, and took the drinks back to his table. It took all of ten seconds before the blonde had her hand on his knee and they were laughing at something together.

I refilled Paul and Philip's pints. 'How'd Reading do today?' I asked.

Paul launched into a play-by-play description of the day's football match. I didn't know the first thing about football, but years behind the bar in a pub had taught me how to look interested when in reality I was completely mystified.

'Wow,' I said, when I judged he'd finished.

He sipped his beer, thirsty after his sporting commentary. 'You haven't a clue about what I just told you, have you?'

'Of course I do.'

'Who won?'

'Reading,' I guessed, because he looked quite cheerful.

'And what was the score?'

That was a stumper. 'Um.'

'I told you thirty seconds ago.'

'It all sort of blurs together,' I said. 'Sorry.'

Paul shook his head and took the drinks over to the table

he habitually shared with Philip. Jerry came out with the student's fish and chips, conspicuously light on the peas and heavy on the chips.

I poured myself another screwdriver. Martha and Maud got up and began to sing an Engelbert Humperdinck song. Horny/Angry beckoned me over and spent five minutes telling me an incoherent joke so he could stare at my tits through my T-shirt.

'This is the whiff of reality,' I told the vodka optic, as if it were the craggy face of my agent. Nobody could hear me over Martha and Maud. 'The one person who's interested in my body only notices me when he's had five pints, and he'll be picking a fight with another punter in the next half an hour, which he'll lose because he's sixty-eight and a chronic alcoholic. And you wonder why my book sucks?'

I downed my drink, and poured another. I wished that something would happen.

I didn't see him come in. The Mouse and Duck had two doors, one either side of the bar, and if I'd seen him come in I would have noticed which door he entered, which would tell me which direction he was coming from. But the pub was unusually busy.

Vodka transformed the karaoke singing and the shouted conversations and the bleeps of the pinball machine into a jumble of sound. I concentrated so as not to spill the creamy head from an over-full pint of Guinness, and spilt it anyway.

'Sorry,' I muttered to the customer, one of the students, but he was drunk enough not to care. He missed my hand when he gave me his money and the pound coins fell into the frothy Guinness pool. I threw a bar towel over the whole mess and went away. Jerry wasn't serving; he was talking with Paul and Philip and drinking his own brandy.

I sloshed wine in a glass for one of the women who'd just finished singing karaoke and when I turned around from the till, there he was.

In retrospect it should have been a cymbal-crashing strobe-lit moment. In actual fact, I didn't register him, much, except as another person to serve. I leaned on the bar in front of him, more heavily than I normally would have done, and smiled, more widely than I normally would have done.

'What can I get you?' I asked.

He looked at me steadily, then took his time turning his head and surveying the pub. 'This place is a dump,' he said.

His words were so exactly what I'd been thinking that I laughed aloud and plonked both my elbows on the bar, making myself comfortable. 'You're not wrong.'

He was in his late twenties or early thirties and had short dark hair and a bit of a moustache and goatee. He smiled, and his teeth were perfectly straight.

'Can I buy you a drink?' he asked.

Now that was something new. Even Horny/Angry at his horniest never bought me a drink. 'Thanks, I'll have a vodka and orange,' I said. 'Yourself?'

'Sounds good.'

I helped us to the premium vodka instead of the House Special and topped both of our drinks with the coloured bendy straws that were Jerry's concession to the world of cocktails. He paid me with a twenty and lifted his glass to me in a toast.

'To dumpy pubs,' I said, and took a gulp. The alcohol was starting to taste very good, and it warmed my body all the way from my lips to the bottom of my stomach.

'To meeting new people in dumpy pubs,' he said, and it was completely cheesy, but I smiled at the line.

'Another couple of pints, Eleanor,' Jerry called, and I turned away from the stranger to pour Stella. I felt his eyes on me as I walked behind the bar. Again, cheesy. But his gaze felt like a light touch on my shoulders, my hips, my behind. The hairs on the back of my neck stirred as if he were breathing on me.

When I glanced up, he hadn't looked away. He gave me half a private smile and sipped his drink.

Warmth grew in my belly. This wasn't Horny/Angry leering at my tits and arse. This guy was young, good-looking, well-dressed and, as far as I could tell, more or less sober.

I checked the corner of the pub. Hugh and his blonde had left. I had a vague memory of him yelling goodnight to me and waving on his way out the door, though it was hard to tell if that was a memory from tonight or from any other one of a thousand nights.

Martha and Maud wanted more gin; the students had decided to do shots of Aftershock; the guy who ran the karaoke machine needed his two bottles of lager. As I filled the orders I glanced surreptitiously at the new man. He wasn't talking to anybody else at the bar. Instead he was sitting quietly, sipping his drink, surveying the action, such as it was. I caught his eyes on me two or three times.

The gloopy noise of the pub seemed sharper, the karaoke beat more enticing. Knowing I was being watched, I traded banter with the punters. My smiles were twice as wide because they were for an extra person.

As soon as I could without being too obvious, I wandered back to the man. 'Ready for another?' I asked him, even though his glass was more full than mine.

Okay, maybe I was being obvious. He was no more subtle than I was, though, because he shook his head and the next words he said were, 'What's a girl like you doing in a place like this?'

I burst into laughter that was more than a little tipsy. 'That's the worst line ever.'

He leaned a little bit more on the bar, a little bit closer. 'Maybe, but I want to know.' He had a nice voice. I couldn't hear all the nuances of it because it was too loud in the pub, but it was deep and it was, at this moment, intimate.

'This is my local,' I said, shrugging, 'and they offered me a job a couple years ago.' As I said it I realised I was wrong – I'd been working at the Mouse and Duck for almost three and a half years. If that fact wasn't pathetic, I didn't know what was.

'Do you like it?' I could catch the subtext even through the noise: Who would?

'I'm not just a barmaid,' I blurted. 'I have a secret life.'

He raised one eyebrow and all at once he looked very familiar, though I couldn't tell why.

'That's intriguing. What's your secret?'

I lowered my head towards him and lowered my voice, too. 'If I tell you, it wouldn't be a secret, would it?'

'True.' Closer, he smelled of aftershave. Something subtle and expensive, not the Lynx that most of the pub regulars slapped on for special occasions.

I gestured to the room. 'Nobody around here knows. It's very glamorous,' I added, although, in truth, writing erotic novels wasn't exactly glamorous. In fact, the whole reason it was a secret from everybody except for Hugh was that I didn't fancy most of Reading knowing I had a filthy mind.

Both his eyebrows went up this time and I pegged it: he looked like George Michael. Not in Wham! – later. When he was going for the urban sophisticated image, without the earring. This guy was rougher around the edges, and I wasn't really sure about the features, not having stared at George Michael since the eighties, but he had the same general look. Except straight, obviously. His clothes were well-cut and expensive, too.

'Hmm,' he said. 'Let me guess. You're a spy.'

'Close.' I raised my own eyebrow, smiled, and realised that I was unmistakably flirting.

Good. I wanted to flirt. I wanted to be someone other than myself, tonight.

'Actually you're right,' I said. 'I'm a spy. Don't tell anyone.'

'I won't.' He lifted his glass to his lips and drained it, then held it out to me. 'Fancy one?'

'Sure.'

My fingers brushed his as I took his glass. The contact seemed significant. In fact, everything seemed significant: the smell of his aftershave that lingered in my consciousness as I turned away, the place on the glass where his lips had touched it, the way that everyone else was wrapped up in their own conversations, leaving the two of us somehow connected.

I stretched to the vodka optic and felt the way my breasts lifted under my T-shirt. I bent to the refrigerator for orange juice and pictured how my backside was outlined by my tight jeans.

I wrote about this feeling all the time. Mostly from imagination and exaggeration. And now it was happening to me.

It even had the whiff of reality.

'You can't come in here and do that, you're all a bunch of fucking cu—'

I recognised the high-pitched, outraged voice right away. I might be in my own little world of sexual tension, but Horny/Angry had turned the corner into rage. He'd seized one of the students, a particularly scruffy one, by the collar and was yelling in his face.

'Here we go again,' I muttered and went around the bar.

Jerry, Paul and Philip got there just as I did. Philip and I each grabbed an arm, Jerry and Paul grabbed a leg, and we hoisted Horny/Angry off his stool and towards the door.

'Time to go home, mate,' Jerry said to him, the same words he'd been saying just about every Saturday night since I'd worked here, and before that, when I'd been a customer. Probably for the past twenty-four years, as far as I knew. Horny/Angry struggled a bit, but he was used to this routine too, and mostly he only breathed his breath, sodden with alcohol and fags, in my face.

'Shouldn't let a woman do this work,' he slurred at me. 'Bunch of fucking cu—'

'You're speaking to a lady,' I reminded him, and that shut him up long enough for us to get him outside into the chill autumn air. Philip and Jerry set him upright and Jerry gave him a gentle push homeward. Horny/Angry staggered a bit, but he took the hint and started moving off, muttering under his breath.

'See you tomorrow, mate,' Jerry said, quite cheerfully, and those words were so depressing I felt like running back inside and downing the rest of the bottle of premium vodka.

'And this is my life,' I said to the night sky and Horny/Angry's retreating back.

As soon as I re-entered the pub I was hit by the wall of sound and smell, like the old drunk's breath, only everywhere. The air outside, cold for September, had hit me like another shot of vodka, the one that made everything clearer; the air inside fuddled my brain, made me feel drunk.

I walked behind the bar and straight to the sexy stranger. Near him, the air was fresher from his aftershave. He watched me.

'Very professional handling of that old man,' he said, his voice amused.

'I can handle all sorts of men,' I said to him, the words coming out without a plan, fuelled by booze and frustration. 'Listen, do you fancy going somewhere else after I close up?'

He smiled. His eyes narrowed and as slowly as he'd smiled, he looked me up and down. I nearly shivered, his gaze was so appreciative.

'Yes, I do,' he said.

'Great.' I seized the bell ringer and clanged last orders. It wasn't quite time for them yet but I didn't feel like waiting any longer than I had to.

The typical last-order rush kept me from looking at my new date for the evening. But I felt him there, like an itch in my side. It was half pleasurable and half torture. My hands were clumsy and when I turned around too quickly I got dizzy and I spilled part of the drinks I was serving. Nobody seemed to care. I wondered why I bothered staying sober, then poured more lager and thought about my date and where I was going to take him, and the itch turned into a gnawing in my stomach because these things happened in my books, but I never did them.

I didn't drink while I was working, I didn't come on to total strangers, and I certainly didn't contemplate taking them home with me and having sex with them.

I whipped my head up from the taps and had to blink hard to focus my eyes.

Was I contemplating taking him home with me and having sex with him?

I pulled the pint glasses from under the spigots. Sloshing cider all over my hands, I shoved the drinks towards the customers, took their money, threw it into the till, and looked for the man I was planning to make a slut of myself with.

He was gone.

His stool was empty, his glass likewise.

'Damn,' I said. Not only had I practically propositioned a total stranger, he had also run away at the first opportunity.

This did not happen in my books.

I tossed the rest of my drink down my throat before it occurred to me that he could have gone to the loo.

Serving drinks while keeping one eye on the men's loo and one eye on the empty barstool wasn't an appropriate task for someone who'd imbibed an uncountable number of screwdrivers. I poured tonic into Maud's gin and promptly dropped it on the floor, shattering the glass.

I knelt down, gingerly poking the shards into a pile. Jerry appeared, as he did whenever there was the threat of breakage to his pub belongings.

'You all right, El?'

I looked up and saw that he was regarding me with something that could be concern on his stubbled face.

'I'm fine, it's no problem,' I tried to say, but something about the change of altitude as I was kneeling on the floor had made my speech centres mushy and it came out as more of a jumble of consonants.

He took my arm and pulled me upwards. I noticed that I had gin and other assorted tipples soaking into the knees of my jeans.

'You look done in,' he said, and even in my state I realised that he was using a euphemism for 'pissed'. 'Why don't I finish up here and you go home and rest.'

'I'm all right.'

'Good. Go home, I can handle this.' He patted me on the shoulder again, as he'd done outside, and turned away to serve the remaining punters.

I went into the back room to fetch my coat and bag. *When I come out, he'll be on the stool again*, I promised myself, but when I came out he was still gone. Jerry was pulling a pint of bitter, and I hovered near his shoulder.

'You want a taxi called?' he asked me.

'No, I—'

What I wanted was for him to go into the men's loo and check to see if my date was in there, feeding pound coins into the condom machine, but I couldn't ask him to do that.

'Goodnight,' I said instead. I let myself out from behind the bar and threaded through the people and noise of the pub towards the door.

Outside, the cold air was like a shot of vodka, but this time I'd already had too many. I banged the door shut behind me and made my unsteady way past the picnic tables in front of the pub, towards the street and my way home.

'Eleanor.'

I whirled around at the voice coming from behind me. A dark figure was in the shadows cast by the pub. I could see a faint puff of condensation from his breath before he stepped forward into the light from the streetlamp, and I saw it was my man of the night.

'I thought—'

'I went outside for a breath of fresh air while you finished up,' he said. He took my hand in his. He was very warm and the contact made me feel even dizzier.

I don't know if I swayed towards him or what, but a second later we were back in the shadows near the pub wall, and I was in his arms. He was a bit taller than I was, broad-shouldered, narrow in the hips, and his chest and arms felt strong around me. The sound of his breathing shocked me, it was so real.

His mouth met mine in a kiss, which was even more shocking. His lips were hot and soft and his facial hair a subtle scratch. He didn't feel like any other man I'd kissed before. He tasted of orange juice and the smell of his aftershave. His tongue touched mine and I clutched his jacket, holding on and letting him in.

I should write about a man with a beard, I thought.

The street and shadows whirled around us, the noise of the pub faded into the background, and I was only conscious of our breathing and the sounds I was making in my throat. His hands were on my waist and his mouth was gentle, demanding, accomplished. When we broke for breath I tried to focus on his face, but couldn't see much except for the gleam of his eyes and the moisture on his lips from our kiss.

'I only live around the corner,' I gasped.

He smiled and I could see his perfect teeth. He seemed to have a lot of teeth, but I wasn't exactly seeing one of anything.

'All right,' he said.

3

I opened my eyes the next morning, and then the sunshine made me close them.

My head was hurting. A lot. I groaned, turned over away from the window, and opened my eyes again. My bedside table came into focus. On it was the bottle of lemon-flavoured liquor that I'd bought a year ago on a cheap holiday to Naxos, and which had stayed three-quarters full for the past eleven months.

It was empty. Here was the reason for my headache. Bad, stupid Eleanor, for drinking dodgy liquor in bed and –

There were two glasses on the nightstand.

Memory teased at the back of my headache. I'd worked down the pub – and met that man – and then –

I sat up in bed, my head pounding and my stomach rolling. There was no man in my bed, and no sign of one in the room. My duvet and pillows were pretty messed up, but that could be because I'd had a restless night.

Except I was naked.

I ran my fingers through my hair, which seemed to be standing on end.

I never slept naked. I wore a T-shirt and knickers. Unless I was in some sort of relationship, which I most definitely was not at the moment.

But that man, last night –

I grabbed the pillow next to me and sniffed it. There was a distinct scent of expensive aftershave.

Right. This meant nothing. Maybe he'd come home with me, we'd had a couple of drinks – comprising most of a bottle of ropey booze – and we'd passed out, after which time, in my sleep, I'd removed my clothing.

'Hello?' I called. 'Is there anyone in the house?'

No one answered.

Good. So maybe he'd had a nap, and then woken up and gone home and I hadn't got naked till after he'd left. Just because I'd never undressed myself in my sleep before didn't mean there couldn't be a first time.

I slung my legs over the side of the bed and winced. My thigh muscles were sore. So were my rear-end muscles and my arm muscles and my stomach muscles – what there were of them. I felt as if I'd done a rather hefty session of callisthenics.

I felt, in fact, very much as I'd described one of my heroines feeling after an all-night orgy session with six or seven virile policemen. Give or take the handcuff marks.

I checked my wrists. No chafing.

'Thank God for small favours.' I hauled myself out of bed, pulling on my dressing gown.

'All right,' I said to myself as I went down the stairs. 'I remember kissing him. I brought him home. We had some drinks. We did some exercises or something. He went home and I took off my clothes and went to sleep.'

Halfway down the stairs I spotted my bra, dangling from the handrail.

Stomach ever sinking, I reached the bottom of the stairs and saw my knickers on the floor. In my living room, my jeans were on the couch, my T-shirt on the coffee table, my socks draped over the stereo.

I hadn't undressed myself in my sleep.

I opened my dressing gown and looked down at my naked body. The skin on my breasts and belly was pink, as if it had been rubbed with something rough. I remembered my date's facial hair, which apparently had been intimately acquainted with a great deal of my body.

And I didn't remember a minute of it.

Someone knocked on the door, and I froze. Him? Coming back to pick up where we'd left off?

I swallowed, gathered my courage, and opened the door. If it was him, at least he could fill me in on the night's events, and let me know whether I'd enjoyed them or not.

It was Hugh.

He was wearing jeans and a sweatshirt, looked as if he'd recently showered, and he was staring at me.

'Morning,' I said.

'Morning, Eleanor,' he replied, and his voice was a little bit weird. 'Are you all right?'

'Great!'

Normally I would have stepped aside to let him in, but I was intensely aware of my clothing scattered around my normally neat living room. Instead I nodded brightly, causing more pain to pierce my head, and repeated, 'Great! How about you, did you have a good night?'

'*You* did,' he said, and he tilted his head in an attempt to see around me. 'Are you on your own?'

'Of course I am. Who would be here?'

'That's what I was wondering.'

'Why would you wonder that?' My attempt at being nonchalant was dreadful, but between the headache and the sick stomach and the lost memories of a completely uncharacteristic one-night stand, I was having a hard enough time remembering how to talk.

Hugh raised both his eyebrows at me. I remembered the guy in the pub doing the same thing when I'd flirted with him. He was also staring at my mouth.

I touched it. My lips were slightly sore, and I remembered the friction burns on the rest of my body. It seemed I'd done quite a bit of kissing, too, beyond the one kiss outside the pub that I could remember.

'I don't think you could make all that noise yourself,' he said.

'Noise? Were we – was I making a lot of noise last night?'

He raised his eyebrows higher.

Hugh's terraced house was next door, and his bedroom and mine shared a wall. It wasn't exactly soundproof.

'Well, I hope I didn't disturb your fun and games with Henrietta.'

'Harriet,' he corrected, and annoyance flickered across his face, though I thought it was unfair of him to be bothered that I couldn't remember the name of his date when he hadn't been sure of it in the first place. 'So who is this guy? I didn't know you had plans last night.'

'Oh, you know, these things just happen.' I shrugged and rubbed my hand over my lips again. Because these things did not just happen to me, and Hugh knew that as well as I did.

He leaned against the doorpost. 'Is he really still there? I'd like to meet him.'

'No.' It came out quickly, the answer to both questions.

'He left pretty early, didn't he?'

Hugh was still looking annoyed, though I had more reason to be annoyed than he did. 'Hugh, I don't need you to play the inquisitor about my private life right now, I need to go and have a bath and take some aspirin.' I ran my hands through my hair again.

Hugh's eyes dropped from my face, and I realised that my action had made my dressing gown gape open a little on my chest. When I looked down I could see the red friction marks. I pulled the dressing gown closed, and gave Hugh a pointed stare.

'So I'll see you later,' I said.

He nodded, his gaze still on my dressing gown. 'Right,' he said, but he didn't move, so I shut the door.

Noise. The mystery man and I had made lots of noise, enough noise to penetrate a brick wall.

I knew from past experience, from trying to get to sleep when Hugh was having fun next door, that every word didn't get through. Only the loud bed creaks. The cries. The screams. Particularly the high-pitched female ones.

I leaned back against the door.

Not only had I had drunken sex with someone I didn't know and forgotten all about it, but it had also been loud, uninhibited, orgasmic, *screaming* sex.

'Shit,' I said.

I closed my eyes and tried to remember. Maybe it was a blessing that I didn't have any memories to be ashamed about. But then again, I hadn't had an orgasm with another person in such a long time that it seemed brutally unfair that I didn't remember this one – or ones, as seemed to be the case.

My eyes popped open. I also didn't remember something else about the sex.

I raced upstairs and dived straight for the bedside table drawer. It wasn't hard to find the box of novelty coloured condoms, given as a party favour at a hen night for a university friend last spring, still pristine and sealed. A brilliant metaphor for my own sex life, up till about ten hours ago.

But there was the machine at the pub. I'd suspected him of going there anyway. I crawled across the bed, grabbed the wastepaper basket, and rifled through it. No sign of wrappers or used sheaths.

Maybe he was a slob. I got down on my hands and knees and looked at the floor, under the bed, in the hallway, anywhere that a drunken man could drop or fling a used condom. Then I went downstairs and looked through the living-room bin, under the couch, between the cushions. I checked the toilet and the sink and the bathroom bin.

It was only when I'd emptied the contents of the kitchen bin on to the floor and was sitting amongst banana peels, coffee grounds and cheese wrappers did I give in to the inevitable conclusion.

I'd slept with a man who resembled an eighties pop star and I hadn't used protection.

It was Sunday afternoon down the Mouse and Duck, and I put on the kettle in the kitchen and put an extra spoonful of instant coffee in my mug. I felt like a rotten tooth.

'Slip a bit of brandy in that, you'll feel better,' Jerry said to me on his way through the kitchen to his flat upstairs.

I shuddered at the thought, and Jerry chuckled and handed me the milk.

'You'll need to put on a braver face than that if you're going to turn into a drinker, girl.'

His voice was full of friendly compassion, and I searched his face for any awareness of what I'd ended up doing last night as well as drinking. He didn't appear to be hinting at anything, so maybe he'd missed my flirting with George Michael man. Maybe that meant that the whole pub had missed it, which would be a considerable relief.

'I'll stick with coffee, thanks, Jerry.'

'You all right down here by yourself?'

'I'll be fine. I've had worse hangovers.' The spoon clunked against the side of my mug and I winced. 'I think.'

He chuckled again and left me to it.

I brought my coffee into the pub and sat with it behind the bar on a stool I'd pulled back there. The Sunday afternoon sunlight was not kind to the Mouse and Duck. It filtered through week-old cigarette smoke and shone on seats leaking stuffing, and tables ringed and scarred and burned. The wallpaper and ceiling and net curtains were tinged nicotine-yellow. The only small bit of beauty was the stained-glass window above the lounge-bar door; blue and purple with the pub's building date, 1923, in red glass in the middle. It threw a puddle of colour on to the worn and gummy carpet.

Paul and Philip had the football on the TV in the corner, but they were obviously aware of my hangover because they had the volume turned down much lower than usual. Paul smiled at me but I didn't catch any knowing wink or nod, so maybe I was safe with them, too.

The left-hand door opened below the stained-glass window and Hugh came in. He was wearing the same jeans and sweatshirt he'd had on earlier, and he was alone. I poured him a pint of Coke and he sat on a bar stool, pushing a cardboard box towards me.

'Thought sugar might help,' he said.

I peeled open the lid. Inside was a whole, perfect, glazed strawberry tart, the size of my palm.

'Gorgeous.' I took it out of the box and weighed it in my hand. It was still warm. 'Is this what you've been making this morning?'

'It's practice for next week,' he said. 'A couple of the other ones didn't come out as well.'

I took a bite of it and closed my eyes as the pastry and fruit dissolved in my mouth and the world suddenly became a whole lot better.

Hugh had quit his latest job in I.T. nine months before to train as a pastry chef at the local college, and I was often his official taster. Or, more often, Hugh had used his latest cake or pastry concoction as a sort of seduction tool to lure yet another young lady into his bed, and I got the leftovers the next day.

Either way, I got to eat quite a bit of cake. It usually made me feel much more optimistic. It made sense to me why women would sleep with Hugh because of his pastry.

That couldn't be the only reason they slept with him, though.

I took another bite and considered Hugh, something I rarely did because I saw him so often. He wasn't exactly a stud in appearance. His brown hair was perpetually tousled, and his body was tall and lanky rather than buff. In many ways he looked like the puppyish first-year university student he'd been when I'd met him, when I'd been a first-year myself, seven years ago.

But he could certainly cook, and, apparently, charm. And with all the practice he'd had, he was bound to be good in bed, I guessed, though his ladies didn't seem to stick around for very long.

I wasn't contemplating having sex with Hugh. I considered the talents of every man I came across, not because I wanted to have sex with them, but because it was an automatic occupational hazard. If you write erotica, you need to imagine different men's sexual styles.

For example, I'd always thought Jerry with his tattoos and shaved head would be a typical bit of rough: macho, demanding, dominant. Though one time Jerry had confided to me that the Mouse and Duck had been named after the tattoos of Mickey and Donald that he had on his buttocks, so maybe there was a softer side to that machismo.

Philip would try to be a manly alpha male – he had the shoulders, the loud voice, and the construction worker's forearms – but he wouldn't quite have the conviction; he'd probably crack a joke at the essential moment. Paul, who was shorter and slighter, would be gentler and more considerate. He would probably ask what you wanted. Philip and Paul never seemed to go anywhere without each other, so I tended to lump them together as ménage material.

Not that I wanted to actually have sex with the Mouse and Duck regulars. God, no. Imagine that orgy: every five minutes someone would take a break for a pint of beer and a fag and Horny/Angry would get overexcited everywhere and then try to beat everyone up.

Yuck.

Hugh . . . well, I'd known Hugh before I started looking at men as research material, so I didn't have first impressions to go on. And now I knew him too well. He was part of the furniture. I imagined he used whipped cream and chocolate fairly often, but I wasn't going to venture much further than that. I had his sexuality thrust in my face (metaphorically, that is) every day as it was.

'Feel better?' He smiled at me and I realised that he was sitting on the same stool that my seducer of last night had occupied. Hugh sprawled on it, though, one foot touching the ground and the other hooked on the stool's crossbar, his arm flung casually on the bar. Whereas the man last night had sat elegantly, his body more compact, more poised.

At the thought, some feeling rushed through me, though it was hard to tell if it was remembered lust, or present dread.

'The tart's gorgeous,' I said, and polished it off. 'Thank you for saving me one.'

'My pleasure. Tell me about the book.'

I sighed. I didn't feel like talking about it, but he'd softened me up with the strawberries and I couldn't refuse him now. The pastry was a winning seduction technique in more ways than one.

'Bryce says it "lacks the whiff of reality",' I told him, keeping my voice low so Paul and Philip couldn't hear what we were talking about. Bryce was my agent.

'What does that mean?'

'Don't ask me. The book's called *The Throbbing Member of Parliament*, for God's sake. It's full of good-looking, sexy politicians getting it on with each other. And he expects some reality in there?'

'Good point. Maybe you can relocate it to another profession? Television stars, models, chefs? The college is a hotbed of lust and intrigue, I could tell you all about that. All the teenage students are dating each other and snogging in the corridors. Makes me feel like a grandfather sometimes.'

I shook my head. 'It's not the concept he's got a problem with. He approved the synopsis and he actually came up with the title himself. It's the emotion. He says it doesn't strike a chord.'

'Well, I couldn't blame you for not getting emotionally involved with politicians.'

I leaned my forehead on my hands and rubbed my eyes hard with the heels of my palms.

'I don't know, Hugh. I didn't feel any different writing this one to when I wrote the others, I don't think. I can't tell. They've all started blurring together now. Maybe seventeen erotic novels is too many and I should start thinking about another career.'

He reached into the box, picked out a crumb of tart, and put it in his mouth. 'Is that what you really think, or are you just discouraged at the thought of revising this novel?'

That was an awkward question. I didn't know what I really thought, except that I was fed up.

'I mean I was talking to a woman the other night,' he continued, 'and she's a novelist, too. She said that she had to do extensive revisions on all of her books, like pages and pages of structural overhaul. You've never had to do that.'

'What does she write?'

He shrugged. 'Some sort of literary stuff. She teaches creative writing at the college.'

'Well, that explains it. She probably has to dig deep into her psyche to come up with some universal human truth or something. In contrast, I write smut.'

'Sex is a universal human truth.'

'Uh huh. That's why my stories are always shortlisted for the Booker.'

'I'm not talking about the Booker,' he said. 'I'm talking about you being so pissed off that you had a little vodka wallow last night.'

He found another crumb and put his finger in his mouth to lick it off.

Hugh had nice hands, I'd give him that. They were long-fingered and capable looking. Maybe he'd stick with the pastry career. He tended to change jobs nearly as frequently as he changed sexual partners.

I, on the other hand, was stuck firmly in my erotica-writing beer-serving rut.

The door opened and I looked up sharply, half expecting

to see a broad-shouldered form, perfect teeth gleaming underneath a pop-star moustache.

It was Martha and Maud. I got down some stemmed glasses for their gin before they had taken more than a step inside the pub.

'So is that why you were indulging in some fun and games last night?' Hugh asked.

'Shhhh!' I hissed, looking significantly at Martha and Maud. Their hearing wasn't great (hence their fondness for karaoke), but it would be just my luck that comments about my sex life would be the thing that cured their deafness.

'Afternoon, Eleanor,' Maud said cheerfully, her white hair turning momentarily blue and red as she walked through the light cast through the stained-glass window. She reached the bar and put her creased handbag on it. 'What's Hugh saying to you that you don't want us to hear?'

I knew it. 'Hugh was telling me about what he got up to last night, Maud,' I said loudly, as if she hadn't just proved she had perfect hearing when she wanted.

'Ah, Hugh, you need to settle down with a good woman,' Martha said to him, waggling her head. 'No more of these blondes and redheads.'

'Say the word and I'm yours, Martha,' Hugh replied. I pushed the gin and tonics towards the two ladies as they cackled at Hugh's remark. They practically minced over to their table, and I swear Maud's hips had an extra sway to them.

'It is always blondes and redheads, isn't it?' I said, struck by what Martha had said. Of course they saw him and his dates every weekend and many weeknights, too; obviously they'd observed more closely than I had and seen a pattern.

'Hadn't noticed.' He tugged at a lock of hair on the back

of his head. 'Anyway, we're talking about you. Where's this new bloke of yours?'

'Don't know.' I began to empty the glass washer.

'When are you seeing him again?'

I shrugged. 'Is this any of your business?'

'You weren't this reticent last time you started seeing someone. I seem to recall you talking about him for hours. And I figure that last night I witnessed most of your passion through the wall, so I'm practically your chaperone.'

'Hugh, I witness your passion through the bedroom wall on a regular basis and I don't poke my nose into your frankly dubious sexual life.'

I was concentrating on lining up pint glasses on the shelf and not looking at Hugh, so I didn't see his reaction to my retort. When he hadn't replied for several moments, though, I poked my head over the bar.

He was frowning and I could see a faint flush on his cheeks.

'Can you really hear it when I have sex?' he asked.

'Don't worry, I'm not there with a glass to the wall or anything.'

He winced slightly. 'You mean you can hear everything when you're lying in bed trying to get to sleep?'

I took some pity on him. 'I can hear the girls, mostly. I don't hear you very often.'

Hugh sat there and drank his Coke for a while as I stacked glasses. I wasn't sure why he was embarrassed. I mean, I knew why *I* was embarrassed – my one-night stand had been completely uncharacteristic behaviour, and Hugh seemed to know more details about it than I did – but Hugh revelled in his active sex life. He certainly never made a secret of it.

Though apparently he'd never known about the sound-transmitting property of our mutual bedroom wall till now.

It wasn't as if I'd never had sex in that bedroom, either. I wasn't an erotic powerhouse like my heroines, but I'd been in a relationship or two over the past four years. Nothing euduring, but they certainly included carnal activity on a regular basis while they lasted. And yet Hugh had never heard anything coming from my side of the shared wall before last night.

I finished replacing glasses and started folding bar towels, my face still averted from Hugh. The reason was obvious. I was normally a quiet sexual partner. I held my breath, I made silent gasps, I left words behind with my clothes. Not like the women I wrote about, women who issued orders and described fantasies and screamed in ecstasy.

I wondered if I'd done that last night – talked dirty, yelled. If, while I was drunk, someone else had taken hold of my body. Maybe there was something about the man I'd been with that allowed me to act that way.

Maybe there was something about me that made me act that way.

'What's his name?'

Hugh's voice nearly made me jump. I looked around the pub furtively, because for a moment I'd expected my mystery lover to walk in the door again, in response to my furious attempt to remember – or maybe it was to forget – what we'd done together.

But no man. No name, either.

I must have asked him at some point, mustn't I? Surely I wouldn't go to bed with someone whose name I didn't even know?

'George,' I said, and as I said it, it struck a chord with me.

As if it might have been the name of someone I'd begged to ravish me and a name I'd screamed out in fulfilment.

Then again, it might just be because he reminded me of the Greek half of Wham!.

Hugh nodded and didn't seem surprised, so maybe he'd heard me saying it through the wall. 'Are you going to see him again?'

The man was going to keep on asking till I told him. I knew what he was like. If I didn't answer him now, he'd be knocking at my door tonight asking again. And in the pub tomorrow night, asking again. His concern would be touching, if it weren't so annoying.

I remembered when my ex, Michael, had chucked me for that barista in Starbucks a couple of years ago. At first I'd loved the fact that Michael was in a band, but by the end I'd been going off him because all he talked about was how they were playing on some obscure stage at the Reading Festival. I hadn't been upset.

But Hugh had followed me around and asked and asked and asked till I had to admit that yes, I was a bit bothered. I mean, Michael hadn't known I was an erotic novelist; only Hugh and my editor and agent knew that. I'd never told Michael because I thought he'd probably compare my real-life bedroom antics unfavourably to my imaginary ones. But even without that knowledge of my secret life, surely pulling pints had to be more rock 'n' roll than making skinny soy lattes.

So my feelings were hurt, even though I hadn't known it, and Hugh had ferreted it out. He seemed to know when I needed him to keep on asking.

But I didn't know the answer to this question. An even more thorough search of my house had revealed no traces of my mystery man – no phone number, no scrawled note, not even hair in the brush in the bathroom. No condom, of course. The bed was cold, and I had no reason to think he'd stuck around after I'd passed out. He'd left nothing behind but lip prints on the glass of some noxious Naxos booze.

'No, I think I've seen the last of him,' I said.

Zero to Three Months: The Whiff of Reality

5

*S*o this is what it feels like to be in politics, Lucy Sharpe thought. She smoothed her hands down her leather-clad thighs, relishing the warmth, the suppleness of her own body. The intrigue. The complications. The battles.

The power. Oh yes, more than anything, the power.

She stalked a few steps in her pointy-toed high-heeled boots, swaying her hips, thrusting out her breasts. She looked good, and he was watching her. From the expression on his face it was with as much fear as desire.

She wanted both from him. She'd never known it till now.

Lucy rested her weight on one leg, her hand on one hip, a pose she knew made her look even more angular and in control. She let her gaze travel slowly over the figure in the chair before her. The black cords binding his arms and legs made his skin look even paler. There were faint red marks where the ropes chafed against his skin. And yet his muscles stood out in sharp relief. So much strength and so much vulnerability.

Especially between his legs, where his cock poked into the air, helplessly virile.

Lucy licked her lips and she saw him twitch. Slowly she approached him. She spread her legs, one thigh either side of his, and bent to rest her weight on the back of his leather chair. The position put her barely restrained breasts on a level with his face and his hot breath.

'You're helpless,' she told him and she saw a tremor shudder through his body. 'You're mine. Mr Shadow Minister for the Environment.' She pronounced the title precisely, letting him know with every syllable that his political position meant nothing here. The only position that mattered was the one she'd put him in.

'Let me go,' he pleaded. She wasn't sure if he meant it. 'I'm supposed to be at a summit in Brussels to discuss green issues. If I don't go, I'll—'

'Shut up,' she snapped. 'You're not going anywhere. You're staying right here and you will do exactly as I tell you. Exactly.'

She lowered her hand and tested the velvety length of his erection.

'Speaking of green issues,' she said, 'when was the last time you got checked for diseases?'

I banged my hands on my desk beside my keyboard. 'Shit!'

Green issue? Diseases? What was going on in my head?

I looked around my office. It was actually the extra front bedroom of my terraced house, furnished and painted entirely in white. White computer, white desk, white chair, white rugs on the white-painted floorboards, a white pull-out sofa bed for the rare occasions when I had guests. It was my blank space. My room where I could come and wipe myself clean of my mind-clutter, sit in front of my computer, and write.

It clearly wasn't working.

For one thing, Mr Shadow Minister for the Environment was supposed to be blond. He'd been blond in the original draft of the book and there was absolutely no reason that he should change now that I was doing revisions. It would create all sorts of continuity problems because of course I didn't only describe his head hair.

But irresistibly, as I wrote him, he became shorter, darker, and gained a moustache and goatee.

For another thing, characters in erotic fantasy didn't worry about prophylactics. The publishers put a warning in the front of the book to tell the readers that in real life they should always use a condom, and then the characters got it on happily for the next three hundred pages or so as if the word 'Durex' had never been coined. Nobody got gonorrhoea, herpes, chlamydia or, God forbid, HIV, because those things are not part of anybody's sexual fantasy (or if they are, I don't want that person reading my books, thank you).

And now I was completely ruining this fantasy by having my heroine ask one of her sex slaves if he'd had a check-up.

I was supposed to be putting the whiff of reality into this book, but that was too bloody much.

There was only one thing for it. It was Wednesday, and I was through with putting off the inevitable.

I shut down my computer and went downstairs to the phone. I knew Hugh was home, and it was more expensive to ring him than to walk out of my front door and bang on his, but ringing was often safer if I wasn't sure what he was doing.

He picked up on the second ring. 'I need you to come somewhere with me,' I said.

*

The clinic was located in a separate unit behind the hospital. The entrance was in a sort of courtyard, overlooked by banks of windows and the main hospital walkway. It might have been purposefully designed so that every single person in the Royal Berkshire Hospital was able to see exactly who'd been a naughty boy or girl and needed a swab stuck up inside them to check for nasty germs.

I pulled my scarf tighter around my face. Hugh, on the other hand, was looking around with great curiosity. When we walked into the clinic he was immediately attracted by the bowlful of condoms on the receptionist's desk.

'Wow, are these for anybody who wants them?' he asked, bright-eyed and cheery-faced, as always, and the receptionist smiled at him and nodded.

'Brilliant,' he chirped and took a handful to shove inside his coat pocket. He was reaching for some more when I leaned over the desk to speak quietly to the receptionist.

'Eleanor Connor and Hugh Gibson. We've each got appointments at eleven twenty.'

Hugh's hand closed on my wrist. 'Hold on. I don't have an appointment. This was for you.'

'I figured I might as well make you one, while I was at it.'

'Excuse us,' Hugh said to the receptionist, then pulled me out of the building to the very public courtyard. His hand was strong on my wrist as he turned me to face him.

'I don't need to be checked for sexually transmitted diseases. I'm careful. Look.' He waved one of the coloured condoms from the bowl inside at me. 'See this? I use them. Religiously.'

'I figured it couldn't hurt, and that you might as well while you were here.'

His brown eyes sparked, and I realised he was angry.

I'd known him for seven years, lived next door to him for four, and for a lot of the three years before that I'd shared halls of residence with him, and I'd hardly ever seen him angry before. His eyes were wide and there was a flush over his cheekbones.

'Don't play the innocent with me, Eleanor. You don't just make an appointment for someone else at this type of place. You've got another reason.'

I had no idea how to deal with Hugh angry. It was like seeing a stranger.

'Honestly, I—'

'What is it, El? I don't assume it's because you want to sleep with me?'

I stepped back, shocked. 'No.'

He didn't let go of my wrist, and his grip got tighter.

'Are you feeling guilty about having sex with that George? Because if you are, go ahead, but don't try to make me feel guilty too.'

'I wasn't trying—'

'I've never once judged you for anything you've done, even when I thought you've made some bloody stupid mistakes. And I never asked you to judge me, either.'

I'd been feeling overwhelmed and uneasy, but that pushed me over into anger, too. 'What bloody stupid mistakes?'

'Every damn so-called relationship you've ever had, now that you've asked me. Including this one with George, apparently.'

'At least I have relationships, instead of picking up a new fuck-buddy every five minutes.'

'Except for last Saturday night.'

'Will you stop bringing up Saturday night? How come it's fine for you to sleep around all you want and when I do the same thing it's a major topic of discussion?'

The blood was pounding in my ears, because this was not fair, no way.

'Because I—' Hugh dropped my wrist and held up both his hands in frustration. 'Maybe because Saturday night is the reason we're both here at this clinic arguing.'

He ran his hand through his hair, throwing it into even more disarray than normal. 'Is it only a guilt thing, or did you not use a condom?'

Shame flooded me, displacing anger. 'I don't think we did.'

My emotions must have shown on my face because Hugh stared at me, and the flush on his cheeks abated.

'Stupid girl,' he said. It sounded more affectionate than angry, and that did it.

'I wanted some company,' I told him, willing the tears not to appear. 'I've never done this before.'

'No, you haven't. Of course not.' He took hold of my shoulder this time and pulled me up against him, my face pressing to the soft cloth of his coat. 'Okay, let's do it.' He gave me a quick hug and a kiss on the top of my head and let me go before I could get any more wobbly. 'But if I have to have something shoved up my old fella I'm going to make you pay.'

Hugh wasn't always the smooth sex machine he liked to think of himself as now. I remember the day I met him. It was the first day of university.

I'd been there for about two hours; the first hour was taken up by moving my stuff from my mother's car to the hall of residence where I was sharing a room with some girl I'd never met by the name of Leena. Her name sounded very exciting to me, as if maybe I was going to meet the kind of person there weren't many of in my small home town of Upper Pepperton, someone creative and exciting and unique. Someone sort of like I'd had in mind when I'd picked my going-to-university outfit, which consisted of black jeans, black top, and lots of plastic jewellery. When I got to my room Leena wasn't there, though I could see she'd dumped her suitcases on one of the beds already.

My mother, Sheila, wanted to stay and look around, meet Leena, check out every aspect of this life that she'd never experienced herself. I wanted her to get the hell out of there and back to Upper Pepperton as quickly as I could hustle her, so I could start living this exciting new life. In my mind, the biggest attraction of the University of Reading was that it was not within easy driving distance of Upper Pepperton. So I talked fast, unpacked faster, practically pushed my mother out the door and back to her car and then rushed back to the hall of residence to see what was going on.

There was a lot going on. Everybody seemed to know each other, for one thing. Some people smiled at me when I smiled at them, but nobody offered to talk to me as I walked up the hallway towards my room.

That was okay. Leena would turn up sooner or later, and we'd meet each other and we'd click together, and I wouldn't have to worry about anything. It was going to be great. I'd been waiting all summer to get out of Upper Pepperton. It had been the most boring summer on record; all my friends and I had tedious jobs and my sister June hadn't visited once.

When I opened the room door, a slender girl stood there with her back to me. She had the sort of cascade of golden hair that they show in shampoo advertisements. She wore white linen trousers and had a pashmina looped around her neck. At the sound of the door, she turned around.

'Hi,' I said. 'I'm Eleanor. You must be Leena.' She wasn't what I'd expected; I'd expected an exotic flower. But she was beautiful and confident, and that promised something. I put out my hand, feeling like her tall, awkward shadow.

'Yah.' She touched my hand briefly, then turned away again to open her suitcase and rummage through it. 'I'm just grabbing my jacket; I'm meeting some friends to go into town.' She snatched up a jacket, pink to match her pashmina, and flashed me a smile that melted away as soon as it had begun. 'See ya.'

The door swung shut behind her and I stood there in the concrete room, alone.

I sat on the bed she'd left me. Everything was going on outside, and I had a suitcase full of clothes I'd picked to be a new, improved Eleanor Connor. The person I'd looked forward to magically becoming as soon as I got to the new promised land of university.

I had no idea how to be her yet.

Was she the kind of person who went out and introduced herself to people? Would she hang out in her room being cool and mysterious till people found her? Would she go and join a society right away and let herself be brought into a world of association?

Or would she sit here, unsure and lonely, almost (not quite, but almost) wishing for her mother to come back?

Someone rapped on my door, a complicated brisk rhythm. I got up and answered it.

A boy stood outside it. Some of the first-year males I'd seen were men already, but this one was a boy. He was tall and very thin, with almost delicate wrists protruding from one of the ugliest tartan jackets I'd ever seen. He wore thick-rimmed NHS-type spectacles and a goofy smile.

'Hey,' he said. 'I'm Hugh. Pleased to meet you.' He stuck out a hand.

I shook it. It seemed like an overly formal gesture, like this boy was pretending to be a grown-up. Then I remembered I'd done the same thing with Leena, and I shifted my weight, uncomfortable.

'Eleanor,' I said.

'Eleanor. Excellent name.' He scratched the side of his head and I noticed that his hair was messy, sticking up as if he'd not bothered to do anything to it since he'd got out of bed. 'Listen, Eleanor, a bunch of us are going to the union in search of food and beer. You fancy coming?'

I looked beyond him to see who the 'bunch of us' were. Three people stood behind him: a boy with acne and an Iron Maiden T-shirt, an overweight girl who was already wearing a University of Reading sweatshirt, and a very thin girl with mousey hair.

'Uh, I don't know,' I said.

These weren't the friends I was supposed to have when I got to university. I was supposed to be with the interesting people, the exotic people, the creative people. These people looked like . . . well, anyone.

'Come on,' Hugh said, and he tilted his head and smiled at me. 'You can help me knock on doors and round up anyone else who hasn't got anything to do.'

The first few hours of your university experience were supposed to be formative. You could meet the people who would be your tribe for the whole next three years. Others would watch who you were with. They would categorise you.

'Come on, El,' Hugh said again. 'We won't bite you. And if you find somebody better to hang out with we won't be hurt.' His smile widened and his eyes actually twinkled behind his glasses. 'Much.'

I glanced downwards. His trousers were too short for him, and he wore dirty canvas plimsolls, with red shoelaces in the left shoe and green shoelaces in the right shoe.

'I wasn't thinking that,' I told him, and stepped out of the concrete room to join this tribe. For now.

'Of course not.' He pointed down the corridor. 'You knock on the left-hand side, and I'll do the right.'

Seven years since then, and he'd never left me alone since. Sometimes I wondered what would have happened if I hadn't stepped through the door and joined him. What kind of person I might have turned out to be.

The guy with the Iron Maiden T-shirt found some other heavy metal fans and joined them right away; I don't think I ever saw him again. The girl with the Reading sweatshirt, Deborah, responded to the pressures of university life by becoming anorexic. Weight dropped off her, she was borrowing my clothes, and then my clothes were too big for her. She swore she didn't want help and then during our first-year exams she lost it.

I found her in the corridor of our hall of residence clutching the wall because she couldn't stop laughing, or crying. It was difficult to tell which. When Hugh turned up (Hugh always turned up) we called the university nurse who called her parents and we only saw Deborah once more after that, in hospital in Basingstoke where she was from, and she was distinctly unfriendly. She got well, but she didn't want to have anything to do with the university any more.

Five years later I named a secondary character in one of my novels Deborah and I couldn't figure out why, whenever I wrote about her, I found myself awash in feelings of guilt. It was only when I mentioned it to Hugh that he reminded me.

Hugh's memory was always much better than mine; sometimes I thought I didn't bother to remember things because I knew he would.

The third girl, Gwen of the mousey hair, was actually still friends with us now, seven years later. Well, we sent Christmas cards. She dyed her hair blue during the first

Christmas holiday and eventually became a divorce lawyer living in the poshest part of Henley. Her hair wasn't blue any more. She worked something like twenty-three hours a day and always sent me and Hugh joint Christmas cards, as if we were a married couple.

And Hugh and me . . .

It's difficult to chart how someone changes from an acquaintance to a friend, and even more difficult to tell exactly when that person becomes not only a friend but *the* friend, your best friend. Sometimes there are great leaps in intimacy, the afternoons leading to nights spent in the student union drinking and talking about your childhood and bickering about books, music, everything. There are shared visits home, crises with papers and exams and roommates, the first book published, the first shared grief. The big events.

And then there's just time passing. All the hours and hours and hours when you look over and there that person is, Hugh, being Hugh, becoming someone I knew so well that I never had to think about what he was like.

Lots of people assumed we were a couple. At first that made me a bit embarrassed because Hugh was such a geek. Holey socks, wild hair, those glasses. He usually looked like he dressed himself in the dark; in fact, I think most of the time that first year he did, because his rugby-playing roommate Tyler was such a drinker that he never got up before two o' clock in the afternoon and growled if the blinds were opened.

I wanted an extraordinary boyfriend: one of the curly-haired poet-types who slouched in the back of my English lectures, or a philosophy student who wore black and smoked cigarettes so intensely it seemed that every puff was an argument. Someone different and exciting who would make me different and exciting, someone sort of like the men my sister June brought home (a new one every time we saw her), only more intellectual. Not someone as comfortable as a pair of mismatched plimsolls.

Hugh, for his part, discovered girls in a big way when we were in our second year. It seemed as if his love life went from zero to sixty miles per hour practically overnight. He even made a play for me, once.

He turned up at my room on a Friday night around a quarter past eight, wearing a jacket and tie he'd tugged to half mast. I looked up from *Ulysses* with some relief when he poked his head around the door.

'I thought you were going out with your mother,' I said. She'd come to take him for dinner to celebrate his birthday, three days early so she could get in there before his father did.

He threw himself down on the single bed beside me and pulled his tie the rest of the way off. 'I did. All she wanted to do was rehearse all the birthday parties she'd given me over the years and all the expensive presents she'd bought me and compare them to what my dad gave me. Year by year, in detail.' He ran his hands through his hair, restoring it to its usual dishevelled condition. 'I said I thought I was coming down with the flu.'

I ruffled his hair too, in sympathy. 'How long have they been divorced? Nine years, ten?'

'Since I was eight. Sometimes I swear they did it because it makes the arguments last longer.'

He looked at the ceiling, drew in a deep breath, and let it out slowly. 'I'm through with it, though. Next time I see each of them I'm saying that they can compete all they want, but I'm not playing. The minute one parent even hints at mentioning the other one, I'm walking out.'

He slapped his hand on my duvet to emphasise his point.

'Good for you,' I said.

'Yes. It's time I took charge of my life. In all areas.' Hugh sat up and smiled at me. 'So it's *Raiders of the Lost Ark* at the film theatre tonight. Fancy it?'

I threw *Ulysses* to the floor. 'Of course.'

But when we got there, having arrived ten minutes late, Hugh had got the dates wrong and it was an art film about Danish wife-swappers.

Hugh had left his glasses in his room because his mother always nagged him to get contact lenses, so it fell to me to read him the subtitles.

' "Do you want to make love to my fair lady?" ' I read in a whisper.

'Is that to the soundtrack or actually to Audrey Hepburn?' Hugh whispered back.

'I think he means his wife, not the musical. Shut up, there's more. "She is very good at giving –" '

I couldn't say it. I dissolved into snorting giggles and the people sitting near us glared at me.

'What?' asked Hugh. 'What is she good at giving? Gifts?'

'You know,' I gasped between sobs of laughter.

'I don't,' said Hugh, although the fair lady had started to do it onscreen and his vision wasn't that bad.

'Shhh,' hissed someone a row or two behind us.

'A bl—'

'Blood? She's giving blood?'

I could barely breathe. 'No, she's giving a bl—'

'Black plague?'

'Shhh!'

Hugh was managing not to laugh; I was clutching on to his arm so hard it probably hurt him, trying not to slide off my wooden seat. Meanwhile on screen two other people had joined the action and it appeared that they were also having a conversation about flower symbolism.

'A blow job!' I cried, and someone else yelled, 'Shut up!' and I put my head on the armrest and laughed as quietly as I could, tears streaming down my face, as Hugh shook with silent laughter beside me.

We snuck out soon afterwards, trying to ignore the dirty looks. It was a full moon and warm for March, so we swung by Hugh's room, picked up a screwtop bottle of red wine, and went to sit by the university lake. There was a log hewn into a bench near some bushes on the bank, the perfect place to drink and watch the moonlight on the water and talk about everything and nothing; the kind of talk you can do with your best friend.

'I never thought sex was funny before,' I said.

'It's inherently funny,' Hugh said. 'Just listen: blow job. Say it.'

'Blow job,' I repeated, and giggled.

And then we lapsed into the kind of silence you can do with your best friend. The lake made lapping sounds on the shore and the moonlight was so bright it seemed as if I could taste it between slugs of wine from the bottle: something as refreshing as water and a little metallic.

It was difficult to believe that hundreds of students were around us, and beyond that, all of Reading; people with cars and televisions and noisy lives. Here it was hushed, liquid, Hugh and me and the smell of damp leaves beginning to grow.

Hugh put his arm around me. This in itself was not unusual. It was warm for March, but it was still March and he was welcome warmth. I took another drink of wine, closed my eyes, and thought about funny sex. The film had been ridiculous, but imagine something that would turn you on and make you laugh at the same time . . .

From funny sex my thoughts inevitably wandered to Rupert, my latest crush. For a moment I allowed myself to fantasise that the arm around me belonged to him.

I knew Rupert through my former room-mate Leena, who moved in remote circles but who still spoke to me occasionally. Rupert was six feet tall, broad-shouldered, floppy-haired, and played cricket. Normally I didn't go for sporty types, but Rupert had something, some sort of confidence and style I'd never seen before. Maybe it was the way he wore those white, white cricket jumpers with no hint of irony. I pictured myself cuddling into Rupert's blinding jumper and looking up to see him gazing down at me in the moonlight. He'd put a finger underneath my chin, lift my face up to his, and kiss me with the same sort of talent he brought to bowling.

The thought made me sigh in romantic lust. I felt Hugh's arm tighten around me, I heard him mutter something I didn't quite listen to about taking charge of his life, and then he took the bottle of wine from my hand. I still had my eyes closed but it seemed as if he drank for a very long time.

When he put the bottle down on the path it made a hollow, empty sound. I opened my eyes and frowned. There had been about a third of the bottle left when I'd last taken a drink.

I leaned forward to pick up the wine to see if Hugh had hogged it all, and at that moment Hugh lunged towards me.

I felt the warmth of his breath, the heat of his lips, on the side of my face near my ear. And something wet that I realised, with shock, was his tongue.

I jumped off the bench, knocking the wine bottle over on to the path. 'Hugh,' I gasped, 'did you just *try to kiss me?*'

I stood in the moonlight and stared at Hugh. He appeared to be as surprised as I was.

A quick calculation told me that if I hadn't moved at exactly the same time that Hugh had lunged, he would have planted his mouth right on to mine.

'You tried to stick your tongue down my throat,' I said, and, as I didn't know how to deal with the idea of my best friend kissing me, I started to laugh.

A duck, roused from sleep in the nearby weeds, splashed in alarm and launched itself into the air, flapping and quacking.

Hugh put his hand to his face and rubbed it. 'I guess I did. Funny, huh?'

It had been a joke. 'What were you thinking?' I asked, relieved.

He stood up and brushed himself off. 'Just practising my aim. I think we can conclude that it isn't very good.'

He went to pick up the bottle, kicked it off the path instead, and went into the bushes to fetch it. I heard him cracking branches and swearing and I started laughing all over again, and Hugh laughed too, and everything was normal, our friendship was the same.

Anyway, obviously the whole episode was caused by Hugh suddenly discovering his sex drive. He began practising his aim on a regular basis, with a succession of female students, and apparently he was getting better and better, because none of the girls went around wiping their ears.

He still had plenty of time to spend with me, so I didn't mind. It gave me something to tease him about. Besides, it left me a little bit of breathing room to look for that extraordinary boyfriend of my own, the one who never quite seemed to turn up – or if he did, he never stuck around.

Five and a half years and two STD examinations later, Hugh was waiting for me outside the clinic. He only wore glasses when he was driving these days, and he no longer bought the majority of his clothes from charity shops. I linked my arm through his and we started walking together.

'You don't look too traumatised,' I said.

'You should have seen me when they got that long-handled swab out. I nearly knocked the door down and came to kill you.'

'You would've had an easy target. A person can't move that quickly when she's on her back with her feet in stirrups.'

'I think the nurse who took my sexual history was intrigued,' he said. 'Do you think it would be tacky to go back and ask her out?'

I kept walking, pulling him along. After a moment of pretending to resist he carried on with me.

'Thank you for coming,' I said.

He shrugged. 'It can't hurt to get a clean bill of health.'

'No.'

'You shouldn't have made me the appointment.'

'Probably not.'

'I do have things that are my own business.'

'I know,' I said, though I hadn't known it before. Hugh had always seemed to conduct his love life (or the non-naked parts of it, anyway) largely in the public eye. He'd never seemed in the least bit private or embarrassed about it. Or about anything, come to that.

'I'm sorry,' I said. I wasn't used to treading carefully with Hugh.

He nodded. From the side his profile looked vaguely hawklike: strong chin, prominent brows, high cheekbones, and straight nose with a hint of a hooky bend at the end. His lips pressed together and reinforced the resemblance.

Funny how in many ways I still thought of him as that gawky first-year uni boy, when for a long time he'd been a man. Habit, I guessed.

Over the years he'd developed some sort of sex appeal for women without seeming to invest much of an effort. I'd watched him on the pull many a time and he was never particularly flirtatious – he was friendly, cheerful, attentive, but he was that way with everyone. He was that way with me. Somehow it made women fall into bed with him.

We didn't have far to walk; our houses were only a few streets over from the hospital, in one of the many nineteenth-century rows of terraces built for workers in Reading's biscuit or brick factories. I kept hold of his arm, but we didn't talk.

The nurse had said I could ring for my results in a week, and I imagined she'd told Hugh the same thing. I had a week to try not to think about what I was going to find out. Hopefully now that I'd made a positive step I would be able to write without my worries intruding. Hopefully.

Hugh finally spoke as he and I rounded the corner to our terrace. 'It could have been a good thing, anyway, getting checked out,' he said. 'Like making a fresh start.'

He cleared his throat. 'Look, El, I need to ask you something I should have asked you a long time ago.'

I opened my mouth to say sure, and then I spotted the figure in front of my house and I gasped.

She sat on my doorstep, too thin, too pale, gorgeous in a tiny slip dress, black tights and tall, tall boots. Her dark, straight hair fell around her face in attractive disarray.

My wild, unpredictable, glamorous older sister June.

She jumped to her feet at the sight of us and ran to us, fast-moving in high heels.

'Ellie, doll!' she cried and threw her arms around me. Her hug was remarkably energetic for someone so skinny, and she never seemed to age, though she was nearly forty by now. I hugged her back.

'What are you doing here?' I asked, delighted. 'I haven't seen you since Christmas.'

Christmas, when she'd shown up unexpectedly in Upper Pepperton with her boyfriend Jojo, who was large and mysterious-looking with designer white-man dreadlocks and a sharply tailored suit. She'd showered expensive gifts on us and my mother had hastily set two extra places at the table. Jojo had sat in the chair I still thought of as my dad's, helping himself to implausibly large amounts of brussels sprouts, and I'd listened to June talking. I drank in her careless words and wondered about her life.

She hadn't stayed long enough; she never stayed long enough. She wound up my mother, probably because they were so different.

'And who is this breathtaking thing?' she asked me, turning to Hugh.

'Hugh Gibson.' He held out his hand. 'I've heard a lot about you.'

'Well, haven't you done well, little sis?' She took Hugh's hand and instead of shaking it, she leaned forward and up and planted a big kiss on his mouth.

Hugh looked surprised, but not wholly unpleased. June had one of those wide, sexy mouths meant to be slathered in red lipstick and wrapped around parts of male anatomy.

'Hugh's my best friend,' I told her. 'He lives next door.'

I'd told her about him before, on the rare occasions I'd seen her, but she obviously didn't remember. Unlike Hugh, who'd heard me talk about the mystery that was my older sister over and over again, and who seemed very interested indeed.

Of course he would be. She was beautiful and charming and lawless. Aside from our hair and eye colour you wouldn't know we were related.

'It's wonderful to meet you, Hugh,' June said, giving him one of her wide, wide smiles. She was fourteen years older than I was, but she had that type of bone structure that made it difficult to tell her real age.

Then she turned to me. 'Ellie, doll, I'm coming to stay with you for a little while! Isn't that wonderful?'

For the first time, I noticed two large canvas duffel bags on my doorstep. I unlocked the door and June wafted inside. I reached for one of her bags but Hugh beat me to it and picked up both of them.

'Your sister is really something,' he said to me in a low voice.

'I know,' I said. 'She's never been to Reading before. I've

never even had a card from her. And now she turns up out of the blue.'

'What do you think she wants?'

'I don't know if she wants anything. June just turns up. That's how she works.'

And whenever she did turn up, she brought intrigue, like a scented whirlwind scattering fairy dust.

'It's nice to see her,' I added, though June was never quite 'nice'.

She wasn't like normal people. She didn't have a steady job and she'd lived all over the globe with all kinds of different men. She didn't own a house and she hadn't finished school. Sometimes she had a lot of money and sometimes she was stone broke and showed up asking my mother for a loan she'd never repay. Today, the dress and boots she was wearing looked expensive-chic, but her duffel bags were Army surplus.

June had already gone into the kitchen. Hugh put down her bags and the two of us followed her. I put on the kettle while Hugh sat next to June at the table squeezed into the corner of the tiny terraced-housed kitchen. She looked incongruous in the familiar surroundings; a bit of wildness in my tidy home.

'So June, what have you been up to?' I asked her, putting on the kettle.

'Oh, babe, what haven't I been up to.' She laughed her throaty laugh and took a packet of tobacco and rolling papers out from somewhere. Her dress didn't seem big enough for pockets, so maybe she'd had them hidden in her knickers.

'Like what?' I asked, taking down some mugs.

'Oh, ups, downs, everything.' She began the delicate task

of rolling a cigarette. She'd always liked to roll her own. When I'd been younger, she'd used liquorice paper and strange-scented tobaccos that filled the house with exotic scents. My mother had hated it.

'How about you,' she said, 'what have you been up to, Ellie? You look so grown-up in your own house. Where are you working?'

'The same place,' I said, and then, when I saw her blank look, added, 'the pub.'

'Oh yes,' she said, although it was clear she hadn't remembered such a boring snippet of information.

'What brings you to Reading?' I asked.

'Well, I would have come a lot sooner if I'd known you had such an adorable house and a good-looking neighbour.' She turned to Hugh, who was sitting perforce very close to her. 'What's going on between you and my little sister?'

'Nothing,' I said. 'We're just friends.'

'Mmm. Got a girlfriend, then?'

June trailed men behind her like puppy dogs. 'He had nine or ten girlfriends, the last time I checked,' I said, dumping sugar into June's mug.

'Eleanor likes to give me a hard time about dating women,' Hugh said. 'I'm not as bad as she says I am.'

'Yes you are.' I finished making the tea and joined the two of them at the table with the mugs. 'So,' I said, before June and Hugh could get too distracted by flirting to pay any attention to me, 'what *does* bring you to Reading, June?'

'Ugh.' June made a face and took a dainty sip of tea before she finished rolling her fag. 'Do you remember Jojo?'

I nodded.

'What did he tell you he did for a living?'

'He owned a nightclub, didn't he?'

June produced a slim silver lighter from somewhere on her slender person and lit her cigarette.

Hugh glanced at me. I had never allowed cigarette smoke to sully the air of my clean house. Whenever I had a party I forced people to stand on my doorstep if they wanted to smoke.

I met his eyes and shrugged. I couldn't explain to him, without interrupting June's story, that the scent of tobacco was as much my sister as her high-heeled shoes and her wide red smile. Yet another way she was different and more glamorous than I was. She'd taught me how to roll a cigarette like her when I was ten, but I could only produce wobbly cones, not slender cylinders like June's. And I couldn't smoke them without coughing.

'He didn't own a nightclub. It was a lie.' June blew a thin stream of smoke out of her mouth. 'He didn't seem to do anything except talk on the phone all day, and then go out at odd hours. And then there were people coming in and out of the flat all the time. Eventually I figured out he was dealing.'

'Drugs?' I asked, and then regretted it as I sounded so naïve.

'Oh sweetheart, imagine my shock. Turns out there were thousands of pounds changing hands every day. And can you believe, most of the time Jojo couldn't even be bothered to buy a pint of milk?'

'Now that is shocking,' Hugh said, amused.

'It really is. Anyway, I was fed up, and Jojo has a temper on him. It was arguments, arguments, arguments, and he likes to use his hands.'

She pulled her tiny dress off one tiny shoulder and I saw a set of distinct bruises on her creamy skin, the size of a large man's hand. Then she gestured to her left eye and I saw, now that my attention was drawn to it, that under her dark make-up there was a spreading yellow bruise.

I drew in a breath of pain and sympathy. June was so very small, and Jojo had been so big. This was the dark side of being a bad girl, of being wild and free. Suddenly I was glad of the bricks of my safe little house around me. Nothing ever happened, but at least boring wasn't scary.

'Oh, June. That's awful.' Her misfortune made her somehow more human, less like the untouchably glamorous wicked fairy figure of my childhood.

Hugh was frowning, too. 'Bastard.'

'I know,' June said sadly. She drew on her roll-up with a delicate breath.

'Well, you did the right thing leaving him,' I said. 'I'm glad you came here instead of staying with someone who's beating you up.'

'Thank you, Ellie. I knew you'd understand.'

She launched herself off her chair in a cloud of tobacco smoke and hugged me. I gave her a hug back, feeling how fragile she was, how vulnerable. She was family, and she needed me. For the first time in my life, sympathy overcame the awe I usually felt towards her.

It had to be traumatic to be assaulted by your boyfriend, and since she hadn't gone into detail about what happened, it was probably even worse than she was telling us.

'What did you do?' I asked her, still holding her. 'Did you call the police on him?'

'Oh, no. I broke his nose.'

She sat back down at the table and drew on her fag.

'Got an ashtray?'

I stared at her. She was still small, still thin, but nowhere near fragile. And in no way in need of my sympathy.

Hugh took a plate from underneath one of my aloe plants and gave it to her to put her ash in. Then he scraped back his chair and stood up.

'Well, it's been a very interesting morning, but I've got to get to work,' he said. 'Catch you later, June.'

'Oh, definitely,' she replied, her eyelids at half mast as she gave his body the once-over from head to foot. 'We are all going to have so much fun.'

I followed Hugh to the door. 'You're right,' he said. 'Your sister is pretty incredible.'

'I don't really know her. Maybe this visit means we'll get closer.'

'That would be good.' He ruffled my hair, shorter than June's. 'I hope you do.'

As he twisted the doorknob, I remembered something. 'What were you going to ask me about before June turned up?'

For the first time since June had kissed him, Hugh looked uncomfortable.

'Oh, nothing,' he said. 'Not important.'

When I was growing up, there was one rule in our house: *Eleanor shalt not act like June.*

No staying out all night partying. No getting a job and losing it two weeks later or starting a course and then dropping out. No sneaking men into my single bed. No starting screaming fights with my mother at two in the morning which left her tight-lipped for days afterwards. No disappearing for days or weeks or months at a time. No smoking, no spontaneous outbursts of affection, no equally spontaneous outbursts of breathtaking bitchiness, no careless beauty or excitement.

Except for occasional weeks between men and jobs, she didn't live with us in Upper Pepperton, but even when she wasn't in the house June was a shadow there, half darkness and half nearly blinding sunlight. She was absolutely, terrifyingly free, and she was my mother's favourite topic of conversation.

My mother's second favourite topic of conversation was the fact that, thank God, I wasn't anything like June. I was a good girl.

A good girl who fervently, desperately wanted to be more like June.

Her freedom, her glamour, were shimmering entice-
ments to everyday good girl Eleanor, who I knew lacked
sparkle next to June. For a couple of weeks when I was
fifteen I'd even tried dressing like her, hitching up the skirt
of my school uniform, painting on red lipstick, frothing up
my neat dark hair with hairspray and mousse. Until I'd
caught a glimpse of myself in the mirror from afar and
realised I looked ridiculous, a bit like a female version of
Robert Smith from The Cure.

I gave up. I was meant to be mundane.

At the moment, this particular mundane good girl was
celebrating the clear results of her sexually transmitted
disease tests by lurking in the corner of the biggest chemist
in Reading, waiting for the family planning aisle to clear so
she could buy a pregnancy test.

My period wasn't even due for two more days. But every
day was another day I couldn't write properly, couldn't think
about anything except for the fact that I'd been so stupid as
to have unprotected sex.

In theory it was great to be wild and free; in reality, if you
were someone like me, born to be normal, it made you
worry so much that it wasn't worth the hassle.

I perused the corn pads on the foot-care display for the
dozenth time. I'd chosen this chemist because I figured I
would be less conspicuous than in the smaller one nearer
my house where I was known by sight. But the downside
was that there were lots of other customers. I made a note
to come back sometime when I wasn't distracted by anxiety.
To an erotic novelist, there was probably inspiration to be
found watching people buying birth control.

But right now those people were blocking my objective
of buying a pregnancy test without being noticed. Two

teenage boys in the blazers and ties of the local public school were loitering in front of the condom display. They were reading the labels aloud, half hushed and half bold, pausing between each one to laugh loudly and self-consciously.

Enough was enough. I turned, marched up to them, took a packet of Durex Fetherlite with spermicide off the shelf and held it out, saying 'I think these will do perfectly fine for you as an entry-level condom, unless of course you need the extra large.'

The boys' eyes went huge and they backed off, muttering something about only joking. Alone at last, I searched the shelves for an early pregnancy test, saw that if you bought two it was cheaper, decided I was never in a million years going to need two because after this experience I was swearing off sex for good, grabbed a pink packet, and legged it to the till. The cashier didn't even give me a second glance.

One problem solved, I thought as I headed back towards home. I'd take the test and it would be negative and I could get back to work. Then that would be a second problem solved, because I could revise *Throbbing Member* and make it realistic. Somehow.

That only left my third problem.

June had been with me for a week and I was still none the wiser about what made her tick. She was an enigma living in my house. Aside from the snippet of information about Jojo, she'd sidestepped all my conversational gambits designed to get to know more about her. She'd offered me charm instead: giggles and 'sweethearts' and vague references to an exciting life lived elsewhere.

But maybe these things took more time, I thought,

fishing in my pocket for the keys to unlock my front door. Just because I was a writer I didn't have an automatic insight into what people were like. Quite the opposite, actually. One of the things that appealed to me about writing was that in fictional worlds, people made a lot more sense than they did in real life.

My house, when I opened the door, didn't smell like my house. June's cigarettes, June's perfume. I didn't notice it so much when I was in the house, but being outside in what passed for fresh air in Reading made the alien scents more obvious. I paused on my way to the kitchen to light a couple of the scented candles on the shelves in the living room.

'Hey,' June called cheerfully from the kitchen. She was at the table, eating what looked like a heap of chocolate with a spoon.

'What have you got there?' I asked.

'Hugh brought it round on his way to his lecture or whatever it is,' June said with her mouth full. 'Coffee hazelnut cheesecake. It's delicious. Want some?' She held out her spoon.

I looked at the cheesecake. June had eaten it haphazardly, reducing what I knew had probably been an impeccably presented dessert into a random pile of cheesecake, nuts, and crust.

'That's okay,' I said. 'I've tried Hugh's cheesecake before.'

Of course, then it had been *my* cheesecake.

'He's really quite dishy,' she said, licking her spoon and putting it back into the pile of cake. 'Tall,' she added, as if I hadn't noticed.

'Hmm.' I put my package, well wrapped in a bland carrier bag, on the table.

'I'm gasping for a cup of tea, doll.'

I turned to put on the kettle, and for the second time that day took my courage in my hands.

'I was thinking,' I said, 'that since you've been here we haven't really had the chance to sit down and have a good talk about things.'

'Oh! You are so right. Tell you what, sweetheart, I'll make us a nice dinner tonight and we'll have a proper natter. I need to find out what you've been doing with yourself, don't I? I'm sure you don't spend all your time working at that ghastly pub.'

'That sounds great,' I said, turning to the tea-making optimistically. I couldn't picture June making dinner. I'd never in my life seen her cook anything herself. She didn't even bother to toast bread before she ate it. But it was nice of her to offer, and we'd spend some real time together.

From behind me I heard a rustle of plastic carrier bag. 'Ooh! Who's been a naughty girl then, Ellie?'

I whirled around; June had the pregnancy test in her hand.

'I think you'd make a divine mother,' she continued. 'So responsible and tidy.'

'That's – I bought that for my friend.'

She raised her eyebrows. 'Oh really?'

'Yes. She was too embarrassed to buy it for herself.' I hoped my flushed cheeks weren't too obvious.

June shook her head. 'Why should anybody be embarrassed about having had sex? It's one of the best things you can do. Releases your natural endorphins.' She licked chocolate off her finger sensuously. 'Everyone should have as much sex as possible, that's what I say.'

'Hear hear,' I said, with a lame little laugh.

June was right. Look at her. She'd had sex aplenty,

probably more sex than I'd had hot dinners. Was she lurking in chemists buying pregnancy tests before she'd even missed a period? I thought not.

I was silly to be worried. Couples who wanted babies tried for months, sometimes years to conceive, and I'd had nothing but a one-night stand. The chances were minuscule. And here I was, worrying about it like a cardigan-wearing school Health Ed teacher.

I picked up the test and put it in a drawer, intending to stuff it in the bin as soon as I was alone.

'So, what have you been up to today?' I asked, putting the mugs on the table and sitting across from her.

'Oh, this and that, faffing around.' She took a sip of tea, and stretched like a satisfied cat. 'Mmm. Tell me, Ellie, you ever get a man coming in your pub who looks like –' She gestured her hands vaguely. 'You know, who was that singer in that eighties group who had all those hits?'

I nearly dropped my mug halfway to my mouth. 'George Michael?' It burst out of me without my thinking.

She snapped her fingers. 'That's it. Sort of good-looking in a weird kind of way. You ever get someone looking like him in your pub?'

I was staring at her; I did my best to look more casual. 'Why?'

'Oh it's a friend of mine who I think said he lived in Reading.' She shrugged. 'I thought I'd ask. It's not like you wouldn't notice him if he came in, right?'

'Uh.' I swallowed. 'No, he'd be pretty noticeable.'

'That's what I figured. Maybe he doesn't live in Reading any more.'

'Or maybe he drinks in a different pub,' I suggested. 'The Mouse and Duck is pretty much a dump.'

'Maybe,' she agreed, though she'd obviously lost interest. She dipped her finger in the dregs of the cheesecake and licked it. 'Mmm. That Hugh is an absolute angel. I wouldn't mind licking this cheesecake off his chest.'

I stood up and searched in a drawer for a Gaviscon; my stomach was queasy as anything, probably because of the conversation. I found one and crunched it.

'I need to get to my desk in your room, so I can do some work,' I said. 'You mind?'

'Of course not, sweetness. You go right ahead and work there all you want. Balancing your chequebook?'

'Something like that.' I dumped my tea into the sink and went upstairs. Before I opened the door to my white room, my office, the pristine brain of my house, I drew a deep breath. Then I surveyed the destruction.

Clothes. Little tiny slip dresses, pairs of tights, eensy T-shirts, lacy bras. At least four mugs, from what I could see. Newspapers, an empty bottle of wine. One of my cereal bowls, full of cigarette ends, was balanced on the end of the unmade sofa bed. My desk was covered with bottles of make-up, brushes and used cotton wool.

Get over yourself, Eleanor, I thought. *You write smutty novels, not works of literary greatness. You don't need a room of one's own; you just need a keyboard and a filthy mind.*

I picked my way through the mess and turned on my computer. There were sticky rings from cups on the top of my desk. They had started to attract dust.

I was never going to be able to work in here till June was out and I'd reclaimed the room. I shut down the computer, picked up a notebook, and went to my own room and shut the door.

Five minutes of staring at a lined piece of paper and I knew it was no good. I was never going to be able to write a new scene for *Throbbing Member*. I wasn't anal or anything. I mean, I'd had people staying with me before. Not long ago I'd had a total stranger in my bed, right?

But I could hear her downstairs, scraping her chair back and singing. She'd probably be going through my bathroom cabinets next, and looking through the phone book for the number of her friend who looked like George Michael. Any minute now she'd light up a fag and I would be able to smell it.

I needed space.

'I'm going out,' I called to June as I went down the stairs, and didn't wait for her cheerful reply before I shut the front door behind me and went next door to Hugh's. I unlocked the door with the spare key I had on my ring and went inside.

It smelled of chocolate in here, and faintly of Hugh's aftershave. 'Hugh?' I called, though June had said he'd gone to college.

I didn't usually let myself in to his house, though in theory I could whenever I liked, and he let himself into mine pretty often. But there was the matter of his girl-friends, and anyway, whenever I wanted him he seemed to show up near me one way or another.

His house was tidy and clean, and my shoulders immediately relaxed. That was one thing Hugh and I had in common: we weren't neat freaks, but we both liked things in place. We used to get teased about it at university, but then again people used to queue up to share houses with us because we would do the washing-up pretty often.

Here, I could probably work. I searched through his CD

collection till I found one I'd given him and that I also owned, and put it on. I settled myself on his brown leather couch, put a couple of cushions behind my back and another on my lap, and settled my notebook on top of it.

Sitting like this, I was facing the shelves of books and DVDs that Hugh had on his wall, and I idly let my gaze wander over them. He had quite a few expensive cookbooks; the rest of the shelves were stuffed with forensic thrillers and funny science fiction/fantasy paperbacks. We didn't share taste in literature; I didn't look through his shelves very often.

Which was probably how I'd missed seeing that one of his shelves held a line of sixteen purple-spined books, every one of them with the name Estelle May on it.

I let out a snort of laughter. Hugh had all of my erotic novels in plain sight, in pride of place, in fact, in his living room.

I put aside the notebook and stood up to take the books down, one by one, from his shelf. He even had them arranged in chronological order, according to their release dates.

I knew where he'd got the first one; I'd given him a copy the day it had come out, because Hugh was directly responsible for it getting published due to his incessant nagging for me to submit the silly manuscript I'd written for fun while we were at university. I flipped open the cover of *A Degree in Carnal Knowledge*, and saw my own handwriting on the title page: *For Hugh, with love and thanks . . . I think. Estelle May.*

I hadn't been used to signing the pen name, and the lettering was awkward. I thumbed through the book, reading phrases and pages at random, remembering how I'd written it between lectures and revising. The University of Reading had become a much more interesting place when I looked at it through the eyes of my heroine Maria, an adventurous graduate student in human sexuality who was writing her thesis on her own experiences of being a total slut.

I laughed out loud when I came to the scene involving Maria, the provost of the university, and two raunchy gardeners in an empty examination hall. I had actually written that scene during a sociology lecture instead of taking notes. I'd rushed off after the lecture to meet Hugh for a pint and to tell him all about it.

I replaced the book and took down the next one, *Temporary Secretary*, a romp about libidinous Jeanette, who had a strange fetish involving photocopiers and a wild imagination when it came to uses for paper clips. I'd written that one while bored out of my mind in a temp job during the summer holiday. I hadn't signed this one; Hugh must have bought it because I didn't remember giving it to him. I picked up my Biro from his coffee table and wrote in it with a flourish: *To Hugh, you're a pervert and should stop reading this filth. Love and kisses, Estelle May.*

Gradually I worked through all of them, signing the front pages. And as I did, something occurred to me, something I'd never noticed before because I'd never looked at all sixteen of my erotic novels at once.

My heroines were invariably beautiful, desirable, independent women who saw what they wanted and seized it without any thought about the consequences.

Every single one of them was exactly like my sister June.

I put the copy of *Cuffed and Collared* back on the shelf next to its sisters. Great. Just great. She wasn't only in my house and in my office; she was here, too.

And how was I going to make my current book any better now that the knowledge was in my head that for nearly six years I'd been writing erotic novels based on my sister?

I sat back down on the couch and toyed with the pen and stared at the lined paper.

I couldn't write about my sister again. Now that I knew, it seemed far too pathetic.

What was I going to do instead – write an erotic novel based on me?

'Another glass of red, doll, and a pint of Stella for Hugh.' June smiled winningly at me and put a crisp twenty-pound note on the bar.

'What happened to dinner?' I asked her.

I wish I could say my voice was calm, and that I was being mature and keeping everything in perspective, but I wasn't. I'd wrestled two hours with my novel, crossing out every sentence I wrote and several I'd written days ago, for good measure.

Every word seemed wrong. Sometimes there was magic in the air; when I wrote my novels, especially at the beginning, the story would flow out of me and I would laugh at my own audacity. But there was no magic today, not in this book.

Maybe there never was going to be any magic with this book; maybe the whole thing was stupid. Maybe I was a rubbish writer who'd never be good for anything except churning out second-rate smut.

When I'd come back home there was nothing in the kitchen except for two used teabags and a lingering whiff of tobacco. I'd been muttering to myself and fuming ever since, too angry to eat, and my temper and my appetite weren't improved by seeing my sister cosily curled up with Hugh in the corner of the Mouse and Duck when I came in for my shift.

'Oh, Hugh came by and said he'd been to the bank,' June said, 'so I figured, why eat when you can drink? Better do me a Jack Daniel's on ice while you're at it, and do you want anything? Hugh's paying.' She showed me the twenty again.

'June, do you ever keep any of your promises?'

My heart was beating like the bass on the pub's ancient jukebox; my body felt as if it were on the edge of a precipice, about to fling myself out of the rules of my own life.

Eleanor is not like June. And Eleanor does not fight or argue. She stays detached and sensible, I thought.

I put both my hands on the bar and braced myself. I'd heard enough arguments over the years, through the walls and floorboards of our house in Upper Pepperton, and sworn never to act that way myself. That I would never get so angry I lost control, lost myself, dissolved into powerless tears and accusations as my mother always did whenever she was confronted with my sister's defiance of the way that the rest of the world behaved.

My face felt stiff and red and my stomach rolled. June blinked at me. At first I thought it was in surprise, and then she blinked again and I realised she was actually fluttering her eyelashes at me.

'Honey, I'm sorry. I'll do it tomorrow night, yeah? It's just that Hugh was so charming and he insisted I come out with him.' She wiggled the twenty again. 'You sure you won't have a drink?'

'No thanks.' I poured her drinks and slapped them down on the bar.

June immediately downed the Jack and held the glass back out. 'Might as well fill that up, save me the trouble of walking to the bar again.'

When I didn't move right away she rolled her eyes. 'Ellie, don't get angry; it's such a bore. I'm a lousy cook. If you knew what you're not missing in my noodle surprise you'd thank me.'

'It's not the cooking,' I said, and tumbled into it. 'It's the way you leave my house a mess, and smoke in it, and never help out with anything, or even tell me why you're here or how long you're staying, and then you promise to do something and take off the minute a man crooks his little finger. Can't you ever grow up?'

My voice, loud and shrill in the pub, suddenly didn't sound like my own. It sounded like an echo of my mother's, through all those floorboards and walls and years.

I stopped.

So it wasn't enough that I'd discovered through my fiction that my secret fantasy was to be more like June. I had to find out that really, I was much more like my mother.

June smiled. It made me clench my fists.

'Eleanor, chill out and have a sense of humour, won't you?'

'I have a sense of humour,' I shrilled.

My sister put her hand on mine. Her fingers were covered with silver rings and she had perfect nails. 'I know you do, honey. That's why I wanted to come and stay with you.' She squeezed my hand. 'And you're right, I haven't been helping, and I haven't talked to you about why I came to visit you. I'll be better, I promise.'

She said it with her eyes steady on mine, and my anger, though it didn't disappear, wavered. She looked so sincere.

'You won't. You never have.' I hated how petulant I sounded.

'I will. Listen, tomorrow we'll have a proper girly chat and I'll tell you everything. Okay?'

I nodded and tried to salvage what was left of my sense of humour by smiling at her. She beamed back and held out her empty glass for me to fill again.

I watched her go back to Hugh; she put his pint down in front of him and slipped under his arm to nestle close and look up into his face with her big green eyes.

No difficulty guessing who was going to be Hugh's latest bedmate, then.

I swallowed a gulp of ginger ale that did nothing to make my stomach feel better and busied myself emptying the glass washer.

My eyes were continually drawn to Hugh's corner, though. I thought he wasn't into brunettes. And I would have thought he'd have the good taste not to get off with his best friend's sister. But apparently Hugh's sexual appetite knew no boundaries of hair colour or loyalty.

June's giggle pierced over the ill-balanced music and I saw her cuddle closer to Hugh. His long limbs and broad shoulders made her seem even more tiny and elfin. Something about the way he was sitting with her made him look protective. As if he were trying to be some knight in shining armour as well as the Don Juan of Reading.

I grunted and poured Maud and Martha their gins. When I turned around from the cash register Hugh was at the bar.

'Hey,' he greeted me with a smile – wide, sparkle-eyed,

guileless, with that one crooked tooth on the bottom left-hand side that only made all the rest of his teeth look straighter.

Well could he smile. For the price of a few pounds he was wining and Jack Danielsing himself into a wild night of sex with June Connor, who no doubt knew a shocking trick or two.

'Nice of you to come and say hello,' I said, grabbing two pint glasses from the shelf and beginning to fill them with cider and Stella.

He raised an eyebrow. 'I waved.'

'Oh, gosh, I do apologise. I should be honoured.'

'Tetchy, are you?'

'Enjoying my sister, are you?'

'Yes, as a matter of fact.' He scratched the back of his head and I noticed that his thick dark hair looked particularly as if someone had been running their hands through it. 'She has some interesting opinions, especially after she's been drinking.'

I nodded. 'I'm sure that opinions aren't the only interesting things she can share when she's been drinking.'

'I concur with your judgement, Ms Connor,' Hugh-as-Sean-Connery replied.

I glared at him. He was trying to jolly me along, make light of the fact that he was going to shag my sister senseless without even asking my permission first.

'Here,' I said, pouring more Jack Daniel's from the optic into a glass, 'this should help you move things along more quickly. Just do me a favour.' I put the glass down in front of him, and folded my arms. 'Try to keep the noise down tonight, will you? I need some sleep.'

Hugh's expressions could change with the swiftness of a

bolt of lighting. His eyes narrowed, his brow contracted, and his smile melted half away. 'El, I wouldn't sleep with your sister.'

I laughed, though I wasn't finding this funny at all. 'Uh huh. Don't try to kid me, Hugh, we both know you'll stick your dick in anybody who smiles at you twice.'

His face transformed again, this time into a wide-eyed, open-mouthed expression of what I'd think was outrage on anybody else, but couldn't be with Hugh, because what I'd said was one hundred per cent true and he knew it. I turned away from him and went into the kitchen to deal with a nonexistent food order.

When I returned to the bar Hugh was back with June in their corner, and they were canoodling or whatever it was you called it when two people couldn't keep their hands off each other. I didn't look too closely.

Instead, I involved myself in a conversation with Paul and Philip where they tried once again to explain to me why footballers deserved to make so much more money than teachers and nurses, and in the midst of our argument I looked up and Hugh and June were gone.

*L*ucy Sharpe licked the end of her pencil and tried her best to concentrate on her shorthand and not to listen to what was going on in the next room.

It was common knowledge in Whitehall that the Chancellor was conducting a liaison with the Minister for Internal Affairs. Lucy just wished they wouldn't perform their internal affairs in the Minister's office, in full earshot of Lucy, her new secretary.

'Harder! Faster!' The words were incongruous enough in the context of a blandly decorated government office; when cried out in the Minister's plummy accent they became, frankly, surreal. 'Oh yes, who's my rearing polo pony of love?'

Polo pony of love? Lucy screwed up two bits of paper and put them in her ears. She felt sick.

If she could work in another office, it would be easier, but the Minister insisted that Lucy work right there with only a thin wooden door separating her from the politicians' sexual shenanigans. She must know that Lucy could hear every thrust, every slap, and every metaphor. It was as if the Minister enjoyed knowing Lucy could hear.

With a great effort of concentration, she managed to finish typing up the minutes of the morning's meeting and was sending the document to the printer when the door opened and the Minister and the Chancellor entered the room, adjusting their clothing.

I paused with my fingers on the keyboard and sighed. The idea had come at about three o'clock in the morning, as I lay in my bed trying to sleep. If reality was missing from my novel, maybe I should, after all, rewrite *The Throbbing Member of Parliament* with the heroine, Lucy Sharpe, being more like myself.

I'd come into my study, filled with June's things, and had started typing.

However, there was a new problem with that solution: as an erotic heroine, I was awful.

For one thing, an erotic heroine would get turned on by hearing other people having sex – even if she didn't want to be – otherwise, there was no point in writing about it. Whereas I had spent the entire night feeling sick at the mere possibility that I might hear Hugh and June having sex with each other. I'd tried sleeping on the couch, out of hearing range, but had had no luck, and when I'd gone to bed out of desperation for some sleep I couldn't stop my ears pricking up at the slightest noise.

Those noises were the wind, or the house settling, or my other neighbour Alice's noisy water heater. There'd been no peep from Hugh's house.

But that didn't mean anything. They could be getting it on hanging from the bathroom ceiling. They could have gagged each other with rubber balls. They could have spent the night having sex in a succession of taxis for the benefit of a succession of voyeuristic taxi drivers.

I should have felt grateful that I couldn't hear them, but instead I was much, much more of a wreck and a prude than Lucy Sharpe.

Downstairs, the front door opened. My heart leapt and my hands clenched on the keyboard. June was home.

Having her home was even worse than having her out, because I was probably going to have to hear about her exploits. I bent my attention back to my lame novel and my lame heroine, who, I was beginning to realise, would be awful in whatever novel she happened to be in.

'Lucy,' said the Minister as she came into the room reknotting her Hermès scarf, 'do you think you could let the Chancellor have the dossier we prepared this morning? He's eager to get the full picture.'

Lucy bit back a sarcastic reply and said, 'Yes, Minister,' instead. Jobs like this one didn't come along every day, and if she had to put up with hearing about amorous polo ponies and the unsavoury images they evoked, it was a small price to pay. She lifted the dossier from the desk and held it out towards the Chancellor.

His fingers brushed hers when he took it, and Lucy looked up at him in surprise. Her embarrassment had been such that whenever he came into the office she'd avoided his eye, but now something compelled her to examine his features.

He was a tall man, surprisingly young-looking for someone in such an important office, and his rangy body filled out the broad shoulders of his tailored suit. From this angle, from below, he had high cheekbones and a strong chin, and a straight patrician nose with a slight bend on the end of it, like a hawk's.

*

'Ellie, doll? I'm home.'

The words only just filtered through because what I was writing had suddenly become interesting.

Lucy, beyond all probability, had started to do unexpected things on her own in the way that fictional characters did when they were becoming realistic, and she had decided to be attracted to the Chancellor, up to that point a minor supporting character, who had, with the words appearing under my typing fingers, abruptly gained a description.

A description that echoed precisely the way I'd described Hugh to myself a couple of weeks before, on our way back from the STD clinic.

'Ellie?' June's voice was closer, at the bottom of the stairs.

What did what I'd just written mean? If Lucy was me, and she was suddenly attracted to the Chancellor, and the Chancellor looked like Hugh, did this mean that *I* was attracted to Hugh?

'Hey, sweetie.' June stepped into the spare room. She was wearing the same slip dress as last night and her long hair had that just-got-out-of-bed tousle. She dived immediately for the desk beside me and retrieved a packet of tobacco.

I couldn't be attracted to Hugh. He was my best friend. I'd known him for years and never once been attracted to him. It was one of the enduring mysteries of my life why all these other women constantly fell at his feet.

But that would explain why I'm so upset about him sleeping with June, I thought.

'Ellie?' June waved her hand in front of my face. 'Are you hypnotised or something?'

I blinked and focused and noticed grey circles under her eyes and a distinctly greenish tint to her skin.

'Hung over?' I said.

'Death warmed up.' She slumped on to the pull-out couch and began rolling a cigarette. 'Make me a cup of tea, will you, doll?'

I saved the document, closed my word processing application, and shut down the computer. 'Make yourself one,' I said, 'I'm going out.'

'Oooh but you'll make me a cup of tea first, won't you? I've got a splitting headache and my back is killing me.' She writhed on the crumpled sheets. 'Must have been in a weird position.'

The word *position* lodged in my brain next to the image of June and Hugh trying out every illustration in the *Kama Sutra*.

'It's your own bloody fault you feel this way, you can make your own bloody tea.'

'Fine.' She stood and flounced down the stairs.

I looked at my computer screen, which was telling me hitherto unknown feelings about my best friend, and then I looked around my unbearably messy spare room. Hours of putting up with my sister's clutter and listening for sex sounds made me feel claustrophobic in my own life. I pushed back the chair, which caught on a pair of tights on the floor, and checked the weather out the window. It was, typically, raining; that greasy, cold autumn rain that washed nothing clean.

I was digging in my closet in my room for my mac when I heard a noise behind me. I turned around to catch June in the act of sprawling over my neatly made bed, her high heels resting on my pale green duvet cover.

'June, I take off my shoes before I lie on my bed,' I said through gritted teeth.

'I'm sure you do. You're so sensible.' From her, it sounded like an insult. 'Hugh and I were just talking about it.'

'Hmm. Yes. I'm sure that's what you and Hugh did all night together. Talked. About me.' I ripped my mac off the hanger.

'We did, actually. He said—'

'Nothing you two talked about could possibly be of any interest to me. And can you get your feet off my bed?'

June shimmied over so that the bottoms of her feet were barely dangling over the edge of the bed. 'God, Ellie, why are you being such a priss? You sound exactly like Mum. Is this how she taught you to act?'

'She mostly taught me how not to act like you.' I pushed my arms into the mac, making my jumper bunch up at the elbows.

June snorted. 'Huh. Not surprising. What did she say?' Her voice raised from its usual husky sexiness into an imitation of Mum's ' "June's a *slut*, June's a *waste*, June's a *problem*. Let's clean the house together, what fun!" I bet you both had a brilliant time slagging me off while I was away having a life of my own, far away from that little perfect house and the little perfect family.'

'Mum never said that.' Not in so many words, anyway. 'And if you'd ever bothered to be around, you'd know that I always defended you.'

'Why would I want to be around? Dad had some life in him at least, but once he popped his clogs there was only Sheila and her little clone.'

She rolled over, incidentally dragging her shoes across my duvet cover again, picked up from my bedside table the mug of tea she'd made, and drank from it. When she put it back down, tea slopped over the edge and spotted on my pillow.

A Sheila clone. Left at home, boring and neat and predictable.

I grabbed the pillow and began stripping off the case before the tea soaked through. 'If you're going to get tea everywhere, at least do it someplace you've already messed up.'

I hated the way I sounded, like an uptight cow.

'And Dad didn't "pop his clogs",' I said. 'He died. But you weren't there for that, either.'

The force of my anger surprised me, but I kept on going, right over that precipice. 'All I ever wanted was for you to be a proper sister. Is that so hard? Somebody you share your life with, somebody you care about? Or can you even care about anybody? Is that too much hassle for you?'

June sat up. 'I'm not your fucking sister,' she said, and she picked up her tea and stomped out of the room.

I stood there, pillowcase in hand, jumper bunched up underneath my mac, shocked at what I'd said. I'd not realised how angry I'd been with her, about all those years, till it had poured out of my mouth.

And then I finally heard what she'd said.

I dropped the pillowcase and ran the short distance across my bedroom and over the landing to the spare room. She'd closed the door but I opened it. June was sprawled on the couch, her skirt and hair artfully disarranged, her face obscured by her mug of tea.

'What do you mean you're not my sister?'

She shrugged and kept on drinking.

I stepped into the room. 'Were you adopted?' That could

explain the tension between her and Sheila, the big age gap, and why she and I were so different. But we had the same eye colour, the same hair colour.

'No,' she said, and put down her mug, empty. 'Listen, forget I ever said anything, okay?' She stood and came towards the door, but I didn't get out of her way.

'I want to know what you were talking about.'

'It's not important, doll.'

'I think it is.'

In her heels, she was as tall as I was. I met her eyes and looked at her steadily. I think it was probably the first time I had ever done that. Close up, I could see that her smudged mascara had collected in the lines around her eyes.

'Why did you say you weren't my sister?'

'I said I wasn't your *fucking* sister,' she said, and she lifted her chin. 'Because I'm your fucking mother.'

I sank down on to the couch, staring at her.

'You what?'

'I'm your mother. I got pregnant with you, I carried you for nine months, I gave birth to you. You're my daughter. *Capice?*' She pressed her hand to her forehead. 'God, have I got a hangover.'

I tried hard to make sense of this. 'But you were only a kid when I was born.'

'I was thirteen when I got up the duff, and fourteen when I had you. I was going to have you adopted, but Mum and Dad said they'd keep you.' Now that she'd dropped her bombshell, June looked almost as if she were enjoying this. 'Whew. You know, it sort of feels good to tell the truth after all this time.'

'You lied to me. You all lied to me. For my whole life.'

June shrugged. 'Well, it was better for you. I don't have a

maternal bone in my body, darling.' She sat down at my desk and began rolling a fag.

I felt numb. 'Who's my father?'

'I don't remember. Some bloke or other. It doesn't matter anyway, you're Sheila's through and through. Might as well have skipped my generation altogether.' She lit up.

I breathed her cigarette smoke. My *mother*'s cigarette smoke.

'There,' she said. 'I've shared something with you. Do you feel better now?'

'I don't know what I feel.'

'Well, I feel bloody terrible. I'm hung over and I need to sleep.' She took a last long drag of her cigarette, stubbed it out in one of my bowls, and stretched out on the bed, ignoring that I was sitting on the bottom of it. She closed her eyes.

'We need to talk about this,' I said.

'Later, doll,' she mumbled and pulled the sheet over her head. 'Close the door behind you, will you?'

'June, talk to me.'

She didn't move or make a sound.

'June.'

I prodded her on the shoulder, but she only pulled the sheet tighter over her.

It was impossible to get June to do anything she didn't want to do. I gave up, went downstairs, and picked up the phone.

Mum had recently bought a phone that had caller display on it so when she answered she started immediately talking to me. 'Oh, Ellie, you can't imagine the problems I'm having with this pattern. I dropped a stitch, it was the tiniest little one, and now nothing will come right, it's all wonky.'

I didn't sound like her. Not really. Did I? I certainly never talked about knitting.

I interrupted her. 'Mum? I need to ask you a question.'

'Of course, darling.'

I didn't know how to put it. 'Uh, you know June's here? And we had an argument this morning, and she's hung over, and you know she'll say anything when she thinks she's cornered, any old silly thing to get your goat, but the thing is she says she's actually not my sister, because she's my mother.'

Sheila was silent. This was not a good sign, so I carried on.

'She says she got pregnant when she was thirteen, but that can't be true, can it? I mean you couldn't all have kept that secret from me all my life? Not without me even suspecting anything, right?'

'I wondered when she'd tell you.'

Her quiet words confirmed everything.

'Why didn't you tell me? Why didn't *Dad*?'

'Well, it wouldn't have done you much good to know, would it?'

'That's not the point.'

She sighed. 'Ellie, I'll come down and see you. How about Thursday – no, wait, I've got the parish council and there's that whole debate over the cake-sale disaster. What are you doing at the weekend?'

Just what I needed, a June and Sheila ticking time bomb in my house while I tried to figure out who I should be buying a card for on Mother's Day. And now I knew why all those arguments had taken place behind closed doors or after I was supposed to be in bed: they were trying to stop me from discovering the secret.

'I'm working at the pub,' I said. 'I won't have any time this weekend.'

'Monday, then? I can cancel my book club and get a train.'

'Mu—' I stopped myself before the old, false name came out. 'I'm fine. You don't have to come down.'

'But I want to.'

'Well, I don't want you to. I'm okay. Really. I've got to go now, I'm due at the Mouse and Duck. Talk to you soon. Bye.'

It was only after I'd hung up the phone that I looked down at my left hand and saw I'd dug crescent moons into my palm with my nails.

'Your sister is your mother?'

I nodded, and took another bite of mushroom omelette. Hugh could certainly goggle when he had the right thing to goggle over, I reflected.

When I'd knocked on his door an hour earlier, Hugh had answered it wearing his dressing gown and a scowl. He gave me a deathly stare, clearly remembering my comment the night before about where he put his dick. It took me ten minutes of begging before he agreed to let me buy him lunch.

'But only because it's Mr Tasty's,' he'd said grudgingly as he'd gone to throw on some clothes.

Mr Tasty's was one of the few cafés in Reading that wasn't either part of a chain or trying to be horrifically fake-upmarket. It had lime-green vinyl booths, chipped beige tables, and, for some reason, it served both greasy British fry-ups and Thai food. Neither cuisine was particularly good, but for years Mr Tasty's had been the place Hugh and I went whenever we had something important to discuss with each other. Partly out of habit, partly because we knew we'd never run into anybody we knew there, because nobody ever went there except for construction workers and Reading's few Thai expats.

Hugh poked his fork into his Pad Thai with extra chillies and peanuts, abandoned it, and went back to goggling at me.

'She's not old enough to be your mother.'

'She's thirty-nine. She had me when she was fourteen.'

Hugh appeared to be even more shocked by this information. 'She doesn't look thirty-nine.'

'Obviously a life devoid of any responsibility whatsoever keeps you looking young and fresh.'

I decided I didn't want to know what Hugh was more shaken by: the fact that June was my mother, the fact that he'd slept with my mother, or the fact that he'd slept with a woman who was nearly forty.

'Why – how – what –' He gestured with both his hands, and then wrapped them around his mug, shaking his head. 'I don't believe it.'

I looked at Hugh's hands. The chunky mug looked small in them. He had artist's hands – long-fingered, competent, strong.

'El? You all right? Why are you staring at my tea?'

'Um . . .' I felt my face flush. Why was I staring at Hugh's hands? I'd seen them before millions of times, but never really *seen* them. Never really thought about touching them, or having them touch me. I wasn't sure if I was thinking about it now.

Did the fact that I was thinking about thinking about it mean that I *was* thinking about it, or was I making myself way too paranoid here?

I gathered my thoughts back to the conversation.

'I didn't believe it either,' I said, 'but after she told me, I called my mother – I mean, my grandmother.' I shook my head. 'Sheila. And she told me it was true.'

'Did you ever have any clue? Has June ever—'

'Acted like a mother? Never. She's not exactly the motherly type.'

'Do you know who your father is?'

'No. It could be any male who attended St Michael's school in Upper Pepperton in 1980. Or someone older than that.'

Without warning, my eyes filled with tears.

Hugh wrapped his fingers around my wrist. 'But there's one person who never was your father. Oh, El, I'm sorry.'

I swallowed. Hugh had never met Stanley Connor, the man I'd thought was my father, because he'd died of a heart attack when I was sixteen. But he'd heard me speak of him, even more than I spoke of June. I had a photo of him in my bedroom and one of his cardigans hanging in my closet. I put it on when I needed extra comfort.

He wasn't my father any more.

'He was your grandfather,' Hugh said. 'He belongs to you that way.'

'Yeah.'

Hugh passed me his serviette and I wiped my eyes.

'Anyway, I thought that was worth a Mr Tasty's lunch.'

'It's worth a whole month of them. So what are you going to do now?'

I wasn't going to eat this omelette, anyway; it was even more disgusting than usual. I pushed it away.

'I don't know.'

'Who are you angriest with?'

Bingo. The man read my mind. He knew exactly what was making my guts roll around and my hands shake and my head feel too small for my brain.

'I don't know,' I said. 'June. Or maybe my mother, I mean Sheila. Or maybe the kid who knocked up some thirteen-year-old girl.' I shrugged and laughed shakily. 'Everyone, I guess.'

'Including me. Eleanor, about last night—'

'Don't.' I held up my hands. 'I don't want to talk about it at all, Hugh.'

He looked at me as if he were assessing me and then he nodded. 'All right.'

He twirled noodles around his fork and put them in his mouth. The end of one of them didn't quite make it past his lips and I watched, fascinated despite myself, as he caught it with his tongue. When he chewed, his jaw became even more defined, and swallowing set the muscles in his neck working in a way I had never noticed before in the million-and-one times that Hugh and I had eaten together.

Or, at least, I'd never consciously noticed.

He licked a trace of chilli sauce from his lips and I wondered what words I would use to describe them. Manly? Sensual? It was always so difficult to describe a man's mouth without resorting to cliché and yet Hugh's mouth was unique, so expressive and so Hugh.

And I was thinking about this because I was planning how to describe the Chancellor in my book. Obviously. I straightened in my chair and looked away from Hugh.

'Where's June now?' he asked me.

'I left her at home, sleeping off her hangover.'

He nodded, then checked his watch. 'I'm sorry, El, I've got an assessment in half an hour.'

'No problem, you go.'

'Are you all right to be alone?'

'It's probably best. I'll go for a walk, clear my head a little.'

We stood and he hugged me tightly. He smelled of soap, and of his woolly jumper. I let myself relax against his chest and thought, *Friendship, Eleanor.*

I kissed him goodbye as I always did, on his cheek, and turned to pay at the till instead of watching him leave.

Reading is not, as a rule, very scenic, but it does have its places. One of my favourites was the walk along the bank of the River Kennet. It started under a damp bridge, and the path eventually wended its way along a dual carriageway and past the site of the former Whitley sewage treatment plant, but in between there was a stretch of beauty, in a peculiarly Reading way.

On one side of the river was the path, muddy in places, and on the other was the back of a row of terraced houses. From the front, these looked like normal Victorian terraces, brick and two-storey, like the ones Hugh and I lived in. But when you walked along the Kennet, you could see that in the back the ground sloped away from these houses to the water. An extra storey was revealed below the road line.

Every garden was different: some cluttered, some landscaped, some overgrown, some overdecorated. In good weather you often saw people sitting in the sun. Most days you saw at least one man huddled at the end of his garden fishing. It was as if from the front, these houses were ordinary but when you looked behind, they were revealed in all their richness.

For whatever the reason, this stretch of scenery helped me think, especially when I was trying to be creative. I hoped it would help me think now.

The greasy rain had slipped into a drizzle and the mud squished under my trainers. On this side it was all yellowing leaves and wilted last-summer's nettles, though over the water, in the gardens, there were still some flowers, as if time passed more slowly over there.

You wouldn't want to swim across the Kennet in Reading; the bottom was likely to be littered with rusting shopping trolleys and rotting fast food. But I imagined what it would be like if I could swim across, and climb out on the other side, into the past. Into, for example, eight days ago, before June turned up at my house. When I knew who my parents were, when my house was my own, when my heroines were (as far as I knew) fictional, when, while most things about my life might be boring, they at least made sense.

I kicked at a wet rope of nettles. I'd *worshipped* June. Had done all my life, even though I was also a bit frightened of her. I'd looked up to her like a little kid blinded by fairy dust, and did she care about me? No. Instead, she'd left me blithely behind, lied to me for twenty-five years, and only shown up to take over my house, sleep with my best friend, eat my cake, and generally make me feel like an old fuddy-duddy.

And she'd taken my father away from me.

Gentle Stanley Connor who let me knot his tie on Sundays, Stanley of the bedtime stories and the piggyback rides and the scratchy bedtime kisses.

Suddenly I wasn't only angry at June; I was furious at her. I wanted to wrap my hands around her swanlike neck. I wanted to drag her down to the Kennet and throw her in, watch her mascara run and her hair become straggles and let her get eaten by the shopping trolleys.

I grabbed a fallen branch from the path and whacked it,

as hard as I could, against a tree trunk. It was about the thickness of my wrist and it made a satisfying crack as it broke.

'I hate you!' I yelled. I hit the branch on the tree again and again till it was in little chunks all over the path, and then I looked up, panting, and saw a huddled fisherman two gardens down staring at me from underneath his waxed jacket hood. He quickly looked away when I met his eye.

I hurried onward, over the concrete bridge where another stream emptied into the brook with a whirl of foam and crisp packets, out of the fisherman's sight.

Got to tell Hugh about acting crazy for a fisherman, I thought, and then I stopped again.

I'd nearly been lusting after Hugh over a Mr Tasty's lunch. What the hell was that all about?

It wasn't as if Hugh had changed. I saw him every day and I'd known for some time that he'd grown out of geekdom. He had loads of girlfriends. He'd always had those artist's hands, that unique mouth, he'd always been tall.

Yet it was as if there had been a missing jigsaw piece in my perception of him that only now was slotting into place, and I could understand that he was sexy.

And now I was just going to have to forget about it. Who else in the world would eat lousy Thai food because I needed him to? Who else in the world knew the right questions to ask, the right things to say? Who else had that hug and that smell and made the best chocolate cake in the world?

Hugh was the only important person in my life whose position hadn't taken a seismic shift, the only constant.

I couldn't fancy him. And that was all there was to it.

The drizzle deepened and turned back to rain. I shoved

my hands into my pockets and turned around. I was cold, I was wet, I had a splinter in my hand, and I was suddenly remembering that if I really didn't want to be like June, there was one more thing I had to find out.

The house was quiet when I got in. I checked upstairs and saw that the door to the spare room was still closed.

I felt hung over myself, though I'd barely touched alcohol since my vodka binge two and a half weeks earlier. I'd been feeling this way for a couple of days, and I'd been putting it down to stress, but there was another, very remote, possibility.

The pregnancy test was still in the drawer where I'd stuffed it yesterday. I was thankful I'd forgotten to throw it away. The rubbish was much more unpleasant these days with all of June's cigarette butts.

I went into the bathroom and read the instructions through twice. It had been a day of revelations. I hoped I wasn't about to be subjected to another.

I peed on the stick and then carefully put it down on the edge of the sink. Wait three minutes, it said, and then look for the number of pink lines.

I wanted to hover over the plastic stick watching every nuance of its changing from white to pink. Instead, I forced myself to sit on the toilet seat and look at the blue bathroom tiles.

Had June done something like this twenty-six years ago – sat and waited in dread? How much had that moment changed her life?

How much had I changed her life?

I stood up and left the bathroom and the pregnancy test. Gently, I knocked on the spare-room door.

'June?' I called softly. 'June, can you help me with something? I'd like your advice.'

When she didn't answer, I pushed the door open.

The room was dark, the curtains were drawn, and it looked less cluttered than it had been that morning. It took me a moment to notice that June wasn't there, and another moment to realise that the room was less cluttered because none of her belongings were there, either.

I turned on the light and had a good look round. Her dresses, her tobacco, her make-up had all disappeared, along with the big duffel bags she'd brought with her.

'June!' I called, although I knew she wasn't anywhere else in the house, and I went downstairs. The stuff she'd strewn around my kitchen and living room was gone, too. There was no sign of a note, no forwarding address or phone number left behind.

My sister had turned up, stayed a week, slept with my best friend, told me she was my mother, and then disappeared.

'Son of a gun,' I said.

I turned around and went back upstairs. The little white stick was still on the side of the sink. From a distance you could mistake it for a toothbrush. I wondered whether in 1980 the pregnancy tests were so small and discreet, or whether June had had to go to the doctor. Wasn't there something about a rabbit dying if you were pregnant?

I realised I was hanging around in the door of the bathroom and made myself go to the sink and pick up the test.

There were two pink positive lines in the plastic window.

12

'Two Mr Tasty's lunches in two weeks,' Hugh commented, tucking into his watery green chicken curry. 'This is a record, isn't it?'

I stirred my Tom Yam Gai. Over the past ten days, in the moments that I wasn't feeling nauseated, I'd had a craving for hot, spicy, citrusy soup. I figured it was my body's way of telling me I had to haul Hugh to Mr Tasty's and tell him about the positive pregnancy test.

But now that I was here, both the soup and the idea of telling Hugh made me feel sick.

'It's been quite a two weeks,' I said.

'So what do you have to tell me?'

I spooned up a piece of chicken and let it fall back into the bowl, scattering drops of spicy broth on the table. I took a paper serviette from the dispenser and wiped it up carefully.

'Do you want me to guess?' he asked.

'You never will.'

'Well, let's see. You've been moody as hell for the past week.'

'I haven't been moody.' In fact, I thought I'd done a pretty good job at concealing my worry: I'd shown up at the pub every night with a smile plastered on my face, and I'd tried to be breezy and normal with Hugh. Neither one easy when the smell of the Mouse and Duck made me want to retch.

'You nagged Jerry so hard that he spent his day off scrubbing floors on his hands and knees, you grimaced all through Maud's karaoke singing of "Careless Whisper", and I actually heard you referring to Reading Football Club as "a bunch of weeds".'

'Well, the floors were disgusting,' I defended myself. 'And not one of Reading Football Club looks good in shorts.'

'Most people judge a football team by other criteria,' Hugh told me. 'I had to remind Paul and Philip that you were female and therefore couldn't be bodily thrown out of the pub on to the street.'

'They should get a sense of humour. Or aesthetics.'

'I found half a slice of my Victoria sponge in your kitchen bin when I made myself a cup of tea yesterday.'

That, I couldn't deny.

'I'm sorry,' I said. 'You're right, I've been moody. It's with good reason.'

'What is it?'

A lock of Hugh's thick hair fell over his forehead. His skin was fresh and smooth-shaven, his eyes bright, his brows raised. He looked so confident and so optimistic and so sexy that I opened my mouth, but I couldn't say the words.

I hadn't told anyone yet. Speaking the words seemed too real. It was as if I thought that this little tiny foetus was sort of hovering outside my body, just waiting for me to tell someone about it, so it could attach itself to me and start growing into a baby.

'I'll guess, shall I?' he said.

I nodded.

'June has shown up again and has told you she had a sex change twenty years ago and she's actually your father.'

I had to laugh at that one. 'No. I haven't heard from her since she packed up and left. I've got no idea where she went to.'

'You've heard from your agent and they're going to make *Cuffed and Collared* into a movie.'

'No. I wish.'

'Me too.' He considered. 'Okay, you've decided to stop fighting your feelings and you're finally ready to tell me you're desperately in love with me because I'm your perfect man.'

I laughed at that, too. A little bit forced, because, to be honest, I'd been looking at his mouth again when he'd said it.

'I *am* your perfect man, you know,' he said.

'Uh huh.' I tore my gaze from his face and toyed with my soup. 'Any more guesses?'

Hugh took a deep breath and let it out.

'I don't know, Eleanor,' he said. 'I think I've proved that I can't read your mind.'

He sounded so tired and fed up, suddenly, that I broke my staring competition with my soup and looked at him again. His face was angry as he forked up rice and curry and chewed it vigorously.

Fear spiked through me. Hugh angry was a new thing. I didn't know what caused it, I didn't know what would come of it. And I needed Hugh, the old familiar Hugh, my friend who knew me better than anyone, if I was going to deal with this.

'You're usually very good at reading my mind,' I said lightly, trying to bring the mood back to what it had been five minutes before. 'Remember all those nights playing drinking Pictionary instead of revising for exams?'

'You know, I've always thought that was wrong,' he said, and I was relieved that his voice was more cheerful, more Hugh-like. 'We always won, but that meant we had to drink less. I think if you win a drinking game you should have to drink *more*.' He ate another bite of curry. 'You know, when I open my own restaurant, I'm going to shoot anyone who produces slop like this.'

'You want to open your own restaurant?'

I'd never thought of Hugh as someone with ambitions beyond transient pleasure. He seemed to drift along, like me; over the years he'd had five or six jobs in various I.T. companies, till he'd packed it in to go back to college and train as a pastry chef. Although he was very good at being a pastry chef, I guess I'd assumed this was a new thing he'd get tired of sooner or later; probably after he'd amassed enough skills and recipes to produce enough cakes to seduce all the unattached (blonde or redheaded) females in Reading whom he hadn't seduced already.

'Of course I want to open my own restaurant. Why do you think I've saved up half of my paycheques for the past two years?'

This was also news to me, but, in case Hugh had told me this information at a time I hadn't been listening to him, I kept my mouth shut about it.

'Anyway. What do you have to tell me?'

The pause to discuss Pictionary and his future restaurant seemed to have restored him to his usual spirits. Of course, since I didn't know what had made him angry in the first place, he could suffer a relapse at any time. So I should get in while I had the chance. No waiting for the perfect moment to drop the news, or creating a perfect moment, as I would in a story.

This was all the moment I was going to get.

'I'm pregnant,' I said.

Hugh's reaction was extraordinary. I'd never seen anything like it.

His body jerked back, as if he'd been kicked in the stomach. For a moment the most intense pain crossed his features. He dropped his fork, half-laden with curry, and it clattered on the table.

'Eleanor,' he gasped, and the thought crossed my mind that maybe he was being poisoned by his lunch.

I jumped out of my chair, my hands outstretched to thump him on the back or something, but before I could reach him he stood up. His chair toppled over behind him.

'You fucking idiot.'

His voice was harsh and angrier than I'd ever heard it before, even when he'd been joking. Cold fear seized me, because I didn't know this man across the table from me at all, even though he was wearing the body of my best friend.

'Hugh?' I said.

'Who's the father?'

I looked around Mr Tasty's. There were two men in yellow high-visibility jackets in the corner smoking fags over their bacon sandwiches, and the Thai cook and waitress. All four of them were watching us.

'Hugh, can we—'

'Who's the father, Eleanor?' He'd put his hands on the table and they were so tense that the fingers were white. 'Was it that bloke I heard you with?'

'I don't want to talk about this here, let's—'

'Tell me.'

His face was not the kind of face that you messed with.

'Yes,' I answered.

'Fucking hell,' he muttered roughly and he stalked past me, through the restaurant and out the door, letting it bang behind him.

It took me a few seconds before I could get my head together enough to go to the till and pay for lunch and follow him out on to the street.

He was quite a way down the King's Road already, recognisable from behind by his height and his ferocious gait. I ran after him.

By the time I caught up I was nearly out of breath. 'Hugh,' I gasped, and realised I had no idea what to say to him. All I knew was that I needed him.

'I didn't mean to,' I said weakly.

'I should hope not.' He kept on striding with his long legs and I had to jog to keep up with him.

'Why are you so mad?'

'Because you are without a doubt the stupidest female in the history of the planet. You have heard of condoms, Eleanor? They did give you sex education in school, didn't they? You do know that sex wasn't invented for fun and erotic novels and there's a little thing called reproduction –'

I stopped jogging.

'I know,' I cried. 'I know I was stupid, I know I should have used a condom, you're not telling me anything new here and you're certainly not helping!'

After half a step, he stopped too and whirled to face me.

'You expect me to help you, you go and get yourself pregnant by a man you hardly know, who can't know you, who can't even know who he—' He stopped, as if he were choking. 'And I'm supposed to be the good little friend and pat your hand and tell you everything's going to be okay?'

'Oh, yeah, you're right,' I spat back. 'How dare I get pregnant so your best friend can't hang out with you in the pub any more? God, I might even ask you to change a nappy or two every now and then. What a bloody nightmare. I'm so selfish to go and get myself knocked up by a stranger, I should have thought of *you* first.'

'What do you think I am, Eleanor?' He nearly shouted it, but then he swallowed and lowered his voice. 'What do you think I am?'

'You're my friend and I need you to talk to me about this, not yell at me in the street!'

For a long moment he didn't say anything. I noticed, for the first time, that we were standing more or less exactly in the queue for the number seventeen bus and that people were stepping around us gingerly. I didn't much care. My stomach was rolling and my eyes were watering and all I cared about was that my best friend was acting in a way I didn't understand.

'I don't have anyone else,' I said.

Stranger-Hugh gazed down at me, oblivious of the bus queue.

'Let's go to the Forbury,' he said. He spun around and started walking again.

I tagged along behind him as he rounded the corner and threaded through office blocks to the iron railings of the park. The Forbury was a Victorian pleasure garden, recently restored, inhabited this clear autumn afternoon by women with prams, pensioners, and a small knot of teenage Gothabees with skateboards and cigarettes.

Hugh stalked past the flower beds to an empty bench near the bandstand. He sat on it, his long legs stretched out in front of him and his hands shoved into the pockets of his coat. I sat beside him and heard him take a long breath in and then let it out.

'How are you?' he asked me.

'I've got a bit of morning sickness.'

'I should have stopped this from happening,' he said.

What an odd thing to say. 'How?'

He looked at me and although he looked more like the Hugh I knew, I couldn't read his face at all.

'If I'd—' He ran his hand through his hair. 'I don't know.'

'You could have chained me up in your loft, I guess. That would have kept me out of trouble. Maybe you could do it now?'

Hugh's ghost of a smile made me feel a little better.

'Does he know about the baby? The father?'

'No.'

'What do you want to do?'

I'd been thinking about little other than this for the past ten days. 'I think I need to keep it.'

'You don't need to do anything you don't want to do.'

'Two weeks ago I would've thought that, too.'

Hugh nodded. 'You're thinking about June, aren't you? You wouldn't be here if June hadn't decided to have her baby.'

'See? You can read my mind after all.'

'But you don't have to make the same decision just because of that. You're not June.'

I snorted. 'Well, I'm twelve years older than she was, and better educated, but I seem to have made exactly the same mistake.'

'Oh, El,' Hugh said, and he put his arm around me, and though that didn't cure anything, it made me feel a whole lot better.

'You're not like her at all,' he said.

'Yes, that's what I've always been told.' I sniffed. 'I bet she didn't get a single stretch mark, and as soon as I start showing I'm going to be like a road map.'

He rubbed my back. I gazed into the park, at the statue of a striding lion on a stone pedestal. Reading legend said that the sculptor of that lion had found out, after the lion was erected, that a peculiarity of the lion's pose meant that its left legs had been sculpted so much longer than its right legs that if the lion were real, it would topple over.

Apparently the sculptor, upon finding this out, had committed suicide.

I wondered what it would be like to have such a life-or-death stake in something you had created.

I didn't think I'd kill myself if I found out that it was impossible to have sex with a dozen policemen at once.

I sat up straighter.

'One thing, though,' I said. 'I'm not letting this kid be raised by anybody but me.'

'Good for you.'

'This kid is going to know who he or she is. It's going to know I'm its mother from the beginning. And it'll have to know who its father is, too.'

'Right,' said Hugh. 'Right. When are you going to tell him?'

'I don't know. That's the thing.' I turned on the bench so I was facing away from Reading's lion, symbol of colossal fuck-ups, and looking at Hugh. 'I don't know where he is. I need you to help me find him, Hugh.'

13

'Estelle! How goes the book, darling?'

I don't know why it was, but my agent, Bryce, invariably rang me when I was doing something not even remotely connected with writing. This time I was dripping from the shower, which I'd got out of when I'd heard my phone ring. He also always called me by my pen name, a habit I never quite had the heart to break him of.

'Great,' I said automatically. Uh huh. As if. I hadn't touched my computer since the day I'd discovered that my sister was my mother and I was pregnant. Lucy Sharpe was still shaking the Chancellor's hand, examining his features, and discovering to her surprise that she found him attractive.

'How are you?' I asked in a transparent attempt to stall for time, wrapping my towel closer around me.

'Oh fine, darling, you know how it is; I'm having lunch with Rose O'Shea in a minute! Have you met her?'

'No.' I never met people in the publishing business because I never went to any of the London networking parties. Partly because I didn't want to introduce myself to people who didn't know my books – 'Hello, my name is Eleanor Connor and I write filth' – and partly because I didn't want to disillusion the people who did know my books, by being so ordinary.

Bryce had become my agent quite at random. I'd opened the *Writers' and Artists' Yearbook* in the middle, swirled my finger around and pointed, and landed on his name. I sent him my first manuscript, *A Degree in Carnal Knowledge*, and when he'd asked me a week later to meet him in London, I went to my first and only publishing lunch.

I was impressed by Bryce straight away. Despite his incredibly camp manner, he was built like a rugby-playing Frankenstein monster. He always wore Gaultier and he always managed to look like a thug, even with a rose in his buttonhole. I figured he would confuse editors into paying me money for my writing, and the theory had worked reasonably well, so far.

'So Estelle, tell me the truth now. How goes the book? Have you sorted out that reality problem?'

'I don't know. I mean, are you sure this book is a good idea in the first place? I'm not sure that anybody will believe that politicians are really sexy.'

'You're joking, darling; politicians are sexy as hell! Look at that Gordon Brown, so divinely rumpled!'

'Uh . . . right.'

'And the title – it will be flying off the shelves! So what's your plan of action?'

'Well, I sort of thought I'd completely change the heroine. Make her a little more' – *boring* – 'human. Tone down the dominatrix angle a bit, at the beginning, at least.'

'I think you're right, Estelle, in the first draft you did leap into the leather rather precipitously. Well, that sounds fabulous, I'll leave you to it, any idea how long it will be? A couple of weeks?'

Now let's see. I was working at the pub, growing a baby, and searching for its father.

'Maybe a bit more than that.'

'Fine, well, we were ahead of deadline anyway, let's see how you get on. Must rush or I'll be late for lunch! Toodle-pip, darling, happy writing!'

Toodle-pip. I towelled off my hair, wondering where Bryce got his ideas of reality from anyway.

I was just going back to the bathroom to retrieve my clothes when the phone rang again. I bit my lip, hoping it wasn't Bryce deciding he needed a definite delivery date for the book, and picked it up.

'Hello?'

'Ellie, how are you?'

It was Sheila. She'd been ringing every couple of days since the June-is-my-mother revelation, wanting to talk about it. However, since I had very little desire to talk about that subject or the other major subject taking up most of my brain, I usually cut the conversations short.

'I'm fine,' I said. 'Like normal.' Or as normal as I could be.

I didn't know how she'd react to the news that I was expecting. It was possible she'd take it in her stride; after all, her daughter had given her the same news twenty-six years ago, so it couldn't be too much of a shock when her grand-daughter did the same.

It was also possible that she'd be disappointed. That was what I was dreading. All my life she'd wanted nothing but for me to be different from June (only now did I fully understand why), and this news could be like a kick in the teeth.

Besides, she'd kept a major secret from me all my life. I could do the same right back.

'I've just got out of the shower and I'm all wet,' I added.

'Well, I thought I would ring you and tell you about the new vicar; you knew that Mr Swallow was retiring? The new one is called Richard and he's ever so nice. Lost his wife about ten years ago. As you can imagine, all the ladies in the parish council are watching him closely.'

'Uh huh. Listen, M—' I stopped myself before calling her 'Mum'. 'I'm dripping all over the carpet here and it's freezing.'

'Oh. All right, then. Have you heard from June?'

'No. Still no idea where she went. I'm not missing her much, to tell the truth.'

'I don't imagine you are, Ellie, but don't be too angry, sweetheart. Oh, and there was another reason I rang; I wanted to know if you were going to come home next weekend for the harvest festival? It's going to be quite something this year, Richard has rallied everyone round and—'

'I don't think so. Anyway, I'm shivering now, so I'm going to go. Love you, bye.'

Don't be too angry. That was easy for Sheila to say. She'd had years to be angry with June. And she hadn't heard my bombshell yet.

'You don't remember anybody talking to me at all?'

Jerry scratched his bristly head. 'Which night was this?'

'Saturday the eighteenth of September.'

'Was that the night you got shitfaced behind the bar?'

I felt myself flushing, but I ignored it. I was going to have to own up to a lot more than drinking on the job, eventually. 'Yes.'

'I remember you helping out with Norman.'

I glanced at Horny/Angry, who sat further down the bar nursing his third pint of the evening. 'It wasn't Norman.'

'What did he look like?' Hugh asked. The three of us were sitting at one end of the bar; Paul and Philip were watching football on the telly and Martha and Maud were at their regular table. There were only regulars in the Mouse and Duck tonight, so far.

'You didn't see him either?' I asked Hugh.

I thought back. I'd tried to remember more of that evening, but it was still a blur. I did recall the blonde, though. 'No, you left with that Henrietta woman before he turned up, didn't you?'

'I walked Harriet home, yes,' Hugh said firmly.

'What did the bloke look like?' Jerry repeated Hugh's question.

'He was about medium height, not that tall, medium build, dark hair and eyes. He had a goatee.'

Jerry narrowed his eyes as if he were concentrating. 'Long hair? Tattoos?'

'No, short hair. No tattoos.' None that I could remember, anyway. For all I knew, he had his full name, address and National Insurance number tattooed on his arse, but as I had no recollection of it, it wasn't helping me any.

Jerry was shaking his head. 'I don't think so.'

'He was wearing a blue button-down shirt and a suit; it looked like it could be designer gear. He—' I hesitated, but anything that could jog Jerry's memory would help me. 'He looked a bit like George Michael.'

Hugh let out an incredulous laugh.

'You are joking.'

I shook my head.

Jerry frowned. 'That guy out of Wham!? Didn't he have blond hair, like in a quiff?'

'I meant later George Michael.'

He deepened his frown. 'I can only picture him with blond hair.'

I got up, walked over to the jukebox, and selected the George Michael's greatest hits CD. 'Like this,' I said. Hugh and Jerry came over and peered at the tiny reproduction of the album cover inside the machine.

'You find that attractive?' Hugh asked me. I shot him a look.

Jerry shrugged. 'I don't remember anybody looking like that. Then again, I don't tend to notice blokes.'

'What music are you putting on over there?' Maud called across the room at us.

'We're looking at George Michael, Maud,' Hugh called back.

'Oooh! I love a bit of George Michael,' Maud squealed. She began wiggling her shoulders in a way that might be considered seductive by an octogenarian. 'I want your sex,' she sang in her quavery voice.

'I wouldn't kick George Michael out of bed for eating biscuits,' Martha agreed.

'Ooh no.'

'They say he doesn't like ladies, though.'

'Ooh, what a waste.'

Hugh nudged me. 'Looks like you might have some competition there, El.'

'Shut up, Hugh.'

'Is it true what Martha says, that he doesn't like ladies?' Hugh persisted.

I ignored the question and went over to Martha and

Maud. 'Speaking of George Michael, I wonder if you ladies remember seeing a man who looked like him? A couple of weeks ago, on Saturday the eighteenth of September?'

Both of them became intent, searching their memories. 'On a Saturday night? Was it the karaoke night?' asked Maud.

'Yes.'

'Did he sing?'

'No.'

'Well, I don't remember seeing anybody looking like that, do you, Martha?'

'No, more's the pity.'

'Who you looking for, Eleanor?' called Phil.

'Some bloke who looks like George Michael, imagine!' Martha answered him.

'Late twenties, early thirties, dark hair and eyes, goatee,' I explained. 'He was in here on Saturday the eighteenth of September, came in quite late in the evening, sat over on that stool.' I pointed to where he'd been. 'Do you remember anybody like that?'

Both Paul and Phil thought hard and shook their heads. 'Why are you looking for this bloke?' Paul asked.

I caught Hugh's eye and gave him a warning look. 'Oh, I made a bet with him for twenty pounds,' I lied quickly.

'What about?'

Damn. I hadn't thought through the implications of this lie, nor the fact that Paul, Phil and Jerry were all regular denizens of the bookies' and harboured a deep interest in all things gambling.

Someone scored in the game on the telly and there was a chorus of cheering.

'On the football,' I said. And then immediately kicked

myself because both Paul and Phil chirped up, obviously interested.

'Eleanor? Our Eleanor? Betting on the football? There's hope for you yet! What did you bet?'

'Uh . . .'

Double damn.

'It wasn't the football, really, it was . . . it was . . .'

Oh God, was there any way I could make this lie credible?

'What Eleanor means is that there wasn't any science to it,' Hugh said. 'She just bet that Reading would draw in the next two games.'

'And you want to find this guy to collect your twenty quid?'

'That's right.'

'Wish we could help you.' Paul and Phil went back to their game, chuckling.

What was this guy, invisible? Had nobody noticed him except for me? Surely someone would have observed our flirting – it wasn't as if I did it often.

My eyes travelled to Horny/Angry.

With a sigh, I went to his end of the bar. It was desperate times, after all.

'Hey, Norman,' I said.

'Eleanor,' he said as his eyes fastened inevitably on my tits.

'Did you happen to see a man with a goatee here a few weeks ago? Talking with me? It was Saturday the eighteenth of September,' I added, though I doubted that days or dates meant anything to Horny/Angry. How could you keep track of time when every day followed exactly the same progression of alcohol consumption and mood changes?

'Bastard,' he muttered.

'I couldn't agree more,' said Hugh, who had followed me to this end of the bar.

I ignored him. 'What do you mean by that, Norman? Do you know him?'

'Bastard,' Horny/Angry repeated, and took a belligerent swallow of his pint.

I assessed him, trying to judge how far he'd gone into Angry mode. He was still eyeing up my breasts, which would normally mean he hadn't crossed the line into far-flung rage yet. But maybe he'd expanded his repertoire to be both horny and angry at the same time.

'Are you saying that this specific man is a bastard, Norman, or are you talking about the world in general?'

'Fucking bastard,' Horny/Angry said. He pushed himself off his stool and shuffled towards the men's toilet.

'What do you think that means?' I watched him go.

'At least he has an opinion,' Hugh said, and we went back to the quieter end of the bar. I refreshed his Coke and sighed.

'So much for that,' I said. 'Thanks for covering my arse with the betting story.'

'You'll have to tell people the truth sooner or later.'

'I know. But I'd rather wait till I've got things sorted out more in my own head.' I looked around the Mouse and Duck. 'I guess I'll have to pack this job in.'

The prospect didn't quite give me the rush of joy I might have expected. Change was scary, I guessed, even if the change was leaving a dead-end job in a manky pub, and I'd experienced far too much of it lately.

It didn't make me happy to realise I was someone who feared change, who gained comfort from one day being the same as the next, but there you go. If you couldn't accept unpleasant truths about yourself when you were up the duff from an anonymous one-night stand, when could you?

'So nobody remembers him here,' Hugh said. 'I guess the next step is trying to find this bloke's phone number. What's his last name?'

'If I knew that, I would have tried the phone book before I humiliated myself trying to invent bets about Reading Football team.'

'True. So the man didn't tell you anything about himself, didn't leave his phone number, didn't tell you his last name. What a prince.'

'He might have told me and I just don't remember.'

'It's still not exactly hero behaviour.'

'Hugh, stop slagging him off. This is the father of my child you're talking about. Besides, you're one to talk.'

'I always leave my number, and ring. Always.' Hugh tapped his long fingers on the bar, a complicated, agitated rhythm. 'At least you know his first name.'

'Um.'

Hugh stopped tapping. 'What?'

'I'm, uh, not sure if he's really called George.'

He stared at me. I squirmed underneath his intense brown gaze.

'You just called him George to yourself because you thought he looked like George Michael, didn't you?'

'Maybe.'

'Jesus!' Hugh clapped his hand to his head. 'Could you possibly be even more foolish, Eleanor Connor?'

I thought about warning him again about glass houses, et cetera, but he did have a point there.

'He might really be called George,' I said.

'Right. Okay. So, basically, we have to find this man and all we know about him is that, despite the fact that he resembles a pop star, he can sit in a pub completely unnoticed. And that his first name may or may not be, and probably isn't, George.'

'And he may or may not be a bastard.'

'I think we can safely assume that he is. Do you know anything else about him? Any distinguishing marks, an accent, anything?'

'He gave me multiple orgasms.'

Hugh winced at that. Served him right.

'I don't think that would help us in a general search, though,' I admitted.

It was obviously half-time in the football game; Paul and Phil came to the bar for new pints. 'Hey, El, you really don't have this guy's number and he owes you money?' Paul asked.

I nodded. 'And I could use it, believe me. Keep an eye out for him, will you?'

'I've got a better idea,' said Phil.

'**H**ard to believe you've never been to one of these before,' Hugh said as we shuffled through crowds of people towards our seats.

I surveyed the stadium, which was full of blue and white around me. Twenty-two thousand people, most of whom were wearing Reading colours, thronged the stands.

'Hard to believe that you and Phil thought going to a Reading football game was a plausible idea for finding George,' I said. 'This place is huge and everyone looks exactly the same.'

'Which is exactly why nobody will notice you staring at them.' Hugh dug into the large bag he'd been carrying. During the bus ride from the station to Madejski Stadium he'd refused to tell me what was in it. Now he handed me a Reading scarf wrapped around something hard.

I unwrapped it. 'A pair of binoculars.'

'You can spend the game looking for George. Unless you'd rather watch the football.'

'I'll look for George. Where'd you get binoculars?'

'My auntie Janice thought I should take up bird watching

when I was thirteen. Put on the scarf.'

I wrapped the blue and white scarf around my neck. 'I feel as if I'm being brainwashed.'

We reached our seats, and Paul and Phil, two rows ahead of us, smiled and waved. I'd never seen them so happy, even when they were drinking.

'This is an astoundingly stupid idea,' I said. 'I'm only going along with it because I couldn't think up anything better.'

'It's unbelievable that you've never been to a Reading football game before,' said Hugh. He was wearing the obligatory blue and white striped shirt; he had the height and build to carry off stripes rather well, I noticed before we sat down.

'I didn't know you were so gung ho about it.'

He shrugged. 'I'm not, I just think it's important to support your local team. It's being part of your community.'

'Yeah, but that community is Reading. It's not the world's most wonderful place.'

'It's a place, and we live here, right?'

'Yeah, but we didn't choose to. We studied here, and then stayed because we didn't have anywhere else to go. It's not much of a reason to live somewhere.'

'It's not why I stayed.'

'Why did you stay?'

'I like it. I like how the town centre is all modern shops and then you look up and the buildings are actually all Victorian. I like how my house was probably built for a biscuit-maker's family and had five or six kids living in it.'

'It sounds grim to me.'

'No, it's not grim at all. I like being reminded that things change, however slowly. I mean, look at this place.' Hugh looked around the stadium, and I took it in again. It was pretty impressive, much bigger than I'd expected.

'This is all right,' I said reluctantly. 'But most of Reading seems like such a non-place to me. It's most famous for its railway station and its jail. People are either stuck here or they're passing through.'

'And which one are you?'

'I'm not sure.' God, unless I moved, my child was going to be born in Reading. How depressing.

'We've had some good times here, you and I,' Hugh said. 'And it's the first place I've ever felt at home. My parents pulled me around so much after their divorce that I think this is the longest I've been anywhere. I mean, I've lived everywhere. London, Luton, Leicester, and that's only the middle of the alphabet. Did I tell you about when I was ten and I had to commute to France every weekend because my dad was working there and he was damned if he was going to miss out on a single second of his contact time?'

'That actually sounds fun.'

'It was awful. The only part I liked was the ferry because I got some peace and quiet.' Hugh looked around the stadium again, though he didn't seem to be seeing it. 'Reading is where I became an adult. That's a good thing.'

'I've always been impatient to get the hell out of most places,' I told him. 'I couldn't wait to leave Upper Pepperton.'

'You haven't left Reading yet.'

'I'm too damn lazy. Anyway, what if I went somewhere more exciting like London or Brighton, and it didn't turn out to be more exciting at all? Reading, at least, is safe in its mediocrity.'

Hugh shook his head as if I'd told him the saddest thing in the universe.

'I'd always thought that writers were supposed to be observant people, but you challenge that belief every day.' He tapped the binoculars. 'Maybe these will help.'

I started to ask him what he meant, but at that moment a great cheer erupted from the stands as the game began and it wasn't worth saying anything. Instead, I lifted the binoculars to my eyes and started to search the crowd.

I decided to take the stadium piecemeal, beginning at the left bottom from where I sat and sweeping the stands upwards, then over. There were quite a few people I couldn't see clearly; some of them were too far away, and some were at the wrong angle from where I was sitting. Still, I had a good view of several thousand people, any one of whom could be the guy I'd slept with.

Twenty minutes later my arms were aching from holding up the binoculars and I'd only looked at a sliver of the crowd. There had been two guys with goatees, but one was Asian and one was ginger. When the stadium burst into cheers, presumably because Reading had scored a goal, I was happy to lower the binoculars and peer at the field through them.

Actually, this football thing wasn't too bad. The men really could move, and watching the ball was much more interesting than looking at a bunch of people watching the ball. Plus, now that I took the time to study them, one or two or five of the players had extra-fine legs . . .

'Any luck?' Hugh asked, and then he evidently noticed where I was looking because he nudged me. 'Eleanor, are you looking at the players' arses?'

'Maybe,' I said.

'You're going to be a parent.'

'I write erotica for a living.'

Despite that cast-iron defence I raised the binoculars again and searched the crowd some more. No . . . no goatee . . . too old . . . too young . . . too blond . . . too female . . . too fat . . .

I shifted in my seat and instantly became aware that in my new position my thigh was pressed against Hugh's.

His leg was warm and firm and it had been pressed against me thousands of times before. I'd sat on his lap, I'd watched films on crowded couches and squished into the backs of student Minis with him.

It had never been like this before. It was as if the side of my thigh had a 'turn Eleanor on' button on it and Hugh was hitting it repeatedly. Heat flushed through my body.

I could shift away. Or then again, I could pretend it wasn't happening, and then I wouldn't have to lose this feeling.

I curled my fingers harder around the binoculars and looked and looked because anything was better than meeting Hugh's eyes by mistake and letting him know that I was enjoying rubbing legs with him.

I skimmed over a group of people waving flags, past a dark-haired man with a goatee, and then stopped and went back.

He was standing on his own, wearing a Reading shirt covered by a corduroy jacket, his arms crossed.

The part of my brain that wasn't distracted by Hugh's leg focused on him.

Was it George? It was hard to tell from so far away, and my memory wasn't that clear anyway. Something about the way he was standing seemed familiar.

I pictured him holding a vodka and orange and making a

half-sarcastic toast. I pictured him holding a microphone and singing 'Jesus to a Child'.

Maybe. It could be.

'Hugh.' I tugged on his sleeve, handed him the binoculars. 'Over there, near the exit,' I said, pointing.

'Where?' He swept around, focused in, and I could see when he spotted the man because his shoulders tensed. 'Is it him?'

'I'm not sure. It could be.'

He lowered the binoculars and stuffed them into his knapsack. 'It's nearly half-time. Let's go over to that exit and we'll be able to catch him if he comes out.'

He launched himself out of his seat; I scrambled after him, over the other people in our row and up the steps to the exit. As we hurried through the concrete corridor at the back of the stands I heard another cheer, and then the unmistakable sounds of lots of people on the move.

The double doors to our left opened and fans streamed out, talking, laughing, hitting each other on the back, jostling. I hung back instinctively, not wanting to get trapped in the flow, but Hugh was on the balls of his feet, impatient and strung tighter than a wire.

'There he is,' he said, and again threw himself forward, into the crowd, parting it with his long limbs. I saw him reach out and grab a man by the shoulder of his corduroy jacket.

People streamed between us; I struggled through them, trying to reach Hugh and maybe-George. I saw Hugh's lips moving and knew what he was saying without having to hear his voice: 'I've got a friend who needs to talk to you.'

The man, whose back was to me, shrugged his shoulder violently, trying to shake Hugh off. Hugh held on and I heard him saying my name.

By this time I was close enough to hear the whole conversation. 'Get the hell off me, I'm not talking to anyone,' the man was saying, and I paused, trying to remember whether George's accent had been quite so Reading.

'Listen, mate, you need to talk with her, it's important, she's over there, look.'

Hugh pointed at me and the man glanced in my direction.

Three things happened next, one following the other with swift inevitability.

The man said, 'I don't need to talk to some slapper.'

Hugh curled his pointing hand into a fist and thumped the guy on his jaw.

And I realised that this wasn't George.

'Hugh!' I yelled, but by then it was too late. Not-George snarled and began raining blows on Hugh, who punched back, and I flung myself towards them and tried to grab Hugh and drag him away. Before I could get there three police officers in helmets and fluorescent yellow protective vests were wrestling the two of them to the ground.

'My best friend, the football hooligan.'

'Shut up.' Hugh pressed the bag of frozen peas closer to his eye. I'd nicked the peas from the Mouse and Duck, which stood between the police station and our houses. Fortunately, I'd remembered to order them this week. 'I'm just glad he didn't break my hands or I'd be out of a job.'

'I'm glad the police only decided to caution you. I wonder if it'll be in the *Reading Post* tomorrow.'

Hugh made a disgusted sound and kept walking down the street towards our houses.

'Who knew that you had so much testosterone flowing through your veins,' I said.

'It's not testosterone. It's honour. The man got you pregnant and then called you a slapper.'

'One quibble, O Knight in Shining Armour: that man didn't get me pregnant.'

'And I wish you'd let me know that before I beat the hell out of him.'

I decided it was best to keep quiet about the number of

bruises Hugh had sustained in this encounter.

'Anyway, you don't need to defend my honour,' I said. 'We're in the twenty-first century.'

'Don't worry, I won't bother any more.' We reached his door, he dug in his pocket for the keys, and opened it. 'Anyway, thanks for the peas.' He began to slouch inside.

'Hugh,' I said. He stopped. 'I'm sorry about this.'

He frowned at me, and then nodded. 'That's what I was waiting for. Come in.'

I followed him inside and into his kitchen, the mirror image of mine, except much more full of actual cooking equipment and food. With his free hand he pulled a biscuit tin from the cupboard and plonked it on the table. 'You make tea,' he said, and took the peas off his face.

It shouldn't be true – I had never been attracted to the rough-and-ready sort – but Hugh with bleeding knuckles, a swollen lip and a blackening eye was so sexy that I couldn't do anything for a minute but try to remember to breathe.

And he was angry at me again, and this shouldn't be true either, but God that made him sexy, too.

Was it his anger that had suddenly made him attractive to me? Had I noticed him as an alpha male for the first time? Like a character in one of my books ... maybe Detective Inspector Becker in *Cuffed and Collared*, or The Boss in *Temporary Secretary*.

I'd have to make the Chancellor alpha. Maybe there should be a villain – maybe the selfish, beautiful Minister of Internal Affairs. She could get one of her henchmen to beat up the Chancellor to teach him a lesson for spurning her, but he could fight back.

I licked my lips, imagining for a moment how Hugh's

bruised lip would be hot and coppery-tasting with blood if I were to kiss him.

No. How the *Chancellor*'s lip would be, when *Lucy* kissed him.

'I'm aware that I look like a bloody piece of meat, you don't have to rub it in by staring.'

I snapped back to reality. 'Sorry. Thinking about my book.' I put on the kettle and took a deep breath.

'I really am sorry,' I said. 'I'm taking you for granted. I always take you for granted. I'm glad you tried to beat up a stranger because he looked sort of like a guy who got me pregnant by mistake.'

'Thank you.'

'You have to promise me one thing, though. If we do find the real George, you can't whip out a shotgun and try to make him marry me.'

Hugh paused in the act of putting a generous pile of brownies on a plate. 'Hold on. Are you considering marrying him?'

'Well, if I do, you and your shotgun will be the first to know.'

He didn't look amused.

'No,' I said. 'I don't even know his name.'

'But you're attracted to him.'

'He's attractive.'

'And you must have liked him.'

'I hope I did.' I thought about it. 'Yes, I did.'

'If you find him and he wants to be part of this child's life, and if you like him—'

'I can't even think about that now, Hugh.'

'I'll think about it instead,' he said grimly, and closed the biscuit tin with a snap. 'You want to like him, don't you?'

'It would make things easier.' I took a brownie and bit into it. As usual, it was delicious, but the twin distractions of Hugh annoyed and Hugh sexy stopped me from appreciating it fully.

This was wrong! It was a huge helping of wrong with wrong sauce and extra wrong for dessert. Was it because of my book? Pregnancy hormones? *What?*

'I mean, maybe this is sort of fate,' I said, trying to force my brain into a more acceptable direction. 'George and I will meet again and find out we really like each other, and this pregnancy will bring us together. It might all turn out rather well.'

He shook his head. 'I always thought you lived in a dream world, and now I know it's true. Guys like that aren't the marrying kind. They're the one-night stand kind.'

'And you should know, I suppose.'

'Eleanor, I have never once slept with a woman and then disappeared. Nor got her pregnant.'

'Hugh,' I said, 'I want this baby to have a father. Are you going to argue with me about that?'

'No. But—'

'So help me find him. Nobody at the pub knew him and the football game didn't work, now we need another strategy.'

He picked up a brownie. 'I have no idea how you find someone whose name or address you don't know. Maybe put a personal ad in the paper?'

I shuddered. 'God, how embarrassing. What would it say? "Can the person who had sex with me on the eighteenth of September please get in touch because I'm going to have your child"?'

'I don't really imagine he's the type to read personal ads, either. How about hiring a private detective?'

'Are there private detectives in Reading? That would imply there were shady and exciting things going on here, wouldn't it?'

'I'm sure even Reading has its dark side.'

I considered it. 'No. It's too weird. It involves telling my life history to a total stranger, and paying him for it. I'd rather try everything else first. How about getting Jerry to have an eighties pop-star lookalike competition to see if he turns up?'

'And you think hiring a private detective is weird.'

'It would be easier if someone knew him,' I said. 'I mean, people can't just appear and then disappear, can they?'

'June seems to do quite a good job at it.' He finished his brownie and took another. 'With your luck the two of them are shacked up together somewhere hot and sunny.'

The image of June and George getting cosy in a deck chair by a pool swam before my eyes. The picture niggled something in the back of my brain that didn't quite feel like jealousy.

'Wait a second,' I said slowly. 'June . . . June said something one day, that she knew one person in Reading and he looked like George Michael.' I widened my eyes and looked at Hugh. 'She does know George. I can't believe I forgot.'

The fact had probably been shoved aside by her revelation that she was my mother, closely followed by my discovering my own impending motherhood.

'Okay, so that means all we have to do is to find June.'

'You make it sound so easy.'

'Well, at least we know her name.'

'We also know that June is a professional at disappearing. She used to do it for months at a time when I was growing up. It drove Mu— Sheila wild.'

I sighed. When she'd disappeared she hadn't only been abandoning the family home. She'd been abandoning her child, as well. Me.

'I'll ring Sheila and ask if she knows anything,' I said, 'though I doubt she will. Did June say anything to you about where she was going?'

'No, she didn't say anything about that.'

Of course, June and Hugh had been too busy getting busy to talk.

I stood up. 'I'll go call and take another look around my house to see if she left anything that might give me a clue.'

'Okay,' Hugh said and he rose to walk me to the door. He always did that, even though the location of the front door was obvious, doubly so because I lived in an identical house to his. It was one of his little politenesses, probably one of the many ways he charmed people.

Because it was charming.

'I'll see you later,' he said, and I stood next to him in the doorway and noticed he had a small crumb of brownie on his upper lip. Just on the curve of it, on the left side, the side that wasn't split.

I lifted my hand and then put it down. Writer's imagination, hormones, whatever: my fingers tingled with wanting to touch him.

Hugh won't notice if I brush it off, I thought. *It's the sort of thing I've done a hundred times before and he never noticed it because I never noticed it. And he won't know that this time, it's different.*

I lifted my hand again. With the tip of my finger I stroked the crumb off his lip. His skin was warm and soft. I could feel his breath on my finger.

The crumb stuck to my finger and without thinking I did

what I wanted to, which was put it in my own mouth. The whole action, the whole idea, was so erotic that I didn't taste the brownie crumb. I tasted Hugh.

For a moment his brown eyes met mine, and of course it was accidental, but for that split second I didn't only taste Hugh with my mouth, I tasted him with my entire body.

I dropped my gaze.

'Okay well, see you later, take care of that eye.' I hurried out of his house and down the street and didn't look back to see if he was watching me.

I needed air. Lots and lots and lots of air, and preferably also a brain transplant. If I kept on this way Hugh was going to notice that something was up and things were going to become awkward.

My mobile rang and I answered it, grateful for the distraction from my lust, till I saw Sheila's number.

'Hi.'

'Eleanor? How are you?'

I'm pregnant, I didn't say. Again.

'I'm fine. How are you?'

'Oh, the usual, the whole cake-sale issue has blown up again, this time it's Mrs Coady on some sort of gluten-free high horse, but Richard says—'

'Who's Richard?'

There was a moment of silence, during which I could picture Sheila's expression perfectly. 'Don't you remember, the new vicar? I told you—'

'Oh yeah,' I said, as if I had no more pressing things on my mind than Upper Pepperton's new vicar. 'Sorry. I thought he was called Roger.'

'Oh goodness no. Imagine. Roger the vicar.'

It was a crack Stanley would have made, and Sheila and

I both laughed. For a split second I wondered why I was surprised about laughing and then I remembered I was angry with Sheila and keeping secrets from her.

'I was just going to call you,' I said. 'I was wondering if you'd heard from June.'

'I was going to ask you that!' She laughed again, but this time there was a stiffness to it. I thought of asking her what was wrong, but it occurred to me that she might be uncomfortable because I was being uncomfortable, and if I asked her questions she'd start asking me them, too.

'No,' I said, 'but I'm trying to get in touch with her. Do you know where she's gone? She, uh, left something of hers behind.'

As I said it the guilt dropped on me. Not only had I gone out and got pregnant like June, now I was flat-out lying to Sheila. Like June.

I was more like June than I'd ever thought. Pity it was only in the bad ways.

'I don't,' Sheila said. 'In fact, there have been several young men who've come round asking where she is. Not that I would ever tell them. And Winnie next door told me she saw someone lurking around the house on Friday when I was at my book club.'

'Did any of them have a beard?'

'Well, yes. Some of them are quite scruffy.'

'Scruffy' didn't describe George. My hopes sank. 'Do you have any of her old phone numbers? Maybe someone there knows where she's gone.' I ducked into a stationer's shop and picked up a pad and pen.

Sheila obligingly went through her address book and gave me several phone numbers and addresses, which I scribbled down in the queue for the till. June had moved around a lot in the past few years, especially considering that she probably hadn't given her mother most of her details.

'Thanks, Mum,' I said, without thinking, after she'd given me the numbers, and then I stopped. 'I mean, Sheila.'

There was a silence on the other end, and then Sheila said, 'I'm still your mum, Eleanor.'

I remembered it all: the cuddles at night, the scrapes kissed better, the meals on the table. The arguments behind closed doors meant to protect me. The teenage fantasies about being adopted, about coming from another, better, more exciting family, a family that understood me. The security blanket she had washed and stitched and washed till I was twelve years old.

She was the only model of motherhood I had; the only model I could follow.

There were no doubts about it: she was going to be disappointed in me.

'I know,' I said. 'Thanks. I'll ring you if I find June.'

I hung up.

16

*T*he Chancellor's brown eyes gleamed at Lucy with a heat greater than the candles that lit the room, greater than the flames that roared in the fireplace.

All her dreams, all her desires were coming to fruition at last.

'Lucy,' he said, 'I want you.'

His beautiful, scarred mouth smiled, and even in the flickering candlelight she could see the shadow of the bruise that blackened his eye. Wounds gained in her defence, for her pleasure.

She lay on her bed, transfixed by the sight of his tall, lanky body.

Slowly, he removed his shirt, his chest appearing inch by inch as he undid his buttons. His skin was golden in the firelight. A sensation grew inside her inexorably, rising from her stomach up into her throat as he divested himself of his trousers and his pants and approached her, gloriously naked, every bone and muscle and inch of skin perfect. His erection, huge, thick and hot, swayed towards her.

Lucy's hands flew to her throat.

'Jesus Christ, will you get the hell away from me with that thing before I throw up,' she gagged, and only just had time to reach the bin before she puked all over her satin lingerie.

I groaned and pushed the keyboard away from me. I tried to take a sip of the ice-cold water that was the only thing I could stand the thought of right now, but the glass suddenly seemed to have a sickening, evil, hitherto-unknown smell of its own.

The mere idea of sex made me shudder. All that touching, and sweating, and panting, and heaving. All that hair and liquid. And why?

So it could get you pregnant and make you feel worse than you'd ever felt in your life.

I stood up and wandered downstairs. It was nine o'clock on a Friday night, a rare weekend night off from my pub job, and although over the past few days I'd been so tired that I could practically sleep standing up, right now I felt too queasy to sleep. I flicked on the television and surfed through the channels, but the movement and the light on the screen made me feel even sicker.

I pushed on my shoes and went next door, on the off chance.

'Hugh,' I said when he opened the door, 'I don't know why they call it morning sickness because it's with me all the bloody time.'

He stepped aside and I came in. The scent of baking filled my nostrils and therefore my being: sweet and gingery. My stomach did a tentative roll, decided it actually quite liked the smell of ginger, and settled back down for now.

'I thought you'd be out,' I said.

'I decided to stay in and make biscuits.' He watched as I dropped heavily on to his couch. Two weeks had healed his face from his encounter with not-George, though the framed clipping from the *Post* on his coffee table commemorated the event.

I spotted something else on his coffee table. 'Your phone's off the hook.'

'Oh is it?' He went into the kitchen, feigning non-chalance, and came back with a plate of ginger biscuits. 'Want one of these?'

I took one and toyed with it till my stomach could decide whether it wanted one or not. 'You're in on a Friday night alone with the phone off the hook?'

'I'm not alone any more.' He joined me on the couch and ate a biscuit. 'Not bad. So how long is the morning sickness going to last?'

'They say it ends after the first trimester, so I've got three weeks to go.' The word 'trimester' felt weird in my mouth. I'd never said it before. I'd only just learned it from a pregnancy-for-idiots guidebook I'd smuggled into my house. I'd been reading it in small spurts, when I felt brave. Mostly it sat under my bed, three hundred pages of mystery and barely formed dread in a yellow cover.

'What does the midwife say?'

'I can't remember. I was too freaked out when I saw her. The whole visit is a blur.'

Hugh frowned. 'Listen, I said I'd be happy to come along with you. I'd be another pair of ears, at least.'

I shook my head. Like 'trimester', 'midwife' was a new word for me, and when I'd made the appointment I'd expected it to be with a large, bosomy woman in her fifties, with iron-grey hair and apple cheeks. That's what the title implied: something like a fishwife crossed with the Wife of Bath. Imagine my surprise when Maggie the midwife turned out to be Scottish, slender, strawberry blonde, and freckled in an intensely cute way. Her ring-less left hand told me that whatever her profession, she wasn't a wife at all.

I could imagine what would happen if Hugh came along to one of my appointments: he'd be flirting with her within five minutes while I sat there like a nauseated nonentity. Not the kind of antenatal care I wanted.

I tried the ginger biscuit. It was nice.

'So who are the biscuits for?' I asked. 'A blonde or a redhead?'

Hugh raised his eyebrows and said nothing.

'Oh, I forgot, you've branched out into brunettes.' I ate the rest of it.

'Do you like the biscuits?'

'They're not bad. I think I read something about ginger helping nausea, you know.' I reached for another. 'Speaking of brunettes, this afternoon I finally got through to the last number on the list Sheila gave me. It was a place June lived two years ago. They haven't heard from her and they want to talk to her about a telephone bill. In fact, every single person I've rung has said June owes them money. I hope you didn't lend her any.'

'No.'

He settled back on the couch beside me, turned on the telly, and flicked through the channels. The activity didn't make me feel ill this time. In fact, I felt a whole lot better – in my stomach, at least.

'Why's your phone off the hook?' I asked. 'Are you trying to avoid one of your women? Or several of them?'

He kept on flicking channels. 'I thought you were spending tonight doing rewrites on *Throbbing Member.*'

'Do you know how impossible it is to write sex scenes when all you want to do is throw up?'

'I can imagine.'

'There might be some people out there who find vomit sexy, but I just don't.'

'I wholeheartedly agree.' He seemed to settle on a programme set in a hospital emergency room, then thought better of it and flicked onwards.

'The thing is,' I said, 'what if I can never write sex again? What if my hormones have permanently changed and my writing career is gone?'

I didn't know where that had come from; it had flowed out of my mouth of its own accord, as if my brain were spitting out its own sick thoughts.

But it was exactly what I'd been worried about. My nausea began to gnaw at me again.

Hugh turned the sound off the television.

'I mean, I could always write something else, but I don't know that I'd be any good at it. And what if I can't write at all once the baby comes? Babies need lots of care and attention and time. How am I going to be able to concentrate?'

Hugh turned the television off.

'And if I can't write, what am I going to do for money? Am I going to end up with the baby sleeping in the back room in the Mouse and Duck while I pull pints and my life goes nowhere? And what if I don't even *like* the baby?'

By now my throat was sore, too, as if I had been violently ill. I felt tears in my eyes and Hugh was looking at me, but I looked at the blank television screen instead.

'My whole life is going to change,' I said, and although I'd acknowledged this before, it was as if I'd never fully realised it till now. 'And I wanted my life to change, but I'm not sure I wanted it to change like this.'

Hugh put his arm around my shoulders and pulled me gently towards him. I leaned sideways and let myself be surrounded by his firm chest, his warm arms, his heartbeat and his breath. He stroked my hair back from my face and I took in a deep, hitching breath and then let out the worry, the fear, the sick-making anxiety in an overflow of tears. They dripped on to his cotton shirt and he didn't move, only held me and didn't say a thing, gave me no answers.

I woke up to the scent of ginger, tears and Hugh. Tentatively I moved my head. I was still leaning against Hugh's chest, but his shirt had dried under my cheek. We were stretched out on the couch; my head was tucked underneath his arm, using him as a pillow. He was half turned towards me and our bodies pressed close together all down their length. He was breathing slowly but his heartbeat under my ear was rapid.

I opened my eyes. It was daylight, which meant that I'd slept here with Hugh all night. The warmth of his body spread through me like a drug and I breathed him in again, so familiar and yet so strange.

When I looked up at his face he was looking down at me.

It was quiet; there was only the sound of our breathing and the soft rustle of our clothes. I'm not sure how it happened because I obviously was not thinking. But I stretched my face up towards his and he bent his face towards mine, or at least it seemed as if he did, and suddenly our lips were touching each other.

It felt as if warm honey were being poured all over me, all through me, sweet and sexy. Then four words forced themselves into my brain with all the comfort of a wailing alarm clock.

I am kissing Hugh.

I pushed myself upright, away from his lips, though my body was still entangled with his so I couldn't get far. My thigh was between both of his and my dirty mind immediately thought about whether he had an erection, because that would mean that he was as turned on as I was – but then again, lots of men had erections automatically in the morning, didn't they, and someone as oversexed as Hugh would probably have an erection after spending the night snuggled up with any female. It didn't have to be because he was turned on by me.

And then what if he didn't have an erection?

I moved my leg down so I wouldn't be able to tell and closed my eyes so I wouldn't be tempted to look. Then, as a wave of panic came over me, I managed to get myself off the couch and on to my two feet.

'Eleanor,' Hugh was saying, but I was at the door already.

'Sorry,' I said. 'That was a mistake. Sorry. I have to go home now because I feel sick again, bye.'

I slammed his door and bolted. I didn't stop walking till I reached the bridge over the canal that led to Reading town centre and I realised I wasn't wearing shoes, only thick socks. My heart was beating like crazy and I felt dizzy.

I dug in my jeans pocket and found a two-pound coin and some small change. What I really needed was a shot of whisky, but more prudently I went into the nearest Starbucks and bought a tall hot chocolate with marsh-mallows. I sat at an outside table despite the chill and tried to look nonchalant to the early shoppers walking by, staring at the posters outside the cinema across from me as if all I cared about was which movie I should see after I finished my drink and maybe put on some shoes.

In reality I was going over those split seconds again and again in my head. I'd reached my head up – I'd wanted to kiss him – and he'd bent his head down. No, he hadn't, I'd reached up all the way myself. And I thought he'd kissed me back, but that was ... what? Illusion, reflex, surprise, kindness?

I tried to drink more hot chocolate, discovered it was gone, and crushed the paper cup in my hands. It started to rain. Of course. I pulled off my socks, stuffed them in my pocket, and headed back home, because I had nowhere else to go at nine in the morning on a Saturday with no shoes. Nobody I knew would even be up yet. Except for Hugh.

'Damn,' I said, and it was so appropriate for what I felt that I said it again, and again; a constant little stream of 'damn damn's all the way back to my terraced house.

It was a measure of how shaken I was that when I got in, it took a moment or two for me to notice that my house wasn't how I'd left it.

The cushions on my couch were scattered and slit, the magazines and books had been pulled off the shelves.

During the night, as I slept in Hugh's arms, destined to make a fool of myself when I woke up, someone had been in my house.

17

You know those heroines in books who are too stupid to live? The ones who go into dark cellars when it's clear that a psycho killer is lurking there, or who think they're too fat and ugly despite men dropping at their feet, or who try to solve a kidnapping case themselves without getting the police involved?

I proved without doubt that I was actually one of those, because instead of immediately picking up the phone and dialling 999, I ran upstairs to my office. My normally pristine, clean, ironically virginal office where I'd reinstated all my writing after June's departure.

I'd had a break-in two years before, when Simon, the punk kid who lived four doors down, had robbed my house to get heroin money (God, I loved Reading), and he'd taken my computer, which had a manuscript on it. A manuscript I'd nearly finished, which was due in two weeks' time, and which I hadn't printed out or saved anywhere else. Fortunately, the police had caught Simon before he had a chance to sell my computer, and I'd got the manuscript back.

Since then I'd had recurring nightmares of it happening

again, and although I did back up my work now on a flash drive, that flash drive was completely portable, brand new, and worth a good tenner for any junkie who wanted to steal it and flog it.

'Simon?' I yelled, hammering up the stairs with no concern for my personal safety. I flung myself into my office and stopped short.

There was someone in there, but it wasn't weedy junkie neighbour Simon. This man was tall and broad with white-man's dreadlocks and a dark well-cut suit. Seeing him reminded me of Christmas and brussels sprouts.

'Jojo?' I gasped.

'Elizabeth,' he said grimly. 'Just the person I wanted to see.'

I noticed that his nose was bent at a different angle to how it had been the last time I'd seen him. The fact was both reassuring and profoundly disturbing. Reassuring in that I knew he'd been permanently injured by someone as sylph-like as June; disturbing in that it reminded me of his propensity for violence against even sylphs.

'My name isn't Elizabeth,' I said, 'it's Eleanor.'

'Whatever.' He waved a well-manicured, paw-like hand in dismissal. 'You're June's sister, right?'

'Well, actually,' I started, and then thought the better of telling a criminal about my convoluted family history. Rather foolishly, I took a more aggressive approach. 'What the hell are you doing in my house?'

He took a step towards me. He was a very large man.

'Where's your sister?' he asked.

'I don't know.'

His big face made it clear he didn't believe me. 'She was here, wasn't she?'

'I'm not telling you that.'

'You don't need to.' He held up the hand I hadn't seen yet, and I saw he was holding a shiny black high-heeled boot. 'I found this under your settee, and I'd know it anywhere.'

Huh. I guessed I hadn't done such a good job cleaning in here. 'What's your point?'

'My point is, you're going to tell me where June has gone.'

'I told you, I don't know where she is. Now go away, because I'm calling the police.'

Jojo seemed not at all alarmed at the idea. He dropped the boot and made for my computer. My shiny, white, state-of-the-art computer bought with royalty money and containing every word I'd written for publication for the past six months. He picked it up.

'What are you doing?' I squealed.

'I'm taking your computer so I can read the messages you've had from June.'

'I haven't had any messages from June!'

Jojo reached down for the plug, my computer under his beefy arm. I grabbed a white ceramic lamp from the shelf next to me and held it up like a club.

'Don't you dare take that computer,' I said in my most threatening voice, brandishing the lamp.

Could I brain someone with a lamp? Would it make any difference to Jojo's thick skull if I did? All I knew was that June had broken his nose, so it was doable. The idea of it made me feel sick.

Jojo paused. He looked at me and he looked at the lamp. He appeared unpleasantly amused by the situation. But he put my computer back down on my desk.

'All right,' he said. 'I won't take your computer.'

'Good.' It came out more of a squeak than a statement, but I held the lamp higher. 'Now get the hell out of my house.'

For a big guy, he moved very fast. I didn't even really see him do it; I felt the lamp snatched from my hand and then there it was in his.

For the first time, this felt real.

What if he hurts the baby? I thought, and the greatest fear I had ever experienced grabbed my stomach and lungs with claws of cold. For a moment I couldn't breathe, I couldn't move, I couldn't think.

'Why don't you open up your emails for me and let me take a look,' he said, his voice calm and somehow even more threatening for it.

I did as he asked, thinking all the time about the baby. I didn't care if having it was going to change my life. It was the most precious thing in the entire universe and if something happened to it I would die.

Jojo stood behind me being large and strong and dangerous. Of course there were no messages from June – she'd never emailed me in her life – but he made me go through my inbox for the past several months, and my address book. When he was satisfied that there was nothing there from her, he pulled my chair back.

'We're going downstairs,' he said. He took me by the arm and manoeuvred me out of the room. The stairway was too narrow for us both to fit, so he walked me down ahead of him, my arm twisted behind my back.

My mind was fuzzy with fear. Surely once he realised that I didn't know where June was, he'd go away without bothering to hurt me, right?

Unless, of course, he thought I was lying about not knowing. I remembered there was a list of phone numbers in a kitchen drawer, headed by JUNE in big red letters.

Jojo pushed me towards the kitchen, away from the living room and the telephone and the main escape route from the house. My back door was locked, but if I were much closer to it than he was, I could unlock it and run out into the back garden before he could catch me. But then what? My back garden was fenced in on all sides.

In the kitchen I felt a rush of relief as I spotted my mobile phone, which was on the counter near the kettle where I must have left it the afternoon before. I tried to reach my hand towards it without being obvious, but once again Jojo was surprisingly fast. He snatched it and dropped it into the pocket of his well-cut overcoat. Then he pushed me into a chair.

'You might as well sit down,' he said, 'because I'm not going anywhere till you tell me where your sister is.'

'Then you might as well sit down too – I don't know where she is, so you're going to be here for a very long time.' I would have been proud of my bravado, if my voice hadn't been shaking all over the place. 'Why are you after her, anyway? I thought you two broke up after she broke your nose.'

Jojo's face got darker and more dangerous. I guessed it was a bad idea to remind him about his nose. I shrank back in my chair.

'If you know about my nose, you know about the money,' Jojo growled, and he put his two paw-hands on the table in front of me and leaned so he was right in my face. He smelled of cologne and onions. 'Fifty fucking grand of my money. I'm sick of your bullshit, now tell me where she is.'

The baby, the baby, I loved the baby and I had to say something to stop him from hurting it.

'If you know June, you know that she is fully capable of staying here and not telling me anything about what she'd done or where she was going,' I said. 'If she had fifty grand, I didn't know about it. She didn't even give me money for groceries.'

Jojo straightened up and stared into my eyes. I stared back, as steadily as I could with my heart beating like a jackhammer and my guts churning liquid. At last, he stepped back.

'When I find June, she is going to pay,' he told me, 'and if I find out you've been lying to me, so will you. I'll be watching you.'

He swiped the kettle off the counter for good measure and as it clattered to the floor, he stomped out of the house.

'Yeah, I can *write* villains scarier than you,' I shot after him as soon as I knew he couldn't hear me. When I tried to walk to the telephone, my legs were shaking so badly I had to hold on to the table so I wouldn't fall down.

I took several breaths, waited till I was calmer, then opened my kitchen drawer, took out the list of June's former phone numbers, tore it into very, very little bits, and stuffed it into the bottom of the bin.

Then I went to the phone. I had dialled half of Hugh's number before I realised what I was doing and stopped myself.

What was I doing? I couldn't phone Hugh. I had just made a fool of myself by kissing him. The last thing I needed to do was get all girly and call him to help me after a big mean man had broken into my house.

I disconnected and dialled the police instead.

18

'Two gin and tonics please, Eleanor dear.'
I didn't know why Martha and Maud bothered to tell me what they wanted to drink; they had the same thing every single night and I always started pouring the gin the minute they walked in the door. But apparently they gained some comfort from the ritual of pretending that one day, they might drink something different.

When I put the glasses on the bar Martha was shaking her head and sucking her teeth. 'A break-in. You must have been scared out of your wits.'

Martha was the taller of the two old ladies. She had grey hair in a permanent; Maud had white hair cut very short. Martha usually wore coordinated polyester trousers and tops in bright colours, and costume jewellery, while Maud favoured beige and subtly flowered prints. Despite their different appearances, their mannerisms were so similar, (probably from years of drinking the same drink together every night), that when I had started working at the Mouse and Duck it had taken me months to be able to tell them apart.

I was quite sure I hadn't told them, or anyone else, about the morning's break-in. 'How do you know about that, Martha?'

'Oh, my grandson Todd is in the Thames Valley Police. He came round for lunch. He does every Saturday.' She sucked her teeth again. 'Did they take much, love?'

'Only my mobile phone.' And one of June's boots, but that didn't seem worth mentioning. 'Does your grandson always tell you about Reading's crime at lunchtime?'

'Oh, no, he knows I know you,' Martha said. 'I'm always talking about our Eleanor.'

Martha talked about me at home? What on earth would she find to say?

'Well, it's nice of you to be concerned.'

Maud, who had been exchanging some words with Jerry at the other end of the bar, trotted over. From her expression I could tell that she had been discussing my break-in with Jerry.

'You must have been frightened to bits, love, finding a strange man in your house like that,' she said to me, 'and especially with you in your condition, you poor thing.' She patted my hand with her soft old lady's hand.

I stared at her. I most definitely hadn't mentioned the fact that I was pregnant. 'How do you—'

She shook her head. 'Don't you worry about a thing, we'll all look after you here, and Martha's Todd says he's unlikely to come back. Is it true it was a friend of your sister's?'

Well, at least they didn't know that June was my mother. 'Her ex,' I told them, figuring it was pointless to conceal anything about this as Todd knew all. 'He reckons she took some money from him.'

They both shook their heads and sucked their teeth and

made general elderly signs of outrage and disapproval with the modern world. Then Martha patted my hand as Maud had done and said, 'Well, you take care of yourself; you don't want any more sudden shocks when you're in the family way', and they went to their usual table.

My suspicions immediately went to Hugh, but I dismissed them. He hadn't told Martha and Maud. In seven years he had never once let slip any of my secrets. He could also be very close about his own life when he chose.

Granted, my being pregnant was probably one of the biggest secrets ever. But old ladies had a sort of sixth sense for detecting pregnancy, didn't they?

I wandered over. 'Can I ask a question?'

'Certainly, dear.'

'How did you two know I'm pregnant?'

'Your hips,' said Maud.

'Your face,' said Martha.

'Oh. Okay,' I said, and went back to the bar none the wiser.

The door opened and Hugh came in. He'd obviously come straight from work because although he wore jeans and a jacket instead of chef whites, he had a streak of flour up one side of his face and through his dark hair. My heart leapt at the sight of him and for a split second our eyes met before I turned away and bent down to rearrange the crisps. I took quite a while debating whether nacho cheese Doritos should be housed next to the cheese and onion crisps because they shared a cheese factor, or whether they should be between Monster Munch and pork scratchings because of the alphabetical order. I decided on alphabetical order, but then I had to decide whether smoky bacon flavour crisps should be under 's' or 'b'.

When I straightened up, he was standing at the bar. I couldn't help it; my gaze went straight to his lips and I remembered in exquisite, torturous detail how it had felt to have him kissing me.

'What's this Jerry tells me about a break-in?' he demanded.

I spied a stray bag of Doritos amongst the cheese and onion and restored it to its rightful position. 'Oh, it was fine, it was June's ex looking for her.'

'June's violent ex?'

'He wasn't violent. We had a chat and he went away.'

'And when did this happen?'

'Just after –' *we snogged*, I thought, and, to my dismay, felt myself blushing. 'Just after I left your place this morning.'

He ran his hand through his hair in the same place where the flour streak was; that was evidently how it had got there in the first place. 'Why didn't you tell me?'

I shrugged. 'Oh, you know, it turned out fine, and I had the police there anyway.'

I couldn't meet his eyes.

'Eleanor, last time the neighbours' cat came in and pissed on your curtains you called me within three minutes.'

'It was nothing. Everything's fine. Do you want a Coke, or a pint?'

He reached over the bar, grabbed my arm, and pulled me towards him. 'Is it because we kissed?' he asked, low enough so the rest of the pub couldn't hear.

'No!' I laughed nervously. 'No, of course not, that was a mistake.'

Hugh's face looked like thunder. It was nearly close enough to kiss me again, a fact I did my best to ignore.

'Yes, evidently it was,' he said.

'I mean, we were half asleep and you obviously thought I was someone else, and I obviously thought you were—'

'I don't want to talk about it.' He let me go and straightened up to his full height. 'Let's never talk about it again. I'll have a pint.'

'Sure.' I turned and began to pour it.

This was a good thing, I told myself. Hugh regretted kissing me as much as I regretted kissing him, which meant we were on the same level, and we could go back to being friends and I could ignore my attraction to him.

And yet a little bit of me – okay, a lot of me – felt disappointed.

Surely if he liked kissing me, even if he hadn't meant to, he wouldn't be so quick to dismiss the whole thing? Surely he'd ask to kiss me again? I mean, Hugh really liked kissing girls, and he hadn't been abstemious about kissing them up till now, when I was the girl.

He must be so spectacularly unattracted to me that the idea was repulsive. I put his pint on the bar, spilling quite a bit of it off the top. Hugh didn't comment; he pushed over the money and took a long drink.

I heard a hammering sound from the other side of the pub. Grateful that something was interrupting the silence between me and Hugh, I looked over to see Jerry hanging a sign next to the other end of the bar. Hand-lettered on white cardboard was the big black command NO SMOKING. Jerry finished nailing the sign to the wall and came over to where Hugh and I were standing. He produced another sign and some nails, and began to ruin the wall over here, too.

'Jerry, this place isn't no smoking,' I said. 'What are you doing?'

He grinned at me. 'Figure it might as well start being. Smoke isn't good for the baby, is it?'

I was dumbfounded. 'But – you said that when they passed the no-smoking law it would be over your dead body.'

'Hey, I got to take care of my own, haven't I? Besides, it might bring in that better class of punter you're always on about.' He finished hanging the sign and went to pound another one in the wall near the entrance. On the way he stopped to speak to two men drinking at a table; they looked disgruntled, but stubbed out their fags.

'News travels fast around here,' I said.

Hugh swallowed half his pint in one. 'Just because you don't want to be connected to anyone in this place doesn't mean that they aren't connected to you.'

He dropped a coin on the bar, reached past me with his long arm to grab one of the alphabetically arranged packets of crisps, and went to join Martha and Maud at their table.

Three to Six Months:
Hormones

*L*ucy Sharpe threw herself down on her chaste single bed. What was the good of passion beyond your wildest dreams if it wasn't going to last?

Her night with the Chancellor had been the most intense, most sensual experience of her life. She'd been thrilled when, afterwards, he'd invited her to be his date at the most glittering, star-studded charity ball of the season. And yet once they'd got there, he'd spent the evening flirting with a succession of women, barely sparing her a glance.

When the ball was over, and they were standing on her doorstep, Lucy tried to appear as seductive as possible, pouting and fluttering her eyelashes. But he left her with a friendly kiss on the cheek.

'What am I doing wrong?' she wailed aloud. The plain walls and dark windows of her one-bedroom flat didn't answer her.

He was out of her league – an important figure in government, while she was a lowly P.A. And he was an accomplished, inventive lover. When they'd been in bed together, Lucy had felt like a blushing virgin: stammering, knock-kneed, uncertain.

But he'd wanted her once. What was stopping him from wanting her again?

Lucy pulled herself to her feet and looked at herself in the full-length mirror that was the only decoration in her bedroom. She wasn't ugly. Her dark hair, though not elaborately styled, was glossy and thick. She wasn't incredibly slim; next to the sylph-like celebrity women at the ball she'd felt clunky and big. But she did have good breasts.

She had to admit, though, that this black dress she was wearing – her only formal gown, bought years ago for a university ball – didn't make the most of her assets. Her breasts, which should have been enticingly spilling out the front, were harnessed by a too-tight bodice. And the colour made her look washed out.

Lucy checked her watch, and then she went to her wardrobe, pulling out a low-cut, bright red top. She chose her best bra and knickers, a short skirt, and the high, high-heeled boots she'd bought on a whim the week before.

If she got a taxi, she could be at the Chancellor's home in twenty minutes. And she'd see if she couldn't make him notice her after all.

I snorted. Yeah, right. Lucy was obviously setting herself up for a horrible, humiliating fall.

I walked away from my keyboard and went into my bedroom. Lucy was supposed to be like me, but she was horribly naïve and pathetic. In contrast with her silly optimism, I knew for a fact that if I turned up on Hugh's doorstep in nothing but cling film, he wouldn't lay a finger on me. He'd compare me to a supermarket chicken and invite me in for some brownies.

My bedroom walls weren't as bare as Lucy's, and my

chaste-ish bed was double, not single. But I did have a full-length mirror, and it showed me that, like Lucy, I needed a haircut. I turned sideways and looked at myself.

I'd lost weight in my first trimester because of sickness, but over the past few weeks I'd started to put it back on again. Still, I wasn't pregnant enough to look definitely pregnant. I looked fat. My normal clothes didn't fit me, and the maternity clothes I'd tried on in the shops looked enormous.

My breasts, however, were fantastic. They strained against the buttons of all my blouses and threatened to pop open my bras till I'd invested in new larger-sized models.

I pulled up my T-shirt and admired myself in the mirror. Now I knew why people who got implants were so happy. It was wonderful to be visited by the Tit Fairy.

Of course, Hugh hadn't noticed them at all.

For nearly six weeks, it had been just as we'd agreed: we'd forgotten all about the kiss and carried on as normal.

Except it wasn't normal. I couldn't stop thinking about him.

When we were sitting around watching television on his couch, I wanted to stretch out with him as we'd done before, every part of my body touching every part of him. When we were walking down the street, my hands itched to hold his. One time we were eating spaghetti and I'd had this whole fantasy about us sucking on the same strand of pasta and ending up kissing, like those two dogs in the Disney movie, *Lady and the Tramp*.

Maybe Lucy wasn't more pathetic than I was after all.

There was one difference, at least: unlike the Chancellor, Hugh wasn't flirting with a succession of beautiful women in front of me. He hadn't brought a single girl into the Mouse and Duck for weeks. No, months.

In fact, June had been the last woman I'd seen him with. Maybe she'd spoiled him for anybody else.

More likely, he was conducting his love life out of my vision and earshot. Which meant that he was trying not to upset me. Which was even worse than if he'd flaunted his love life in front of me, because it meant that he thought I would be bothered by seeing him with other women.

Which probably meant that he was thinking about the kiss as much as I was, except that he was thinking about it in an 'Eleanor-has-gone-off-the-rails' sort of way.

Of course, that was the same way I was thinking about it, but I'd prefer it if he didn't share my diagnosis.

I sighed noisily and pulled my T-shirt off. I grabbed a red, low-cut top and put it on. It made my breasts even more amazing.

At least Horny/Angry would appreciate them.

I went back to my keyboard and Lucy Sharpe. It was a lot easier to write sex scenes now that the morning sickness was gone. In fact, I seemed to be even more interested in writing them; the scene with Lucy and the Chancellor had ended up taking five whole chapters.

According to my how-to book, the second trimester of pregnancy was supposed to considerably enhance a woman's sex drive. That was probably why I was obsessing so much about Hugh and sex in general. Pregnancy was obviously making me insane.

Lucy Sharpe, though, was another matter. She didn't have an excuse for being so naïve. She was acting foolishly and she was heading for a fall.

Jerry's new no-smoking policy didn't seem to have cost the Mouse and Duck any customers; in fact, there were several people I didn't recognise drinking at the tables around the room. The pub, without its customary haze of cigarette smoke, looked slightly brighter, though that made it easier to see that the walls and ceiling were stained tobacco yellow. At the moment, the worst of it was obscured by Christmas tinsel and a wonky artificial tree in the corner by the television. Jerry had started talking about a new paint job, which I would believe when I saw it.

Then again, with the way things were going, it was a possibility. He'd even let me do the entire weekly food order and didn't say a single word when I added frisee to the side salad.

I was just wondering if I dared go down to Woolworth's and buy a few new Christmas decorations to replace the ones we'd been using for years when Hugh came in with half a dozen people I recognised as some of his fellow chefs-in-training from the college.

He waved to me before he went to exchange a few words with Paul and Phil, who had gained a new respect for him since the *Reading Post* had labelled him a football hooligan.

All the other students were teenagers – these six, four boys and two girls, were the only ones old enough to drink. Whenever I met with them I felt ancient and horribly uncool. How did they know how to dress in the latest style, get the latest piercings, and how did they discover the music they put on their iPods? I was only in my mid-twenties and I seemed to have lost that ability – in fact, I didn't think I'd ever had it. And now I was about to be somebody's mother. There was no hope.

Among the boys, Hugh was a man. He stood half a head taller than them and wore a white shirt, a tie loosely knotted, and a suit jacket with jeans.

I tried to recall when, exactly, he'd stopped dressing like a geek. I seemed to remember it happening sometime during our last year at university, but I couldn't remember the precise time or way it happened. Had he grown to fit his clothes, or had his clothes changed to fit him? I happened to know he still had the plimsolls with red and green laces, because I'd seen him wearing them while gardening. In fact, he still had that horrible tartan jacket, too, in his closet.

Anna and Brigid, the two girls of the group, came up to say 'Yo Eleanor' before going off to the ladies' loo together. They were both willow-waisted and had impossibly fresh skin. Anna had a boyfriend who was learning how to be a paramedic and Brigid was a brunette and Hugh had never got off with either of them. I'd asked.

'Evening, El,' Hugh said cheerfully when he came up to the bar. 'Did you hear the one about the horse walking into a pub?'

'And the landlord says, "Why the long face?"' I put his pint on the bar and then I leaned forward. The action pushed my breasts forward and upwards. My red V-neck top strained and outlined. The cleavage effect was, from my point of view at least, quite spectacular.

Hugh laughed. He took his pint and drank a bit, his gaze never once dropping lower than my chin. 'The old ones are the best. So I heard from the Harris hotel, and they said they definitely want me as a pastry chef. Starting next month.'

The Harris was the best hotel in central Reading, and an excellent career move for Hugh. I hugged him over the bar. 'That's brilliant, Hugh.'

My breasts flattened against his chest; my bare skin tingled where it touched his warm cotton shirt. Again,

Hugh didn't seem to notice at all. He hugged me back, let me go, and raised his pint.

'I'm celebrating tonight. Will you get gins for Maud and Martha and pints for Paul and Phil and Jerry and Norman? And whatever this lot want?' He gestured towards the students. 'And you can push the boat out and have an orange and lemonade to toast me, can't you?'

'I can,' I said, and went to get the drinks, disappointment weighing down my limbs despite Hugh's good news.

I wasn't trying to seduce him, because sleeping with Hugh was a very bad idea. But it would be good to have him notice me somehow, at least acknowledge that I was an attractive woman. Or a woman at all. Just to make my ego feel better at a time when my clothes didn't fit and I felt like a crone and my hormones were making me crazy horny.

Hugh and I distributed the drinks and everyone, including the non-regulars, joined in a toast to his new job. He was smiling hugely and his eyes were shining with happiness and he was about the sexiest thing I'd ever seen.

To check whether my tits were indeed as good as I thought, I casually leaned on the bar next to Horny/Angry as I wiped up a beer spill. His squinty eyes grew to the size of saucers and his breathing sped up considerably.

Then again, Horny/Angry could get turned on by a couple of unsliced lemons.

How did you seduce a man, anyway?

You'd think that after sixteen published erotica books, I'd know how this whole thing worked. But in fiction you could engineer situations. You could make the sexy man look at the heroine's suddenly astounding cleavage and fall to his knees begging to take her right there and then, and if there was some spanking involved, too, that would also be nice.

But I seemed to lack feminine wiles. As I collected glasses I tried to remember how I'd managed to seduce the men I'd slept with in the past.

I'd hardly done anything with George except get drunk, and that avenue was closed to me at the moment.

In the heady early days of infatuation with my former boyfriend Michael, I'd spent hours listening to him strum his guitar and read his own poetry aloud. I remembered trying something similar with David, who was this super-genius philosophy student, except I was listening to him expound on Kierkegaard or suchlike. Eventually, they'd stopped talking or playing and got around to taking my clothes off, enflamed by my superior listening skills.

Both of those relationships had fizzled out at about the time I realised I wasn't actually that interested in what they were saying after all. Their special, god-like talents had shrunk once I got to know them, and I guess once I stopped listening to them, they stopped being turned on by me.

In fact, most of my relationships seemed to go that way. I got disenchanted. I didn't know whether this was because the men I chose weren't all that great in the first place, or because I had impossibly high expectations. I wanted someone extra-special, and it seemed that men who were mega-talented or super-intelligent or uber-handsome or ultra-successful all knew that they were. And a big ego automatically made a man *not* extra-special.

Or maybe I just didn't have sticking power when it came to relationships. In any case, all of this was another good argument for me not starting up anything with Hugh.

Nevertheless, I went and sat beside him after I'd collected all the glasses. He was talking to Paul and two students about his interview with the head chef at the

Harris, a story I'd heard already, immediately after it had happened.

I listened, though. I listened hard. I tilted my head and turned my body towards Hugh.

'He wanted to know why I'd spent so long in I.T. if I wanted to be a chef,' Hugh was telling Paul, 'and I told him about an epiphany I had, in a team meeting about the roll-out of a new software initiative. It was an impossible project. Management were putting pressure on us to get it done, while at the same time blocking any actual ideas we had about how to get it done, and everybody in that room had been working twelve-hour days at least. We were all angry and fed up.'

I arranged my face into an expression of sympathy and concern. I laid the tips of my fingers on Hugh's wrist and made a subtle 'tsk'ing sound. He glanced at me in surprise and then went back to his story.

'In the corner of the boardroom there was a table, and on that table was a box of macaroons that one of the team had brought back from their trip to France. That box of biscuits was the only spot of joy in that room. They were broken and the box was a little crushed from where the bloke who'd brought it back on Eurostar had dropped his carry-on on top of it, but they were perfect macaroons. Like a feather, and delicious.'

I rolled my eyes in sympathetic ecstasy about how perfect those macaroons must have been. 'So how did that affect you?' I asked him.

Hugh turned to me. 'Are you all right, El? You've heard this story before.'

Dazzling smile. I was a supportive listener. The best, and sexiest, listener Hugh had ever had.

'But it's such a good story, I love hearing it.'

Hugh's gaze was deep and intense. Lust spiralled up through my body. Desire surely made my eyes sultry, my lips lush.

'Are you all right, mate?' Hugh asked. 'You're not getting morning sickness again, are you?'

What hope did I have if desire made me appear both nauseated and insane?

'Must be the beer fumes,' I mumbled, getting back up and going to the bar.

That was it. I'd used up all my natural resources. Considering half of my DNA came from June Connor, those resources were very scant indeed. I didn't know how to be coy, or how to shimmy and flirt, and it didn't help that I wasn't built like a delicate female flower. Even the tits I'd been suddenly blessed with were balanced out by a rapidly expanding belly.

Horny/Angry motioned for another pint, licking his lips as he did so; the inevitable and only result of my pathetic seduction attempt. I sighed and brought his pint to him.

'Having a good night tonight, Norman?' I asked.

I didn't usually make small talk with Horny/Angry. This half-hearted question made him sit up a little straighter. Or maybe it was because he could see down my blouse better like that, I wasn't sure.

'Not bad,' he said, and smiled at me, his eyes firmly fixed on my breasts. He had the red, pitted skin of a habitual drinker. The tips of the fingers of his right hand were stained yellow. Since Jerry's non-smoking edict, he had been shuffling to the door to smoke outside every half an hour or so. Maybe the extra exercise and fresh air made him metabolise the alcohol more quickly, but he seemed less blurry than normal, though equally as horny.

'Norman, do you remember a while ago when I asked you if you'd seen me talking to a man here in the pub? On the eighteenth of September?'

He rolled his eyes in the semblance of someone who was thinking hard. 'Don't remember,' he said finally.

'You said he was a bastard,' I pursued. It seemed a shame to waste one of his rare lucid moments, especially as I was making the effort to talk with him.

'They're all bastards,' he replied. For a moment his face was hard with anger, and then he seemed to change his mind and smiled at me again. 'You look beautiful,' he said.

Well, hell. I'd been about to abandon him if he couldn't give me any leads on George, but now I felt guilty.

'Thank you,' I said, and then, so he knew he didn't have a chance with me, added, 'I'm sure you've heard that I'm going to have a baby.'

'Loved it when my wife was expecting.'

The sentence was accompanied by a rasping, hawking clearing of the throat that three weeks before would have sent me running for the ladies' room. But there was something else in his voice besides smoker's phlegm.

'You have children?' I asked. I didn't dare ask about his wife, because I strongly suspected that a man who drank alone every evening from four till he was kicked out of the pub could not be married any more.

'Two sons,' he said. 'Joined the army.'

'Really?' I said brightly. 'You must be very proud of them.'

His face darkened, and I could see I'd said the wrong thing. 'Fucking bastards,' he growled. He grabbed his packet of cigarettes and shoved himself off his chair to stomp towards the door.

Well. My listening skills weren't even good enough for Horny/Angry. I let one of my hands settle on my stomach.

This baby was hardly a bulge; in the drawings in my how-to book it still had a definite resemblance to an alien. But once upon a time, even Horny/Angry had been like that: innocent, new, floating inside his mother. What had happened to him to make him who he was? A lonely, bitter man who spent his entire life drinking in a place where the people merely tolerated him up till the point where he became obnoxious enough to be tossed out on his arse?

I rubbed my stomach. 'It's not going to happen to you,' I whispered.

Hugh leaned on the bar across from me. 'Are you all right? Has Horny/Angry been bothering you?'

His face was flushed with success and having drunk two pints quickly. He still didn't spare a glance for my chest.

'Did you know he had kids?' I asked. 'Two sons.'

Hugh nodded. 'He hasn't spoken to them since 1989, when his wife left him.'

'How do you know this?'

'I talked to him one afternoon.' He shrugged. 'That's one thing my childhood gave me; I can talk to anyone. Had to, or I would've been alone.' He gave me a crooked smile. 'Guess I'll have to thank my mum for that next time I ring her.'

I was probably vulnerable anyway because of the baby and Norman's sad life, but Hugh's crooked smile zoomed straight into my heart and twisted it round.

I was being stupid trying to seduce him. Not because it was never going to work, but because if it did work, I might lose him. And he was too precious to me. I wanted him in my life, and I wanted him in my baby's life, too, because this baby needed as much love as it could get so it would not turn out like Norman.

'El? Are you okay? Why are you staring at me like that? You look terrible.'

So that was the outcome of my seduction attempt: I looked terrible.

Good. That was much safer.

'I was just thinking about my book,' I told him. 'The relationship in it isn't working out. I think my heroine's going to have a lot of evenings alone with the sex toys.'

Reading was hell at Christmastime. Hundreds and thousands and millions of people all descending on the town centre to do their shopping, queues of traffic clogging up the roads, and car parks practically bulging at the sides.

I didn't have to drive to get to the high street, but I did have to squeeze my way through crowds of screaming children and grumpy shoppers whenever I walked into a shop, a task made even more unpleasant by my growing belly, threatened by other people's sharp elbows and unwieldy shopping bags. At one point I had to leap backwards to keep my foetus from being stabbed by a man carrying a fake Christmas tree. In my rational mind, I knew the baby couldn't be hurt by a jostle or two. But my rational mind had little to no influence over me when it came to being pregnant. My mind erected an imaginary two-foot safety barrier between my belly and strangers, and when anyone breached it, I felt ready to kill.

And a weird thing: there were pregnant women everywhere.

What had happened? Had there been some sort of

massive fertility boom in Berkshire in the past nine months? Or had there always been so much breeding going on around me and I'd just never noticed till now?

There were dozens of them. Waddling, sway-backed and rounded. Looking tired, or distracted, but mostly serene. As if the world could go crazy around them, it didn't matter, because inside their wombs there was something perfect.

I didn't feel serene.

I fought my way out of the Oracle shopping centre, holding my shopping bags full of presents like a shield, and ducked down Duke Street towards one of the only oases of calm and civilised behaviour left in Reading at this time of year: Jackson's department store.

I wasn't sure how old Jackson's was but I did know it was the only large shop in Reading that wasn't a chain. It inhabited a corner (known as Jackson's Corner) between the library and Market Square, just out of the orbit of the frenzy of capitalism that was jostling and bumping up Broad Street. The shoppers here were local and had been patronising Jackson's for years, buying wool and embroidery floss, school uniforms, and clothes that knew not the vagaries of fashion.

Hugh and I had a long-standing tradition, much like Mr Tasty's lunches: as a Christmas gift every year we had to buy each other something that had featured in Jackson's window display at some time in the past twelve months. I'd had my eye on a jaunty felt hat that had been worn by one of the stiff window mannequins in November, or possibly a pair of driving gloves that had been draped, neatly labelled with price, in the window last spring.

Jackson's departments were laid out on different levels, each one a small microcosm of shoes or workwear or towels.

I visited Men's Fashion, made my purchases, admired the system of overhead tubes that delivered my change, and wandered up and down steps, browsing. It was busy here, but nowhere near like the bigger, flasher shops. I relaxed my hug-hold on my shopping bags and perused a rack of women's slippers. One of my pregnancy books said slippers were necessary for the hospital.

'James!' A voice pierced over the contented hum of Jackson' s shoppers. 'Come back here, please!'

It sounded familiar. I craned my neck over the slippers and saw a young auburn-haired woman clad in layers of jumpers and looking hassled.

'Roisin,' I greeted her.

She spotted me and came round the rack of slippers. 'Eleanor, I haven't seen you in an age.' She gave me an air-kiss and then shouted again, 'James!'

A curly haired toddler poked his head out from behind a bin of socks. He grinned at Roisin and then ducked back out of sight.

The last time I'd seen James, he'd been a crying baby, looking much like all crying babies. After Roisin and her boyfriend had become parents they seemed to drop out of our social circle. Not on purpose – they were both fun, and used to come down to the Mouse and Duck and drink everyone under the table. But once Roisin gave birth her talk inexorably turned to nappies, breastfeeding and school catchment areas. I hadn't rung her in months. Maybe longer.

Guilt tickled me, and then dread. Was that what happened when you had a baby? You lost all normal twenty-something conversation?

'James, come back here NOW.' James didn't come back,

and Roisin turned back to me. 'That child is driving me nuts. So what have you been up to?' She looked me up and down and then her eyes widened. 'My God, are you expecting?'

What was it about women who'd had children, did they have a special talent for detecting pregnancy? 'In June.'

She gave me a big hug this time. 'Eleanor, that's great. Please tell me it's Hugh's. That man needs a baby in his life.'

'It's not Hugh's. We're just friends.'

Roisin blushed furiously, all the way to the roots of her red hair. 'Oh, of course. I'm sorry, Eleanor, I'm out of the loop these days.'

'Don't worry about it. God, imagine Hugh with a baby. He wouldn't know what to do with it. I'm the one who's having it, and I don't know what to do with it myself.'

'You will,' Roisin assured me, 'at least till it learns how to walk. James!' She leapt in an unexpected direction behind a row of winter boots and came back with James wriggling in her arms. 'You are a monkey,' she told him. He grinned at me with his tiny teeth.

'You're a gorgeous one,' I said to him, touching my belly instinctively. This baby inside me would be that big one day. Walking. And talking. And everything like a normal little person.

'So fancy meeting you in Jackson's,' Roisin said, wrestling James more comfortably into the crook of her arm. 'We came in for some crafty-type things for James's granny. How about you?'

'The books tell me I need slippers,' I said. 'For the hospital or something.'

'Oh God, don't bother with those, I never wore slippers in my life. You only bleed on them anyway. Get cheap socks and plenty of them.'

'You bleed on your feet?' I swallowed. It wasn't only the baby I didn't know about. It was bleeding, and slippers, and cheap socks, and the whole frightening trauma of giving birth, and then the years afterwards of being avoided by my friends because I had changed into a different person.

It was everything, every single life-shifting thing.

Roisin put her free hand on my shoulder. 'You'll be all right,' she said. 'Are you going to classes?'

'Um—'

'Listen, I wasn't going to bother with the classes this time because I figured I'd already done it once, but if you want to, we can both sign up and go together. Men are useless at these things. Would you believe, Jimmy nearly fainted when he saw the dolly go through the model pelvis?'

I laughed shakily, and Roisin laughed with me. She'd always had this fantastic dirty laugh.

'Thanks, Roisin, I appreciate it, but I don't think – hold on.' Now that I looked, those jumpers could be hiding something. 'You mean you're pregnant too?'

She nodded. James gave a mighty squirm and dropped to the floor. Within a split second he had pulled six pairs of slippers off the rack and was banging the heel of one of them on the floor.

'See, it can't be that bad if I'm going through it all again,' she said. 'James! Put those away, please, and we'll go and get a milkshake. James! Did you hear me?'

Roisin knelt on the floor and took the slipper from James, who instantly made a grab for another, got the rack instead, and pulled the whole thing down on himself. He burst into tears, covered with slippers.

At that moment, pregnant Roisin looked as far from serene as it is possible for a woman to get.

She swept him into her arms and did a lightning check for injuries. Then he buried his head in her shoulder with his chubby arm around her neck. She patted his back and rocked him, and when she caught my eye she laughed her fantastic dirty laugh, which hadn't changed at all.

'See, the childbirth is the easy part,' she said. 'So shall we go to the classes?'

'Definitely,' I said.

21

'Oh, thank goodness. I thought you'd got fat.'

Four hours on a delayed train to Upper Pepperton on Christmas Eve, fretting all the way about how Sheila was going to react to her granddaughter-and-fake-daughter repeating her real daughter's fate, and this was it?

I pushed aside my tea. 'Did you miss something here, Sheila? I'm pregnant. Out of wedlock.'

'I wish you'd keep on calling me "Mum".' Sheila refilled my cup, as if I'd asked for more, and replaced the cosy on the teapot. The cosy was pink and green and hideous, the product of her knitting club. Sheila was a joiner, especially since I'd left for university and not come back. Besides the knitting, she belonged to book, bridge, bowls, and bingo clubs; she took courses in ceramics and garden-ing; she volunteered to fundraise for just about any local cause. She said it filled her days. It also filled her house with paperbacks, wonky vases, tombola tickets and courgettes.

Despite this joining mania, it was easy enough to see how I'd passed for Sheila's daughter for twenty-five years; I

resembled her a hell of a lot more than I resembled June.
Pear-shaped hips and all.

'Unless you're going to start calling June "Mum"?' she
added.

'I couldn't possibly imagine,' I said.

It was the same as our usual Christmas Eves together:
tea and mince pies and then we'd go to the carol service in
the church down the road. When Stanley had been alive
he'd drunk whisky instead of tea, and come with us to sing
in his big bass voice. It was a time of year when I always
missed him. June, when she was there, would nip from the
whisky and skip church. There was no sign of her this year.

'How far gone are you?' she asked.

'Sixteen weeks.'

She nodded. 'It's a little girl,' she said. 'I knew when I
had June, and I knew when June was carrying you. Your
bump's spread out a bit. She's active, I bet.'

'She – it hasn't moved yet.'

'She will, soon.' Sheila kept on nodding. 'So are you and
Hugh planning on getting married?'

Ah. The key to her mysterious lack of horror.

'It's not his baby. And Hugh's never going to get married
and settle down.'

'Are you sure?'

'Yes. He tells me so every time he gets drunk. It has
something to do with his parents getting divorced and using
him to fight with each other for years. Anyway, didn't you
hear me? The baby isn't Hugh's.'

'Oh. Are you sure?'

'Since I've never had sex with him, that seems like a
pretty good indication.' I took a breath. There was no point
getting annoyed with Sheila; this was all my own doing.

'Whose is it?'

That, of course, was the question. 'I'm trying to find him.'

'Good for you. I know you'll do the right thing.'

'Hold on,' I said. 'Aren't you going to lecture me about having unsafe sex? About getting pregnant by mistake?'

'I've done that already, with June. I cried and I yelled and I lectured. It didn't do any good.' She smiled at me. 'Knowing you, you've already done it to yourself anyway.'

Yes. It was good to know that the woman who raised me knew I was naturally guilt-ridden. But why wasn't she upset?

I didn't want the lecture, yet I felt cheated by not getting it. During the whole four-hour journey I'd dreaded telling Sheila, and at the same time looked forward to it. Finally, I was going to get the sort of attention that June always had. I was going to feel as if I'd been transgressive, made an impact. And now Sheila couldn't be bothered to do anything but remember how she'd lectured June. As if June had got all the credit for my mistakes, too.

'By "do the right thing", do you mean marry the father?' I asked.

She shrugged. 'Well, that's what I did.'

'Oh, God.' I buried my face in my hands. 'Are you saying this runs in the family? Did your mother get pregnant before she got married too?'

'She never talked about it. They wouldn't, back then. Her wedding dress in the photo is very loose, though. Anyway, your fath— Stanley was a wonderful man, so I did the right thing. He loved you more than anything, you know.' She took my hand and patted it. 'I know you'll get through this, you'll find the father and tell him and you'll be very happy.'

'That would be nice,' I said doubtfully.

*

Sheila knew pretty much everyone in Upper Pepperton and she lingered inside the church after the service, catching up with people as if she hadn't seen them in weeks. I knew she'd most likely met up with them in one club or another in the past few days, but people in small towns didn't take long to build up trivia to talk about.

For the first couple of conversations, I hovered at her shoulder watching her like a hawk. I'd asked her not to reveal that I was pregnant yet, but Sheila got carried away sometimes. When it became clear that she was going to stick strictly to other people's gossip and last Wednesday's bridge results, I slipped off to wait for her outside.

The damp settled into my clothes as I hopped from one foot to the other. It was only marginally colder outside than inside the church. I took up my usual post beside the lych gate, where I'd spent countless hours as a teenager kicking the ground, sulking, and failing to look cool while I waited for my mum.

She finally emerged in a chorus of 'Merry Christmas'es and joined me walking down the road back to our house.

'So it's true,' she said to me as soon as we were out of earshot of the rest of Upper Pepperton, 'Ian and Nancy's son Quentin is gay. He came home yesterday with that Colin fellow he'd claimed was only his friend and they announced they were getting married or getting a civil partnership, or whatever it's called, right in the middle of decorating the tree. Nancy is all right with it but Ian is in a state of shock. I wouldn't say it to them, but what did they expect? Nancy was always talking about Colin's taste in decorating, she saved up the Christmas tree for him every year especially. This year it's a fruit theme. Of course she couldn't finish hanging the baubles, she had to comfort Ian, but Colin finished it up. Winnie says it looks gorgeous.'

I usually let these torrents of information pass right through my head and out the other side, but I perked up at this one. Not because Quentin was gay; I'd known that since we were in primary school together and he'd actively encouraged the nickname 'Queen Quentin'.

'People must have talked about us,' I said. 'When June got pregnant. Wasn't it embarrassing?' Full realisation struck me. 'Oh God, all of these people must know that you're not really my mother. They must have known all about it when I was growing up.'

My face flamed hot despite the cold, and I frantically tried to remember if I'd been given knowing looks by the neighbours throughout my childhood. I didn't remember any but that could be because I'd received so many of them that I thought it was normal.

'Oh, it died down eventually. And then you were such a beautiful child, and so good.'

'Jesus.' Every single person in that church probably knew one of my deepest secrets, and in a few months' time, they'd know another one. All I had to do was reveal that I wrote dirty books for a living, and my humiliation would be complete. That would drive Quentin and Colin into second place for gossip, for sure.

'Everyone knew we wanted another child anyway. We'd had June so easily that we thought another one would come along soon, but it didn't. And everyone loved your father so much, they rallied round.' Sheila linked her arm with mine. 'Do you remember that Christmas Eve when it snowed and Stanley carried you on his shoulders to and from church? And you insisted he walk back in his own footprints so the snow wouldn't get more disturbed?'

I remembered. It had snowed while we'd been in church and his footprints were rounded and partly filled in with snow. I'd felt tall and invulnerable, Empress of the Winter.

'I really miss him,' I said. The damp settled deeper into my bones. 'I wish he were my real father.'

'So did he.'

She linked her arm in mine. 'What did you think about Richard?'

'Richard who?'

'The new vicar,' she said, elbowing me. 'Remember you said hello to him after the service?'

I cast my mind back. 'He seems nice. Good sermon,' I guessed.

'Don't you think he looks just like Michael Parkinson?'

'Sheila, he's bald.'

'Yes, but Michael Parkinson without the hair.'

I tried to picture Michael Parkinson in white robes with the light of the altar candles gleaming off his scalp, and couldn't. 'Hmm.'

When we got in we had our usual post-church cup of cocoa and then Sheila made me go and shake the presents under the tree, as I'd done ever since I was a little girl. As I'd got older, the presents were easier to guess. This year I was getting a CD, probably something like Il Divo, who Sheila thought were the next step down from gods, something squishy which was bound to be a hand-knitted jumper, and something lumpy and hard which was most likely a hand-thrown fruit bowl. I pretended to be stumped, then kissed a delighted Sheila on the cheek and went upstairs.

My mobile was on my bedside table. I picked it up and considered ringing Hugh to wish him a merry Christmas and tell him that I'd unknowingly spent my entire childhood as the object of the town's gossip, but I remembered that Hugh usually turned his phone off at Christmas so that the parent he wasn't spending Christmas with wouldn't ring him at a time calculated to upset the parent he was spending Christmas with. He was with his father this year, and he'd call his mother from the callbox on the corner after lunch tomorrow, and then he'd call me.

My room was pretty much the same as it had been when I'd left for the University of Reading at the age of eighteen, though Sheila had taken down the moody music posters. Sometimes when I visited I felt as if nothing had ever changed and I was still that teenager wondering who the hell she was.

I put my hand on my bump, wishing that the baby would move and I would feel less lonely. He or she stayed put. Or maybe the baby was doing acrobatics and I couldn't feel anything yet because he or she was too small.

How had June felt about the whole town talking about her? I knew she wouldn't have felt the humiliation and shame that crawled through me. Was she defiant? Pleased with herself?

I got up off my bed to walk down the hall. June's room was at the end, and it had long been converted into Sheila's sewing and craft room; she slept on the pull-out couch when she visited. I opened the closet, packed with June's things that Sheila had never had the opportunity or the bravery to throw away: tiny discarded cardigans, a fake fur coat, shoe boxes stuffed with old post and photographs.

There were plenty of pictures of June with boys, and later men. I settled on the floor, the shoe boxes spread before me, and scrutinised each of the photos. There was one of June kissing a gelled-haired boy in a photo booth, which looked as if it could be from the right year, but I couldn't see his face. The boys in her whole-school photograph from 1980 were blurred pale and brown circles, some smiling, some looking away from the camera. I looked at every one of them in turn, touching their faces with my finger, and wasn't hit by any bolts of recognition.

A pellet of much-folded lined paper lay at the bottom of one box, shaped like those notes everyone had folded at school for maximum discretion. *Peter*, it said on the outside, in scratchy handwriting that was only slightly more rounded than the way June wrote now.

I unfolded it:

Its OK my mum and dad say their going to keep it, do you want to meet at station tomorrow and hide in loo of London train? Jxxx

I turned the misspelt note over in my hands. Was I the 'it'? Was Peter my father? Why did June still have the note?

I stared at the note for a long time, till my bottom was sore from sitting on the floor, and then I went to my childhood bed.

I didn't suspect anything was wrong till Sheila insisted on going to church on Christmas morning.

'It'll be fun,' she trilled as I blearily pulled on my coat. My sleep had been dogged by faceless boys ducking into trains, and village halls full of whispers. To top it off, I'd woken at four o'clock from the dream about going to school to sit an exam and discovering I was naked. Since then I'd been lying in bed, watching the clock tick the minutes by, till Sheila had bustled in with a cup of tea and a crumpet and told me we were going to the morning service.

Outside, Upper Pepperton was soggy with rain. It dripped off the wreaths on doors and off the Christmas tree on the common.

We never went to church on Christmas Day. We were a Christmas Eve sort of family. Christmas Day was for lounging in pyjamas and maybe making a fire and gradually opening presents, not for huddling on a hard bench at the mercy of every cold draught in England.

'Isn't this fun?' Sheila whispered to me again when we entered the church and slid into our pew, and for a moment I wished I was wherever June was, even if it meant I had to live in screaming chaos.

'It really is,' I said, and hunkered down to read the order of service.

We were halfway through 'O Little Town of Bethlehem' when I spotted it. Sheila's eyes were not on the hymn sheet. Instead she was gazing straight ahead and upwards with a strange light in her eyes.

Sheila was a churchgoer and, by most people's standards, a good Christian, but she'd never been the shiny-eyed, behold-the-altar-in-adoration type, even when it was a holiday and there were a lot of flowers around. I followed her line of vision and saw nothing but the vicar, singing along, putting enough spirit into it that the large poinsettia arrangement beside him was wobbling slightly.

And then the carol finished and the vicar sat down to let Nancy Morley do a reading. She appeared quite stoic despite her son Quentin coming out of the closet. But Sheila didn't look at Nancy, though the rest of the congregation were raptly observing her for any signs of distress. No,

Sheila's gaze stayed right where it was, and her eyes kept on shining, and I understood what was going on.

Sheila fancied the vicar.

I watched her all through the service and she went on fancying him. At the end she hustled me over to where he stood and introduced me. Or rather, reintroduced me; she'd introduced me last night but I hadn't been paying any attention then.

I was paying attention now.

He was tall, but not as tall as Stanley had been, and he had a slightly timid smile. And of course he was bald except for a fringe of brownish hair around the sides. He looked at Sheila warmly but who knew if that meant anything. After all, he was a vicar and it was in the job description to be nice to parishioners, wasn't it?

'I'm sorry we didn't have a chance to speak last night,' he said to me.

Since I'd been the one who'd sloped outside as soon as possible, I could only nod. Why did he want to speak with me? Was it out of a normal vicarly interest in the offspring of his flock or was it because he was trying to worm his way into Sheila's affections?

'I've heard you work in a pub in Reading,' he continued. 'That must be enjoyable. You must meet such interesting people.'

I considered telling him about picking up a strange man in the pub and getting pregnant by him.

I considered telling him about my real job, writing salacious stories that featured every available kind of adultery.

Instead I nodded again.

'I have a friend who has a parish near Reading, perhaps you know him, Timothy White in Wargrave?'

I didn't have the stamina to be rude enough not to respond to a third conversation attempt, so I said, 'No, I'm sorry, I don't.'

There was a pause. I glanced over at Sheila. She was glowing steadily. I couldn't believe I hadn't noticed it last night.

'I'm looking forward to spending Boxing Day with you,' Richard the vicar said, and this time I caught a definite glance exchanged between him and the woman who had brought me up. A complicit glance. A glance that said 'You and I have made plans'.

Then Sheila glanced at me, and this one was a worried glance, and I knew why. We never had guests on Boxing Day. It had always been a day for family only, eating turkey sandwiches made to Stanley's exacting recipe, watching films on television and maybe finishing off that bottle of port.

I knew why she'd invited him. She wanted the two of us to get to know each other, for us to get on like a house on fire, so that I would blithely accept it when he and Sheila embarked upon whatever kind of red-hot affair people their age managed to have.

'I'm sorry,' I said, 'I won't be around for Boxing Day. I have to get back to Reading for work.'

Which was true. I had a book to rewrite, after all. Time was a-wasting, and I'd rather spend it with a blank page than watching Richard and Sheila make googly eyes at each other.

'Oh, I am sorry,' said Richard, and I said my goodbyes and left them to it, hanging out in my usual spot outside to wait for Sheila.

I was kicking at the moss at the base of the lych gate when she came out, looking flushed.

'I didn't know you had to go back to Reading tomorrow,' she said.

'Didn't I tell you? It's annoying because there aren't many trains, but it can't be helped.' I started walking towards home.

'Richard is a wonderful man,' Sheila said, hurrying to catch up.

'I'm sure he is. A man of God and everything.'

'He's really made a difference in this parish. He's full of exciting ideas.'

I hunched my shoulders against the drizzle. Didn't she realise she was supposed to be boring and always stay the same?

'And he's so interesting. I've never met a man so intelligent.'

And last night we'd walked along this same road talking about Stanley.

'It's his intelligence you're interested in, is it?' I asked.

I felt rather than saw Sheila bristling. 'Eleanor, I am fifty-eight years old and my life is far from over. I understand how you feel, but your father has been dead for nearly ten years, and—'

'It's okay,' I snapped. 'He wasn't my father.'

I lengthened my steps to leave Sheila behind.

How powerful it felt to hurl a hurtful line. How freeing just to walk away. What an adventure, not to care, not to imagine the consequences of your actions.

But I couldn't be like June, even if I tried. I slowed, waited for Sheila to catch up, and hugged her.

'Let's have a merry Christmas,' I said.

22

I wasn't going to go to Hugh's annual New Year's Eve fancy dress party, but he bullied me about it from Boxing Day onwards till I gave in.

I dressed as a nun, of course, flowing robes being desirable objects at this point. I planned to spend most of the evening in Hugh's kitchen scoffing the cakes and trying to avoid talking about being pregnant or watching people get drunk. Hugh, however, forced me to dance in his front room to music that became inexorably more awful as the night went on. At midnight we spilled out into the street, as usual, to watch fireworks pop up all over the sky.

'What's your resolution?' I asked Hugh, as I did every year.

'Patience and fortitude. Not to mess things up,' he said. 'And you?'

I thought about it. A single mother, with no idea how to give birth to or raise a child, a large number of whose genes were a complete mystery.

'Patience and fortitude sound good to me,' I said. 'And

finding George, obviously. And I should write my damn book, I guess.'

The next morning, probably the first time in years I'd seen nine in the morning on New Year's Day, I sat in my office and tried to summon patience and fortitude. It was a new year, a new heroine, a new start.

I flexed my fingers. Outside, it was the kind of eerie quiet you only get when everyone else in the world is hung over. I began to type.

Two days later I rang my agent in despair.

The original plan had been to have Lucy Sharpe sleep her way to the top of modern politics. I'd envisaged a massive orgy scene in the secret pleasure basement of Number Ten, with Lucy helping each cabinet member to indulge his or her own private kink.

But my new heroine only wanted to sleep with one person: the Chancellor. I'd attempted to write a scene where she'd spanked the Home Secretary, but she'd ended up chatting with him about stretch marks and haemorrhoids.

I was doing a lot of cutting.

And yet when I tried to write about her having sex with the Chancellor, I couldn't do that either. I ended up in such a frenzy of sexual frustration describing his tall, lanky, yet muscular body, that I was sorely tempted to peg it next door and fling myself into Hugh's arms.

I needed more time. Hence phone call to agent.

Bryce answered the phone with an exuberant 'Estelle! Happy New Year! How's the book? Nearly done?'

'Um, not quite.' I crossed my fingers for luck. 'Actually, I'm pregnant.'

'Really! How marvellous! I love little bitty babies!'

I tried to imagine Bryce with a little bitty baby, whom

he could probably crush with a curl of one finger.

'Um, yes. So, the thing is, I've had a lot on my mind.'

'Of course, darling, of course. Hormones. Et cetera. Oh God, this doesn't mean the book is going to be late?'

'I'm afraid so.'

'How long do you need?'

'As long as I can have.'

'Let's see.' I could hear him flicking through his diary. 'Well it's due to be released in May, so I can ring Duane and beg for the beginning of March?'

Two months to finish the book, and February a short one. I crossed my fingers harder. 'Okay. I think.'

'Well, try your best, darling, that's all anyone can ask of you.'

'All right. Uh, Bryce?'

'Yes, darling.'

'What do you mean by "the whiff of reality"? I mean, all my books are completely improbable sexual fantasies.'

'That's the thing, darling, that's why I signed you when I read your first novel. You have this fantastically dirty mind but there's something about your writing that's so *you*, and that's what makes it realistic.'

'So *me*?' I was in more trouble than I'd thought if Bryce thought my June-wannabe heroines were so *me*. What was he going to make of Lucy Sharpe?

'Yes. So relax, darling, let your feelings shine through. You'll be fine! Must dash, off to lunch, byeeee!'

I was glad to have extra time, but the phone call didn't help at all. In the days that followed I avoided my computer and watched daytime telly. Mostly chat shows, *Judge Judy*, and episodes of *Friends*. Except the episode where Phoebe has to give up the triplets she's carrying for her brother. The idea of giving away a baby made me cry so much that I'd had to go straight out and buy two pints of ice cream and eat them both in order to regain my equilibrium.

I was lying on the couch in an old pair of stretch track suit bottoms and a Status Quo T-shirt I'd bought ages ago, watching the episode where Joey buys the V volume of the encyclopaedia from the tall half of Penn and Teller. My hand rested on my stomach beneath my T-shirt, because it was getting to be quite a satisfying shape. Then I felt it.

It was like a little finger inside my belly poking upwards. Then a flutter. And another poke.

I sat up straight, holding my breath, both my hands on my belly. There was a bit of an uncertain roll.

I jumped up from the couch and ran outside to pound on Hugh's door. In the minutes before he answered it, I felt the baby moving twice.

'I felt the baby kicking! I felt the baby kicking!' I cried as soon as Hugh opened the door.

His eyes got wide. 'Really?'

I rushed inside his house and flopped down on his sofa, belly-up. 'Quick, feel before it stops.' I pulled up my T-shirt.

Hugh sat beside me and put his hand on my stomach.

Warm hand. Warm hand and big, big enough to span my bump and make what I'd thought was enormous look small and delicately rounded. His skin was slightly darker than mine.

I could not breathe.

'Where did it kick?'

I nodded at where he touched me. 'There,' I said, though it came out more like a hiccup.

He stared at his hand. I stared at him. He was intent, focused, eager, gorgeous.

Long moments passed.

'I don't feel anything,' he said, almost in a whisper.

You're feeling me, I thought.

'It was going crazy before.'

He waited some more. My heart was beating so hard I was surprised he didn't think it was the baby kicking. He must be able to feel it. And the shortness of my breath. And the heat from my skin.

His hand shifted. Only slightly, but it was so like a caress that I bit my lip.

'You're really starting to show,' he said, still quietly, still with his gaze focused on my stomach. Slowly, he drew his thumb along the curve of my belly.

Before I could stop it, a small moan escaped my mouth. Hugh looked up quickly from his hand on my stomach and our eyes met.

Instantly he knew it. My weeks of hiding my desire from him were completely worthless because his pupils dilated and his lips parted and I could see that my emotions were written all over my face and he had read them.

No use saying anything. I stared back.

'El,' he said. He swallowed and said my name again. 'Eleanor.'

It wasn't quite the same as he'd ever said it before.

'Hugh,' I said back, quietly.

This time there was no mistake; Hugh was the one who leaned forward, his face towards mine. But when he reached me I was ready for him and I kissed him, open-mouthed and wanting. Our tongues touched and Hugh leaned into me. His hand was on my belly, stroking me with the same cadence as our kiss.

This is Hugh, I thought, and unlike the last time we'd

kissed, the words weren't an alarm bell. They were sexy and correct.

And he was such a good kisser. He was ardent and gentle but he felt as if he could get rough whenever we wanted to. He was lying half on top of me, his chest a solid weight against my gorgeously aching breasts, and this time there was no avoiding the fact that he had a huge erection pressed into my thigh.

It's not just me, he feels it too, I thought in a burst of joy. I buried one hand in his hair and pulled him closer.

That made him lose a bit of his gentleness. He rasped his teeth against my lip and his hand slid up and around one of my breasts through my bra. I moaned into his mouth, fumbled with the buttons at the top of his shirt, and slipped my hand inside to his hot, bare skin.

Hugh tore his mouth from mine and stared into my face, breathing hard.

'Eleanor, this isn't –'

My hand wasn't listening to my brain because it had found Hugh's collarbone and the soft hair at the base of his throat. It was greedy and touched him and touched him.

'Eleanor.' His voice was hoarse. 'Stop it.'

I stopped. But couldn't withdraw my hand, or keep my hips from arching up towards him. 'Why?' I was crazy enough to say.

'Because – oh, good Lord.' He took his hand away from my breast, wrapped it around my wrist, and lifted my hand from his chest. Then he sat up.

I had to look: his erection was visible as a thick ridge beneath his jeans. Who knew what I'd done, but whatever it was, it had worked.

'We said we wouldn't do this,' Hugh said.

'Actually, we said we shouldn't have kissed that time,' I corrected him, my mind still swimming. 'We didn't say we wouldn't snog and grope each other.'

I was sprawled on the couch with my belly and bra showing. My mouth burned. Hugh shifted so that he wasn't touching me.

'You're pregnant,' he said.

'And you don't find pregnant women attractive?'

Hugh raised his eyebrows. He gave his crotch a significant glance.

'You find pregnant women attractive, but think it's too kinky to do anything about?'

'I find *you* attractive.' He reached towards me and I melted, but he only tugged down my T-shirt to cover me up. 'But we need to keep things uncomplicated.'

I forced myself to sit up. 'I thought you didn't like brunettes. What's changed?'

'Nothing's changed.' My leg was brushing his; he moved so it wasn't. 'We're friends. This is a bad idea. Do you want to get out, or do you want a cup of tea?'

'Neither.' I put my hand on his thigh. 'Hugh, I think we need to talk about this.'

'So help me God, Eleanor, stop tempting a desperate man.' He took my hand off his thigh. 'We don't need to talk about this. It's obvious. We can't have sex with each other.'

I couldn't argue with that, much as my body wanted me to. After my weeks of unsuccessful seduction attempts, though, I needed to know a little bit more. 'But you want to have sex with me?'

'You've written sixteen erotic novels, and you don't know the signs yet?'

I took that as a yes. 'Is it because of my breasts?'

Hugh ran his hands through his hair. 'What? No. Well – no. It's because of you. Can we stop talking about this now?'

'You have noticed my breasts, though, right?'

'I'm not going to answer that.' He stood up and opened his front door. 'Go away. I'll see you tomorrow.'

I got up, and felt a little thump. 'The baby just kicked again.'

Hugh reached towards my stomach, then stopped and put his hand on my shoulder instead. 'I'll feel it later,' he said, propelling me out the door. 'Goodbye.'

I went back to my own house, my hand curled around my belly. Feeling the rolls and flutters, under skin made alive by Hugh.

I spent that night writing the most torturous scene of sexual tension I had ever created, topped off with a description of the best kiss in the universe. Lucy Sharpe hardly knew what had hit her.

I finished at four in the morning and then went to bed and slept till noon. My dreams were full of Hugh and the Chancellor, morphed into one person. When I went downstairs my head was blurry and my body was exhausted. I picked up the post from underneath the door and took it to the kitchen table to read while I had tea and porridge.

It was less than exciting. Bills and a magazine from the Society of Authors, whom I'd joined in a fit of optimism, though I hadn't attended any of their events. I leafed through the magazine anyway, trying to avoid thinking about Hugh and what I was going to say to him today. Once I'd exhausted the interest in the magazine I opened the bills, one by one.

I cast a cursory glance over my phone bill, started to toss it aside without reading it, and then stopped. There were many more itemised calls than I usually made. I scanned down it, checking the numbers and the times, and then I went to the phone and called Hugh.

'Get over here, I have something to show you,' I told him, and hung up.

He let himself in the front door with his key and looked me over from top to toe. I was wearing mismatched flannel pyjamas, thick woollen socks and Stanley's bobbled cardigan. My hair was probably sticking up, too, and I hadn't washed my face yet.

'I'm happy to see that you didn't order me over here to seduce me,' he said.

'June made a bunch of calls from my phone,' I told him, holding up the itemised bill. 'Look. I didn't make these calls because I don't know the number. It's a Reading one, though. And she called it twice on the day that she left.'

Hugh took the phone bill and peered at it, 'So?'

'So June told me that she only knew one person in Reading, and it was someone who was the spitting image of George Michael.'

He sat down beside me. He smelled good, as if he'd recently got out of the shower. 'Do you think this is his number? Your mystery George?'

'I don't know.'

He pointed to the telephone. 'Ring it.'

I knew he'd order me to do that, which was one of the reasons why I'd told him to come over. I took the phone and carefully punched in the number.

It was picked up after two rings. 'Hello?' a male voice said.

A wave of panic went through me and I hung up.

'What?' said Hugh. 'What happened?'

I looked at the phone. 'I freaked out.'

'Was it him?'

'I don't know.'

'Did it sound like him?'

'He only said "hello". I don't remember George saying "hello" to me. I have nothing to compare it to.'

'I'm not punching anybody else unless I know it's the right bloke. You'll need to call him again and ask him.'

I dialled in the Reading code, and then I stopped. 'What do I say? "Hi, remember me, you made me pregnant"?'

'That would work.'

I put down the phone. 'I don't know that it's him. I would be much more certain if I could find out his address and go there and see him. Is there any way we can do that?'

'I tried once to find someone's address from their phone number. It's not as easy as it sounds.'

'A woman?' I decided I didn't want to know. 'Never mind. How do you do it?'

'I think there are Internet sites. But listen, El, you shouldn't have to sneak around for this. It will be a lot easier and more direct if you just ring him again. If it doesn't work, we can try to find his address.'

I took a deep breath and punched in the number.

'Hello?' The voice was definitely male, deep, and a little bit irritated. I tried to picture it coming out of George's goatee-surrounded mouth.

'Hi,' I said. 'Um, I'm not sure if I've got the right number or if you know who I am, but this is Eleanor Connor, and I—'

'Eleanor Connor? Oh, hi, Eleanor, yeah. I know who you are.'

Hugh was watching me, his eyebrows raised in enquiry. I screwed up my face, trying to figure out if I recognised the voice.

'I, uh, listen, I know this is weird, but I really need to talk with you about something important,' I said.

To my surprise, he said, 'Okay. Can you meet me this afternoon at four?'

'Uh. Yeah. Sure.'

'I'll be in the Railway Tavern near the station. See you then.'

'Um – okay. Just one thing, though?'

'What is it?'

'What's your name?'

I heard him snort a laugh. 'John,' he said. 'My name is John. But most people call me George.'

He hung up and I buried my head in my arms on the arm of the sofa.

'Eleanor? You okay?'

'That was probably one of the most humiliating things I have ever had to do,' I said to the sofa. 'The guy was clearly not interested in seeing me again after that one night and I've just rung him and asked him his name.'

'The guy's a dick,' Hugh started, and then evidently remembered this was the father of my child. 'Sorry. I mean, he should have told you his name when you met him and he should have called you after you slept with him. It's not your fault. You shouldn't be embarrassed.'

'Well, I am. He said to meet him at four o'clock in the Railway Tavern.' I looked at Hugh pleadingly. 'Will you come with me?'

'I don't think—'

'Please, Hugh. This whole thing is too weird. I want you there so I don't freak out and run away. You can go as soon as I've sat down with him.'

'I don't really fancy being chaperone to you and your lover.'

'You won't be a chaperone, you'll be my moral support. I'll tell him you're my brother or something.'

Hugh sighed. 'If there's one thing last night proved, it's that I'm not your brother.'

Heat went through me at that, and I squirmed in my flannel pyjamas.

After a moment of silence, Hugh stood up. 'All right. I'll come. You owe me several thousand pints, however.'

I stood outside the Railway Tavern, shifting from foot to foot.

It had taken me two hours to figure out what to wear. On the one hand, I didn't want to appear so pregnant that George would take one look at me and run out the back door of the pub. On the other hand, I didn't want to not look pregnant, or else he might not see the urgency of the situation. I finally settled on a loose tunic-y dress over maternity jeans. This had the added bonus of slightly more than hinting at my wowza cleavage, just to remind him of a possible reason of why he'd slept with me in the first place.

Now I wished I'd invested in a balaclava, as well. Anything to spare me the embarrassment of marching into that pub and announcing to a man I didn't know that he was the father of my child.

'What are you waiting for?' Hugh asked.

'What if I don't like him?'

'It never stopped my parents from having a child together,' he said. 'You, however, would have the good sense to be civilised about it. You'll be fine. Now get going.'

'What if he doesn't want to know?'

'Then your problems are solved. You'll bring up the baby without him and its Uncle Hugh will help you out.'

I looked at him. 'You'd do that?'

'Of course I bloody will, whether George is involved or not. I'm your best friend, I'm not going to abandon you.'

'Yes, but you've never shown any signs of wanting anything to do with kids.'

'Well, this one's yours.' He gave my shoulder a slight push. 'Go inside, it's ten past four.'

I hung back. 'I've thought of something. If George is a friend of June's, maybe they've known each other for ages. Maybe they've slept together.'

'So?'

'Well, I know it didn't seem to bother me last night when I was getting all hot and heavy with you, but in cold daylight the thought of having sex with someone who's slept with my mother is sort of gross.'

Hugh exhaled sharply in irritation. 'Eleanor, even if you pick a fight with me, you still have to go in there.'

'I'm just saying that if he knows June, he probably had sex with her. She believes people should have as much sex as possible.' I paused. 'Of course, you know that already. You have that in common.'

'Eleanor, I'm not on a mission to have as much sex as possible.'

'Ha!' I said. 'Now that's a lie. You never turned down sex in your life.'

'Actually, I have. As you should know.'

He had me there.

'Now stop having a go at me and get inside,' he said.

I didn't move, because something else had occurred to me. June's note to a Peter didn't necessarily mean anything.

'What if he's my father?'

'What? You're joking. Is he old enough?'

I considered. 'I thought he was in his early thirties, but men don't always show their age.'

'Or act it,' he muttered, then shook his head as if to stop himself. 'Sorry. Well, there's something else for you to talk about, to avoid awkward silences. "You're the father of my child, oh, and by the way, are you my father too?" It could be a double family reunion.'

'It could also be seriously incestuous and illegal.' I shuddered. 'You don't think he is, do you?'

'Eleanor, I think you are very stupid and very unlucky. But I don't think even you are stupid and unlucky enough to sleep with your own father by mistake. Now go talk to George, because you're starting to annoy me.'

'Right. Okay.' I took a deep breath and marched forward.

As soon as I opened the door, I felt very, very sick. I stopped so abruptly on the threshold that Hugh walked into my back.

'I'm sorry,' I said, 'but there's one more thing. I can deal with the humiliation, and I can deal with whatever he wants to do about this, for myself. But I'm afraid for the baby, Hugh. I'm afraid he'll reject the baby, and the baby doesn't deserve it.'

Hugh's annoyance melted away in a moment and he hugged me in the doorway.

'If you feel that way,' he said quietly into the top of my head, warming my hair with his breath, 'then the baby is very lucky, no matter what George does.'

That fortified me. I broke gently away from him and went into the pub.

The Railway Tavern was a popular pub and therefore it didn't quite have the extent of nicotined dinginess that the

Mouse and Duck achieved. But it wasn't the upmarket place I would have pictured George to frequent, especially as he'd thought the Mouse and Duck was a dump.

I stood looking for him. The clientele was mostly people having a quick drink as they waited for their train. But my eyes skipped over old men drinking the afternoon away, and tired-looking women thin from booze and cigarettes. There was the usual group of teenagers trying to look older, the boys with bottled lager and the girls with alcopops. Four women on a shopping trip chatted over large white wines. A dodgy-looking transvestite with colourful dreadlocks was sucking down a pint of Guinness in the corner.

'No luck?' Hugh asked behind me.

'Let's go get a drink,' I said, 'maybe he's late.'

'The first of the many, many pints you owe me.'

I was handing over the cash for Hugh's pint and my orange juice when I felt a tap on my shoulder.

'Eleanor?' a vaguely familiar voice said.

24

U p till that moment, I hadn't thought it was possible for my stomach to both sink and leap at the same time.

I turned around. Behind me stood the dodgy dreadlocked transvestite. He wore full make-up, rather smeared around the edges, and a black hat perched at a jaunty angle on top of his beribboned hair.

'Are you Eleanor?' he repeated.

'Yes,' I said. This wasn't George, was it, concealed underneath the make-up and hair?

No. This guy was shorter, and thinner, and even my fuzzy memory could tell that his features weren't the same.

'I thought so,' he said. 'You look like your sister.'

That was the first time I'd heard that. 'Who are you?' I asked.

Against all reason, he said, 'I'm George.'

No you're not, I was about to say, but I remembered at the last moment that that would probably make me sound insane.

'June's friend?' he prompted. 'You rang me earlier?'

He evidently thought I was insane anyway, but I rallied

enough to nod and offer him another Guinness.

'Don't worry, this isn't him,' I muttered to Hugh as we followed George to the corner table.

'Why did you think it was?'

Good question. I stared at the back of George's head, trying to remember the conversation I'd had with June, and the answer hit me.

'Oh my God. Who does he look like to you?'

Hugh looked. 'Someone who's had a fight with a paper shredder?'

'No. Boy George? Culture Club? The hair, the make-up, the hat?'

Hugh looked again. 'Maybe if you squint. Why is this relevant?'

'June said he looked like an eighties pop star, and I said George Michael. She must have got them confused. George Michael? Boy George? They're quite similar, I guess.'

Hugh had to stop for a moment and lean on a table in silent laughter.

'Thanks for coming, I really appreciate it, but you don't have to stick around,' I told him, and went to the corner table without him.

'So, Eleanor, what was the important thing you needed to talk to me about?' George asked when I sat down.

Oh, shit. I'd said that, hadn't I?

'I'm looking for June,' I said. 'She was staying with me, and she disappeared, on the same day she rang you twice. Do you know where she's gone?'

George looked cagey underneath his make-up. 'Why do you want to know?' he asked.

'Mainly because she's family and I love her and we want to make sure she's all right. But also because her violent ex-boyfriend broke into my house a few weeks ago trying to track her down.'

George nodded. The motion made the ribbons in his hair bob.

Hugh slid into a seat next to me. I gave him a look that clearly said, *I told you to go away* and he gave me a look back that clearly said, *I'm going to stay and hear every word so I can take the piss out of you later.*

'I drove her to Heathrow,' George said. 'She had a flight going somewhere; she wouldn't say where or when she was coming back. I got the impression she was going abroad.'

Going on a holiday with the fifty thousand pounds she'd stolen from Jojo? – typical. Also typical that she got her friend to drive her to the airport rather than spend any of the fifty thousand pounds on a bus.

'Okay,' I said. 'Thanks for meeting me.'

I started to stand, but then I stopped. I was here, so I might as well ask.

'Just out of interest, you didn't happen to have slept with June sometime in 1980, did you?'

George laughed, and while he was laughing he didn't look like a former pop-star wannabe with questionable taste. He looked like a nice, cheerful bloke.

'I would have been seven years old,' he said. 'Quite apart from other considerations.'

'Okay,' I said, and this time I did stand up. I held out my hand and he shook it. 'Thanks.'

25

The clock was institutional, dull white like everything else in the room, and it had a jump to its minute hand. We'd been waiting thirty-eight minutes for the technician to call my name. It felt as if I'd been doing nothing but waiting lately.

For example, it had been three weeks since kissing Hugh and it was driving me absolutely crazy.

At first, I'd tried to convince myself that I'd only wanted Hugh to show an interest in me to gratify my ego, to prove that I could still attract a man if I wanted to. If that were true, I should have been satisfied with knowing that he wanted, despite his better judgement, to have sex with me. I should have made a note of his erection after our kiss (appreciating its dimensions purely on an aesthetic level) and gone blithely on my way, able to ignore my own feelings of desire for him.

But it wasn't that way. My ego felt a little bit better, sure. But my libido felt a hell of a lot worse.

At least I hadn't heard him having sex with any of his lady friends, nor had I seen him with any, although I saw him nearly every day. So I didn't have to deal with jealousy as well. I had the satisfaction of believing that he was as sexually frustrated as I was.

We didn't talk about it.

At the present moment, instead of talking about it, we were at the Royal Berkshire Hospital together for the second time, except this time we were sitting in a waiting room in the maternity block rather than in the STD clinic. Hugh had volunteered to come to my twenty-week ultrasound scan with me.

'It should be an interesting show,' I told him, my hand on my belly where the baby seemed to be doing cartwheels and star jumps all at once. 'This child never stops moving.'

Hugh nodded. He was taking my word for it, because he hadn't laid a hand on my belly since the kissing incident, even though Martha, Maud, Jerry, and Paul had all felt the baby kicking. (Phil claimed he had watched *Alien* too many times and the whole idea made him feel sick.) He looked tense, even though it had been his idea to come with me.

I was tense, too. 'Damn happy couples,' I muttered to Hugh under my breath. The waiting room was full of them. 'Why do they have to look so smug?'

'I don't think they mean to.'

It was a testament to the power of the hormones passing through my body that I was sexually aware of Hugh even though we were both sitting on hard plastic chairs, surrounded by people and *Auto Car* magazines, only minutes away from looking at my insides.

'Eleanor Connor?' the technician called, and we both got up and went into one of the ultrasound rooms. She was a tiny, round lady with tightly curled hair. 'If Mummy wants to lie on that couch and get her belly bare,' she said, 'Daddy can sit in that chair over there.'

'I'm not the daddy,' Hugh said quickly. 'I'm just a friend.'

Thanks, Hugh, I thought. As if it would have hurt him to pretend for fifteen minutes that we were a normal couple instead of a flaming harlot and her studmuffin neighbour. I toed off my shoes, climbed on to the couch, and pulled up my shirt. My belly gleamed large and pale in the dim light.

'Do you want to know if you're having a little boy or a little girl?' the technician asked.

'I don't know.' It seemed wrong, somehow, to know what gender of baby I was having when I didn't know the father's name. On the other hand, it would help me pick out clothes.

'Tell me if it's obvious,' I said.

'This will be a little cold.' The technician squirted some clear gel on my stomach and I flinched at the temperature. Then she put the scanner on my belly and I saw grey and white shadows on the screen.

A head, immediately. I saw two eye sockets, the cheekbones, more like a skull than a face, but then the scanner moved and I caught a swift-moving glimpse of nose and lips.

'Oh my God,' I said.

The words were totally inadequate.

There was a hand, waving slowly in the fluid world, catching at a foot. A precise, geometric spine. A strong, throbbing heart. A leg jerked at the same time I felt a kick.

Hugh's hand curled around mine.

'That's my baby,' I said.

'I know.' He sounded awed.

'It's all looking fine and normal,' the technician said. She moved the scanner quickly, too quickly for me to focus or fully understand the pictures, but sometimes the ghostly images would coalesce into my baby, and my heart would leap. 'It's got its legs crossed, I'm afraid,' she added.

'Sensible child,' I murmured. But there were tears in my eyes and the words had to be forced out past a lump in my throat.

A few more sweeps, and we were done. Too soon. She handed me a black-and-white photo, not as clear as the other images I'd seen. 'That's its hand and its face and its arm,' the woman said, though I could only actually see the hand. I wiped my belly and got up off the table.

I stared at the photograph all the way out of the room, down the corridor, and out of the hospital. My heart was pounding, my hands shaking.

'It was perfect,' I said. 'It's going to be a perfect baby.' I hadn't known I was frightened till now, when I felt the relief.

Suddenly I was laughing and throwing my arms around Hugh. The sun was high and bright and there was life everywhere, and Hugh was laughing. There was only one thing to do and so I did it.

I kissed him. He swept me up, pulling my feet off the pavement, and kissed me back. At first it was purely joyful, part of the sun and the birds singing and the laughter and the kicking healthy baby.

And then it became about us.

He broke the kiss after a small eternity, but he didn't put me down.

'This not having sex with each other thing is doing my head in,' he said.

'Let's go home.'

Thankfully, my belly was still small enough so that I could half run, half trot next to him through the streets of

Reading to our houses. The sun was everywhere, my hand was in his, and even though it was still winter, I swear that flowers burst into bloom as we passed.

'Whose house?' Hugh asked, panting, as we turned into our street.

'Mine is closer.'

My neighbour on the other side, Alice, was going into her house as we got to mine. She opened her mouth to speak to us, but I unlocked the door and pulled Hugh in after me so fast that she couldn't get a word out.

And then we were kissing again, with no pretence of it being anything other than pure sexual desire. As soon as we were through the door I grabbed his jacket and tugged it off his shoulders so I could feel how his chest felt against my palms, through the cotton of his shirt. He took hold of my top. For a brief moment we had to separate so he could get my shirt over my head.

'God, you can kiss,' I gasped.

'I can do a lot of things,' he said, and he began pushing me through the living room and up the stairs, me walking backwards, my face towards him so I could kiss him some more. My feet, my belly and my arms got in the way, but then we made it upstairs and into my bedroom.

I'd had an elaborate fantasy of undressing Hugh bit by bit. I'd written about Lucy doing that to the Chancellor. I'd wanted to fully appreciate his body, properly look at him for the first time ever.

Not a chance. My hands were too eager: they pushed and tore and tugged, and at one point I think I even used my teeth to unfasten a stubborn button. Every time I exposed an inch of skin, I tasted it with my lips and tongue. As he was pushing down my maternity jeans I bit his shoulder to test the sinew and bone. I touched and touched and touched him as if I'd never touched a man before and I wriggled to help him remove my clothes and then I saw his eyes and I stopped.

He was looking at me, his expression even more naked than his body.

I'd been too frantic to think but, with that look, I remembered who I was. Plain old, good, foolish Eleanor Connor with her pregnant belly, Eleanor Connor who had no idea how to seduce a man, and who was about to shag her best friend.

And I nearly glanced back over my shoulder to see who Hugh could be looking at in that way, because every little bit of his expression said, *You are the most beautiful woman in the world.*

'What?' I said, because he couldn't be looking at me like that.

'I'm just appreciating you.'

'I don't usually look like this.' I gestured at all the round bits.

'You're gorgeous.' He touched me gently above my navel, moulding his hand to me, and then, with the tips of his fingers, my breast.

'What, have you got some sort of perverted desire to make love to a pregnant woman?'

I hated the way I sounded: defensive, abrasive, and insecure. Hugh just smiled.

'I've got a perverted desire to make love to you,' he said. He picked me up, he laid me down on the bed, and he lay beside me.

I have a very good imagination, and a lot of experience in writing about sex. But what Hugh did to me with his hands and his mouth and his body was indescribable. The man had a talent.

And it was *Hugh*. The subject of my fevered fantasies for the past few months. The person I was closest to in the entire world.

Hugh's body was lean and muscular; he had the perfect amount of hair on his chest and legs and his erection was even more impressive than the Chancellor's.

He touched me all over, following his hands with his mouth. I started out gasping and ended up screaming.

When I opened my eyes after my third orgasm, I saw him kneeling beside me, flushed and smiling, pushing a damp lock of hair out of his eyes.

'I've been wanting to hear you doing that while I was in the same room,' he said.

'And I've been wanting to try out one or two things that I've written about,' I said, and I sat up and pushed him on to his back on the bed.

When I'd made him moan, and shout, and beg, and swear, I pushed my own dampened hair out of my eyes and climbed up to straddle his hips.

'Do we need a condom?' I asked him.

He shook his head. And a moment later, as Hugh and I were making love at last, I learned that trust was the most potent aphrodisiac in the world.

E xcept when I opened my eyes later that evening, all I could think was, *Oh shit*.

Hugh was lying beside me, naked. His arms and one of his legs curled around me, holding me tight. His skin and the rhythm of his breathing felt like heaven and home all mixed up into one.

He was asleep, but his face held a hint of his sunny smile. I remembered every moment of having sex with him; I was never going to forget it in my life.

I wanted to press a kiss on his forehead and wake him up. I wanted to trail my hand down his spine and curve it around his backside. I wanted to nestle up against his chest and feel the hairs tickling my nose.

I'd never described anything quite like this. I thought about how Lucy Sharpe would be feeling after she'd got the Chancellor into bed at last. She'd be exultant and confident. She'd feel she was entering a new and exciting stage of her life where she could act out all the fantasies she'd never known she'd had. She wouldn't be thinking about her friendship or her unborn child or the fact that she looked like a beached whale.

How strange it was to be envious of a fictional character I'd invented myself, and who was supposed to be like me.

I gently lifted Hugh's arm and slid out from underneath his leg and rolled off the bed. I grabbed my dressing gown and put it on. Early evening light still filtered through the window. I reckoned we'd been asleep for two or three hours, enough time for me to get some perspective on what we'd done.

I wondered how I was going to get him to leave.

Hugh stirred. He opened his eyes and looked up at me where I stood beside the bed.

'Hello, you,' he said, his voice full of satisfied affection. Without a hint of self-consciousness he stretched out long and wide on the bed.

I stared at him. He was still Hugh, but I had learned so much about him.

I had especially learned why he was so popular in the sack. It wasn't because he had a gorgeous body, though he did; it wasn't because he knew how to pleasure a woman, though he knew that, too.

It was because he made the women he slept with feel special, and different, and cared for. That had to be the most seductive ability a man could have.

'Morning,' I said, though it was evening, because I was feeling morning-after all over.

His smile reached full wattage. 'El, that was fantastic,' he said. He stretched again, curling his toes in contentment.

God, he was so used to waking up in women's beds that this didn't even faze him.

And how often did he wake up in any of those beds more than once?

I swallowed.

For years I had found Hugh's string of conquests amusing. They came and went, while I stayed and watched.

But I was one of them now.

'It was pretty unbelievable,' I said, cautiously.

'You're unbelievable,' he said, rolling on to his front and reaching underneath the hem of my dressing gown to run his palm up the back of my thigh. 'You're a wildcat, Eleanor Connor.'

'Wildcat in heat,' I said, and tried to laugh. 'These pregnancy hormones are really something. Listen, do you want a cup of tea?'

'I want you back in bed with me.' He tugged at my leg, but I stood fast. There was no way I was taking off this dressing gown now that the scales of uncontrollable lust had fallen from our eyes.

'How did it compare?' I asked, trying to keep my voice light.

A ghost of a frown flitted over his sunny face. 'Compare with what?'

'Oh, you know, the sixty million other women you've slept with. I only ask out of curiosity,' I added quickly. 'This sort of thing comes in handy for my writing.'

'Eleanor, I'd never compare you to anyone. You are one hundred per cent unique.'

I bet I was. He didn't even like brunettes.

'I think I'd like some tea,' I said.

In an instant, Hugh sat up, wrapped his arm around both my legs and swept me into bed with him. 'Shut up and kiss me.'

The command was extremely tempting but the rational corner of my brain was reminding me once again that when faced with a semi-naked woman in a bedroom, men were automatically programmed to demand sex, even if that semi-naked woman was nearly five months pregnant and happened to be the man's best friend.

Even if that sex was going to mess up their friendship.

Men had a talent for ignoring considerations like that. They listened to their dicks. I'd been watching Hugh listen to his dick for years now.

I squirmed out of his embrace, which wasn't easy. 'Let's talk for a minute,' I said.

'I have things on my mind other than talking.' He reached for me again.

'Of course you do, but we need to sort a few things out.'

'What's there to sort out? This is great. Come here.'

I planted myself on the edge of the bed in such a way that it would be clear even to the most ardent of dick-listeners that I was not going to budge.

'I think we need to talk about how our relationship is going to change because of – what we've done together.'

Hugh sat up in bed. 'How do you want it to change?' he asked, his voice cautious.

The caution was what did it. It was so clearly the habitual response of a single guy trying to avoid any female getting her hooks into him.

He said he didn't compare, but really he thought I was the same as his other conquests. One shag and he'd forgotten all about what our friendship was like.

'*You're* asking *me*?' I said. 'Come on, I'm not the only one who's done an about-face here. One day you don't even like brunettes and then bang, the next day Eleanor is attractive. It occurs to me, it happened after you heard me and George together, didn't it?'

He frowned. 'Don't be ridiculous.'

'I'm not being ridiculous, it makes sense. Think about it. For years now you've been banging every girl in sight and you haven't even glanced in my direction. Not that I wanted you to, I mean we didn't have that sort of relationship, but then all of a sudden we do. I'm trying to understand it. The only thing that's different is George.'

'Don't bring George into this, Eleanor.'

'I'm not bringing him in, he's already here,' I said, getting into my stride. 'I'm pregnant with his baby. And ever since you heard me and him together you've been different. You've been getting angry, for a start, and every chance you get, you insult him. And then out of the blue, you're interested in me sexually. You know, I think you might be jealous of him.'

'It has nothing to do with him. It's about us.'

The thunderclouds were gathering in Hugh's face and I kept on talking anyway, out of a compulsive need to remind him that this wasn't only down to me, that it was complex, that we were playing with fire.

'But there was no us before there was him,' I insisted. 'I mean, is it like a male thing? I'm sort of your territory and you have to claim me back?'

'That's the most insulting thing I've ever heard,' he roared, and it was nearly a relief to hear him get angry because it meant he wasn't being cautious any more. 'I haven't slept with you to prove anything, I slept with you because I wanted to.'

'Okay, fine,' I said, 'have it your way. It wasn't from any deep dark motives, we were just scratching an itch, getting it out of our systems. That's cool.'

Hugh got out of bed. There was only one thing that could

distract me from his naked body, and that was his furious face.

'Getting it out of our systems?' he repeated.

'Exactly. It's been a distraction, hasn't it, and now we can go back to normal. Right?'

'Are you trying to tell me that you see this as some sort of one-night stand?' he said.

'Well, it was the afternoon, but that's the essential gist of it, yes.' I fluttered my hands and kept my voice cheerful. 'We're friends, and I'm pregnant with another man's baby. Nothing's changed. Right?'

He was staring at me and suddenly all the fear that had been swirling around inside me came to a head and I could barely breathe.

'We are friends, aren't we?' I asked.

Please say yes, I begged silently. *Please tell me I haven't messed everything up*.

He didn't reply for a long moment.

'Of course,' he said finally, and then he broke eye contact and picked up his boxers and jeans from the floor where I'd thrown them.

Some of the fear left. Not all of it, but enough so that I wasn't frozen in one place.

'So, do you want some tea?' I asked.

'No. I've got to go.'

'Oh, okay, I should get to work anyway; I've got to finish the rewrite of this book in the next three weeks or I've got to give back the advance,' I said, aware I was babbling to fill the silence while Hugh wasn't looking at me, 'so I really need to spend all day today slaving away on it. And tomorrow.'

He buttoned his jeans. 'Yeah. At least I've given you something to write about.'

Whoops. I'd forgotten that Hugh read all my books.

'You know I don't write about real life,' I said, deciding to give the Chancellor flaming red hair.

'Uh huh.' Hugh pulled on his shirt. I'd never seen anybody get dressed so fast. He probably had a lot of practice in the quick escape.

'See you later,' he said, and left the room. I heard his footsteps going down the stairs and then pause while he picked up his jacket, and then I heard my door slam. A moment later, I heard his slam, too.

27

He had given me loads to write about. I typed furiously all that night and the next day, and only just managed to tear myself away from the computer to get to the Mouse and Duck for my shift the next night.

Hugh wasn't there. I hadn't heard a peep from him all day. He was angry with me, I knew, but I also knew I'd done the right thing. Sex was sex, but a friendship was irreplaceable.

I tried to ignore the two little voices in my head, the breathy, excited one that whispered, *But that wasn't just any old sex* and the shrill, anxious one that fretted, *But what if the friendship's been ruined already?*

Jerry brought himself and his glass of brandy round to my side of the bar. 'You're looking worried, El.'

'It's nothing.' I refilled Norman's pint and gave both him and Jerry a fake smile. Norman looked happy enough to get it, but Jerry wasn't fooled.

'I've been thinking,' he said. 'How long have you been working here, Eleanor?'

'Three years, maybe a little more.'

'You must be worrying about money and that with the baby on the way. It's about time I gave you a pay rise, eh? And, you know, if you want more hours before the baby comes, we can give you those.'

He was intensely uncomfortable, his face and scalp red and shiny under his buzz cut. Jerry didn't talk about money much, but I knew how much he took on the nights I worked, and he was in no position to offer me a rise. Since he was the main bar staff aside from me, if he gave me the hours he normally worked, he'd be essentially paying me out of his pocket.

'And I was thinking after the baby's born, you don't have to stop work if you don't want to. We've got a spare room upstairs, we can put a cot in, and you can have one of them baby monitors behind the bar. The little one'd be fine of an evening.'

I leaned over and gave Jerry a hug. He looked both startled and pleased.

'Jerry,' I said, 'you are a prince among men.'

'Oh, well,' he sputtered, 'it's the least—'

'You don't have to,' I said. 'I can keep working here till I get too pregnant, but I've got another job I can do with a baby at home.'

'You do?'

'I've never told anyone here this, but I write books. Erotic novels.'

Jerry's face got redder, if it was possible. His eyes were wide and he broke into an enormous grin.

'Erotic novels? Is that like porno?'

I'd kept this secret for as long as I'd been writing, dreading that exact question. But when it came to it, it wasn't that bad.

It was actually a bit of a relief.

'Not exactly. I mean, they don't have pictures, and really they're comedies. But they do have a lot of sex in, yes.'

'And you've got them published? I could buy them in a shop?'

'I'm working on my seventeenth to be published, and yes, you can buy them in a shop. My pen name is Estelle May.'

'Paul! Phil!' bellowed Jerry, immensely pleased. 'Our Eleanor writes porno!'

Of course, after that I was the centre of a crowd of all the regulars and quite a few of the other punters, bombarded with questions and innuendo. Did I make it all up? How much did it pay? Was it hard to get published? Did I *really* make it all up? Could Phil show me a few tricks he knew? How about a story Martha knew about a friend of a friend and how he tied his girlfriend to the bed and dressed up as Superman and then got up on the dresser to jump and—

'Why did you keep it a secret for so long?' Maud asked me.

I looked at the smiling, curious, enthusiastic faces around me.

'I'm not really sure,' I said.

The door opened and Hugh walked in. He had a blonde with him.

My buoyant mood vanished.

'Hugh!' Paul called to him. 'You'll never guess what Eleanor has just told us!'

I saw suspicion flit into his eyes right away.

So much for that trust thing I'd been thinking about.

'What sort of scandal has she let loose now?' he asked carefully, already (I could see) readying his good-humoured expression as he approached the bar with his blonde. She wasn't one I remembered, though that wasn't saying much. They tended to blur together.

'She's written seventeen por— I mean, erotic novels,' Jerry told him gleefully. 'Who would have guessed our El was a sex guru, eh?'

'I certainly never would have guessed it.'

'Hugh knows, he was the one who made me send the first one to a publisher,' I said quickly. 'I don't have any secrets from Hugh.'

Like the cold tone in his voice, the look he shot me escaped everyone else. Then he thawed instantly as he turned to his blonde.

'What will you have to drink, Gail?' he asked her, as if she were the most special person in the universe.

A ball of flames swirled in my chest. I got the drinks for Hugh and his blonde with the bare minimum of communication and eye contact and then I tried not to watch as he took her to his usual Hugh-and-girl corner.

'Tell you what, we should keep those novels of yours away from Norman,' Jerry said conspiratorially.

'Either that, or we should buy him a stack so he has something to do with his hands,' Phil said. They all laughed.

I stayed inside the circle of regulars and tried my best to bask in their warmth, their fond teasing. I laughed and I shot around some witty repartee and I recounted the plots of one or two of my books to a very appreciative audience. I proved that I did not care that Hugh was here with a date, just over twenty-four hours after he and I had ripped each other's clothes off.

Until he came up to the bar for another drink.

'That's one less secret you and I have to keep,' he said

lightly, drumming his long fingers on the bar.

'Nice to see that you've got your social life back on track.'

'Jealous?'

I was so jealous I couldn't see straight. 'No. I'm used to you banging every bimbo in Reading.'

'Didn't you say something to me about being disparaging about people I didn't know?'

I couldn't think of a snappy answer to that. Especially as per my own remark, I was one of the bimbos.

I got him his drinks.

'Are you sure that nothing's changed?' he asked me when I came back.

'I think you've just confirmed it.'

He inclined his head, and held his pint up to me like a toast.

'Here's to one-night stands,' he said, drank, and then went back to his blonde.

I laughed twice as hard at everyone's jokes. I made twice as many of my own. When Hugh and his blonde stood up to leave, I couldn't take it any longer.

'Jerry, I'm popping to the kitchen,' I said. I went straight through the kitchen, out the pub's back door, and through the concrete back beer garden to the alley round the side of the pub. When I got to the end of it I could see Hugh and the girl standing in front of the pub, talking.

It wasn't dignified, but I flattened myself against the wall of the pub in the shadows, watching them. I tried to plan what I would do if I saw them kissing. Tackle them? Cry 'fire!'? Get a grip and admit I'd made a horrible mistake by letting myself fancy Hugh?

I tried to hear what they were talking about, but they were speaking low and I was too far away. The girl giggled and nodded and I clenched my hands into fists. Hugh put his hand on the small of her back to walk with her and I tried to decide how the hell I could interrupt them without looking like a psycho jealous ex-girlfriend.

They went to what I could see was a mini-cab and Hugh opened the door for her. I poised myself to sprint forward and somehow leap into the cab between them, belly and all, and then Hugh shut the door behind her without getting in himself. He waved to the cab as it pulled away.

I sagged back against the wall with relief and watched him walk, hands in pockets, down the road towards our houses, alone.

I was kidding myself. Something had definitely changed.

28

'It's normal,' Roisin said as soon as she picked up the phone.

I'd been expecting a 'hello'. 'What's normal?' I asked.

'Whatever you called to ask me about. I don't need to know what it is – if it's strange, it's normal. You're pregnant.'

I slumped back against the lime-green vinyl seat of my booth, the mobile phone to my ear.

None of this was normal.

My sister was my mother and was on the lam. My mother was my grandmother and fancied the vicar. All of the Mouse and Duck regulars were pointing me out as a local celebrity, and half the time when I looked in the mirror I expected to see Lucy Sharpe.

My best friend had become my lover and was now, apparently, my ex-friend, as we had been avoiding each other for two days. I hadn't seen him, talked with him, or even heard anything through the walls since The Blonde Incident.

'I don't think it's the pregnancy that's causing this weirdness,' I said.

'Believe me, it is. Last night I had a peanut butter and bacon sandwich.'

'That's not too strange.'

'It is when it's dipped in porridge. So what is it with you? And what's that noise in the background?'

'I think the tea urn is broken.' I looked around the café. The tables were sticky, the seats were lumpy, the food on my plate was congealed. The tea urn made a sound like the beginning of the theme tune to *The X Files*.

Everything was exactly the same as it always was, except the seat across from me was empty.

'I'm in Mr Tasty's,' I said.

'Ew, really? Now that is a strange craving.'

I wasn't craving food. I wanted familiarity.

But the familiarity only emphasised how much everything was different. And exactly how big that hole was that I'd kicked in my life.

The hell of it was, the only person I wanted to talk with about my situation with Hugh was Hugh himself.

I bit my lip and the baby moved.

'I wanted to talk to you about those childbirth classes,' I said. 'I feel like I want to understand at least one part of what's happening to me.'

'Great! You'll love the role plays. Hold on, I'll get the schedule.'

Ten minutes later I'd agreed dates with Roisin, and when I said goodbye I felt a little bit better. Maybe it was unlikely that I could have a child without messing it up, but at least I'd made a step towards doing it right.

There was one more step I could take towards doing the right thing. I went up to the counter and ordered another cup of tea. 'And do you happen to have a *Yellow Pages*?' I asked.

The girl working there handed it over without the faintest trace of curiosity, and I took it back to my table, pushing my nearly untouched breakfast aside to make room. First I looked under P for 'Private', but there was nothing there, so I tried D.

By the time my tea arrived I was scrutinising the ads for detective agencies.

Three days later, I was sitting at the most isolated table in the furthest corner of Coffee Republic, across from a small, neat woman in a business suit.

Sophie Tennant had had the least elaborate listing in the phone book, a good thing as far as I was concerned; the large ads about surveillance and marital infidelity in the *Yellow Pages* made me feel as if the whole thing were even more sordid. I was also glad she'd asked to meet me in a central, brightly lit place, the sort of place you would never think anything sneaky was going on. She was friendly and matter-of-fact and had asked me to call her by her first name.

She'd also reassured me with her physical appearance. Sophie was pretty but understated; she didn't appear to be the sort of person who would pull out a gun at the smallest opportunity. I could picture her maybe doing a bit of lurking, but she wouldn't be eating doughnuts and making dirty remarks while she did it, if that makes sense. If I was going to go as far as hiring a private investigator, it was nice that she wasn't a cliché.

'So you don't know the name of the father of your baby,' she said, sipping at her skinny latte.

'Well, I thought it was George, but that might be because I thought he looked like George Michael.'

'And you know nothing about him.'

'No.'

Sophie didn't regard me as if I were the kind of ditzy bimbo you expect to forget to ask the name of the man who's impregnated her. Instead she was nodding, taking my story in her stride, as if she heard things like this all the time. I liked her even more. I'd thought this would be the ultimate in humiliation, but actually it was sort of a relief to be talking about this to someone.

'Forgive me for intruding,' Sophie said, 'but why do you want to find him? Do you want child support, for example, or is there a medical issue?'

'No, it's nothing like that.' I looked at Sophie's light brown hair, held back in a rubber band, and her hands, which were small and had fingernails bitten to the quick. I decided I could be honest with her and if she judged me, at least she wouldn't let me know.

'I recently discovered that the man who raised me wasn't really my father. I have no idea who my real father is. I don't want my child to feel like I do, as if they don't know who they are.'

'Some people would say that nobody really knows who they are,' Sophie commented dryly.

'True.'

'Do you want me to find your father for you as well?'

That surprised me, and I had to take a drink of my decaff to consider. I thought about the way June had laughed when I'd asked who my father was, and the screwed-up teenage note to 'Peter' in her closet. Then I thought about Stanley's bobbly warm cardigan.

'No, thanks,' I said. 'Finding the one father will be enough.'

She shrugged. 'All right. Well, you haven't given me much to work with, quite frankly. If I were the type of agency who kept performance records, I wouldn't take your case, because it would stand a good chance of messing up my one hundred per cent success rate at finding missing persons. Fortunately for you, I'm my own boss, and I don't give a stuff about performance records.'

'One hundred per cent is impressive,' I said.

'It is, if you didn't know I'd only been hired to find four people in the past five years.' A quick grin lit up her face, and then subsided. 'It's mostly infidelity work these days. In any case, there are some things we can try. First, I'll do a bit more of an interview with you.'

It took most of another latte and decaff before Sophie stopped firing questions at me and looked, if not satisfied, then at least thoughtful.

'What do you think?' I asked.

'You really don't remember much, do you?'

'I'm not a good drinker.'

'Evidently. Well, I've got a lead or two, though I think they're pretty slim. I'll follow those up, and meanwhile I know an artist who does witness impressions, so we can have a likeness to show around.'

I nodded. Despite her admission that she didn't handle many of these cases, she seemed to know her stuff. I wondered if my next novel should have a private investigator heroine.

'That's much better than the idea of holding an eighties lookalike contest,' I said.

Her laugh, like her grin, was brief. 'I don't hold out much hope, quite frankly. After the baby's born you can try where DNA testing leads you, if you want to spend a lot more money. But I'll do my best. Is this urgent? I've got some other cases on at the moment and I'm a one-woman agency.'

I gestured to my belly. 'I've got about nineteen weeks to go.'

'There's a little bit of time, then. One more thing: how are you going to feel when I find him?'

Again, I was surprised by her question, but not half as surprised as my first reaction to it: *If she finds George, Hugh will kill me because I've been to a private detective without him. He would love this sort of thing.*

Stupid.

'I'll feel very relieved,' I said as convincingly as I could, but Sophie narrowed her eyes at me and I could tell I hadn't done such a good job.

'Hmm. All right then.' She stood. 'I'll be in touch.' She held out her hand and I shook it.

'Thank you,' I said. 'What do I need to do?'

'Not a lot. I'll arrange for you to meet with the artist in the next couple of days, and then all you have to do is sit back and figure out how you're going to break the news to the guy.'

Lucy huddled in the corner of the darkened office. Her ears strained to hear, over the hum and buzz of the Westminster traffic outside, the final click of the exit door The sound that would tell her that the Minister was gone, and she was safe.

She was safe, but the Chancellor wasn't.

Her guts churned with fear.

How was she going to warn him about the Minister's plan, when he wasn't even talking to her?

I stretched my arms up high and wiggled my fingers. I'd been typing for hours, non-stop for the past week, and a bout of RSI could put a major dampner on my writing career.

Then again, so could not giving in this book on time.

The day was unseasonably warm for February and the windows were open, and all afternoon I'd been smelling the most amazing scent of chocolate coming from Hugh's house. It was clear that he was making something incredible. It was just as clear that I wasn't going to be offered any of it.

My stomach rumbled for the millionth time that day, and

I got up and went downstairs to my kitchen. If I'd thought being pregnant made me hungry, that was nothing compared to being pregnant and smelling Hugh's baking. I rifled through my cupboards in search of chocolate, but didn't find any, which was hardly surprising, because I'd eaten the last bit of chocolate in the house the previous night. It had been a sachet of mint-flavoured hot-chocolate mix. It had been revolting. I'd eaten it all with a spoon, anyway.

I found a bag of prunes and was deciding I was desperate enough to dig in when the phone rang.

'Hello?' I answered, my mouth half full of prunes, hoping it was Hugh offering to come over with some cake, but knowing it wasn't.

'Estelle!' It was Bryce. 'How's the book going, darling?'

I shoved another prune in my mouth. 'Um.'

'Because I've had four people from your publishers ringing me in the past two days asking when it will be finished.'

'It'll be finished on time.' *If I can figure out how the hell it will end.*

'Good! You know what publishers are like, they need time for copy-edits and typesetting, et cetera et cetera; they're saying they're going to miss bound-copy date, so you'll have it done, right?'

'It's nearly done,' I lied. 'I'm just polishing it up so that it'll be perfect.'

'Good girl. What are you eating?'

'Black forest gateau.'

'You lucky thing, you get to eat whatever you want because you're pregnant. I'm on this diet, it's driving me mad. Celery and cottage cheese, and that's it.'

I looked at my rapidly expanding stomach, and tried

to picture Bryce with a stick of celery in his ham-like hand.

'Oops, I must go, Estelle, I'm late for a meeting, but you will get this book in on time, right?'

'Of course.' He rang off and I ate five prunes at once.

Prunes weren't going to do it for me. I needed proper calories if I was going to finish this book on time. I grabbed my keys from the table and went out towards the neighbourhood shop.

Going in to that shop was always a bit confusing because the owner appeared to have a split personality. Sometimes she would be friendly and chatty, talking about the weather and local news while you paid for your bread and milk; at other times I'd greet her and refer to our last conversation about Reading's one-way system or whatever, and she'd look at me as if she'd never seen me in her life. I'd adopted the strategy of saying a cautious yet bright 'hello' when I went in, and gauging her mood before saying anything else.

I'll have to ask Hugh what he does, I thought, and then I remembered and I felt sick. This kind of thing kept happening.

The minute I walked in I spotted him.

He had his back to me, surveying the papers and magazines, but I knew Hugh when I saw him. I froze in indecision as to whether I should ignore him, or turn around and walk right back out again.

But I wanted chocolate. It was bad enough that Hugh was taunting me by baking a cake; he wasn't going to stop me from buying my own sweets, too.

I rushed to the chocolate display, grabbed two bars of Dairy Milk, and threw them on the counter, digging in my pocket for change so I could pay for them fast and get out of the shop before Hugh saw me.

'Hello, Eleanor, how are you today?'

Just my luck that the owner was in one of her chatty moods, when I needed her to be sullen. I looked up from counting my money, intending to answer as quietly and briefly as good manners would permit, but I stopped in the middle of whispering 'Hello'.

There were two of her behind the counter. One smiling, one scowling and rearranging the cigarettes on the shelf.

'You're twins!' I cried out before I could stop myself, and then it was too late to be discreet because I could feel Hugh at my elbow.

The friendly twin was grinning and nodding. 'You didn't know?' she asked, taking the money I was holding out to her.

'No, but I wondered why—'

The other twin turned to Hugh and took his money, and I noticed for the first time that she had short hair, while the happy twin had long hair.

'Oh,' I said, and felt very foolish.

Hugh tucked his newspaper underneath his arm. My choice was either to walk out with him and suffer the awkwardness or stay here and explain how silly I'd been to think for all this time that two shopkeepers were one person.

I went out with Hugh. And then, of course, we were going in the same direction, so we had to walk together.

I have never known a silence so loud. Hugh's newspaper crackled under his arm and my chocolate wrappers crinkled in my hand.

I'll wait for him to say something, I thought. *After all, he's the one who's been producing blondes.*

He didn't say anything. We rounded the corner to our houses.

I heard the jingle as he got his keys out of his pocket.

From this direction, his house was first. Like mine, it had a postage-stamp garden in front and a short walkway to the front door. If he turned in and went into his house without saying a word to me I was going to explode.

He seemed to pause, or maybe that was wishful thinking on my part. Then he turned in and put his foot on to his walkway.

'This is stupid,' I cried.

He did pause this time. For a moment I thought he was going to continue right on up to his door, but then he slowly turned around to face me.

He still didn't say anything, but he looked at me.

'We can't go on like this,' I said.

He raised his eyebrows in agreement, but still didn't speak.

'You're going to make me say it, aren't you?'

He waited.

'I really miss you.'

He nodded, but that was all.

'I'm still attracted to you and I'm sorry I picked a fight with you and kicked you out of my bed.'

Finally, he smiled.

'That's better,' he said. 'What are we going to do about it?'

'Ignore it?' I said hopefully.

'I don't think that's going to work.'

I considered him. He was wearing his glasses and a Dinosaur Jr. T-shirt that he'd had in university and which was nearly threadbare from so much washing. I wanted him more than I'd ever wanted any chocolate in my life.

'No, you're right, it isn't,' I said.

Hugh nodded. 'Want to come in?'

I followed him inside his house and into the kitchen. I didn't even look for the cake. Hugh sat down and I sat across from him.

'You were right when you said I was jealous of George,' he said. 'But you were wrong when you said that jealousy was the reason I wanted to sleep with you. I've been attracted to you for a while.'

'Really?'

He smiled at how incredulous I sounded. 'I'm not bad at keeping secrets,' he said.

'You really kept that one.'

He shrugged. 'I never thought there was any point in letting you know. You never seemed interested.'

I mulled that one over.

'I've got something to admit, too. I was jealous of your blonde.'

'That, I knew already.'

He sounded so smug that I couldn't help bristling. 'Oh yeah? How?'

'Pregnant women aren't so good at lurking in shadows.'

'Damn.' Heat flushed my face.

'I was flattered. Once I stopped being angry.'

'So what are we going to do?'

'What do you want to do?' he asked gently.

I thought about it, and decided that, on balance, the truth was a wiser path at this point.

'I want to drag you upstairs and shag you senseless. Or better yet, shag you senseless here on the kitchen table, if I could be certain it wouldn't shatter under my weight.'

Hugh laughed.

'So it's more than a one-night stand after all,' he said.

'It was really the afternoon. But yes, it's more than that.'

After the uncontrollable passion we'd had last time, I sort of expected Hugh to take up my offer of shagging him senseless there and then, as quickly as possible. Instead he leaned his elbows on the table and looked steadily and thoughtfully into my face.

'But you're still pregnant by another man. That hasn't changed.'

'No. But George hasn't made any signs of appearing.'

'Sleeping with you doesn't make your baby mine.'

I frowned. 'I never said I expected you to be the baby's father, Hugh.'

He shook his head. 'No. You haven't.'

He was still looking at me, making no move towards me, as if he were trying to read something in my face, though I couldn't tell what.

Then he stood up and held out his hand to me, without taking his gaze from my eyes. I went to him and laced my fingers with his. I stood on tiptoe and I kissed him.

It was the first time I'd kissed him not half-asleep, not overcome with frantic lust. The first time from a cold start. It was warm and tender and deeply sexy. It tasted of everything that was sweet about Hugh.

When it was finished we didn't rip each other's clothes off, though I knew that was coming. We wrapped our arms around each other and stood there in the kitchen holding each other tight.

'Your friendship is too important for me to lose,' I told him. 'These past few days of not speaking to each other have been horrible. I even went to Mr Tasty's on my own.' I shuddered.

'So we're friends?'

For a moment I worried, because he'd put that as a question, as if our friendship were in doubt, but when I saw his face I knew I needn't have worried. It was full of affection as ever.

'Best friends,' I said.

'Friends who have sex with each other.'

'Sex friends,' I agreed.

'Friends who have lots and lots of sex with each other.'

'Oh, yes.'

And that was when I decided that we'd talked quite enough and it was time to put the sex part of being sex friends into practice. Knowing how rubbish I was at subtle seduction, I unlaced my hands from Hugh's and let one cup his perfect bottom through his jeans, and let the other creep round to grasp his perfect erection, which rapidly went from half-mast to full mast in my hand.

'Upstairs or the kitchen table?' I asked.

'Let's leave the kitchen table for after you've had the baby.' Hugh pulled me rapidly to the stairs. 'Likewise carrying you up these, I think.'

I was picturing another frantic stripping episode. But when we got to his bedroom, Hugh took off his glasses and we just stood there for a minute, looking at each other and smiling.

'This should feel weirder than it does,' I said. 'I should feel as if I'm about to have sex with my brother. But I don't.'

'That's reassuring, I think.' Hugh pulled my T-shirt over my head. Underneath I was wearing maternity jeans, the really unflattering kind that had elastic more or less all the way up to my armpits. 'I'm glad you've set me a challenge here.'

I started giggling as Hugh pretended to try various ways

of peeling the elasticised jeans from my body. And then he started tickling. After seven years of nonsexual wrestling with me on couches and floors he knew all of my ticklish bits and, of course, I knew his. By the time we had finished we were both lying on the bed, panting and laughing, me in my knickers and bra and him in his boxer shorts, and it flashed through my mind that he'd somehow managed to undress me without my feeling self-conscious about my pregnant body at all.

Then he undid my bra and began kissing my breasts and my panting was with pleasure rather than with laughter.

'Thank you, Tit Fairy,' I gasped.

Hugh looked up from my right breast, his eyebrows raised.

'Are you calling me a Tit Fairy, or is this your normal prayer during foreplay?'

'The Tit Fairy is who visits you when you get pregnant,' I explained. 'Not only have I gone from 34B to 36D, but I have about a zillion more nerve endings in there.'

Hugh was delighted. 'Really? So it feels even better when, for example, I do this?'

He ran his thumb over my nipple in thrilling circles and I moaned, 'Yes.'

'What about this?' He licked it and then blew on it, hot liquid and cold all at once.

'Definitely.'

'And this?'

He did something so spectacular that I couldn't even define what it was, just buried my fingers in his hair and held him there so he could do it again and again and again.

'My God, Hugh,' I squeaked.

He dropped a kiss on the tip of each of my breasts and

propped himself up on his elbows next to me. His lips were moist and his face was bright and boyish.

'Or you know what we could do,' he said, as if we were in the middle of a completely different, non-breast-related conversation. 'We could get married.'

Languishing in ecstasy as I was, it took a moment for me to hear what he'd said, and another for me to understand the words.

I sat up. 'What?'

'We could move in together, the baby would have a father; it might be a good idea.'

His voice was cheerful and casual, as if he were talking about the weather or a recipe for Victoria sponge.

I laughed. 'You're joking. That's ridiculous.'

'Why do you say that?'

'Well, aside from the fact that this baby isn't yours and that you've sworn up and down that you'll never get married, don't you think marriage would put a serious dent in your social life? The blondes and such?'

He shrugged and began tracing around one of my breasts with a finger again. 'Ah, well, there are more important things than blondes.'

His finger went down the top slope of my breast, around the nipple and over the top, zigzagging down the underside, then around the curve back up to the top again. It was very distracting, to me, and, apparently, to him, because he was intently following his finger with his eyes.

'Well,' I said, 'it's very kind of you to offer to make me an honest woman, but it's not necessary.'

'Are you sure?'

I remembered his caution after we'd slept together that first time. This was typical Hugh kindness, and the best apology I could have. I leaned over and kissed him.

'You can stop it with the knight-in-shining-armour rescue, Hugh. You're a nice guy, the best guy I know, and you've just proved it. But you don't want to marry me, and I don't want to marry you. That's all there is to it.'

He met my gaze briefly and there was a strong emotion on his face, evidently relief that I hadn't taken him up on what he'd felt obligated to offer.

He looked as if he wanted to insist further, so I wriggled closer to him, wrapped my arms and legs around him, and pulled him down to me.

'Now didn't we mention something about shagging each other senseless?' I murmured in his ear as I nibbled on it.

'We did.' He gave me a smile that was pure Hugh, and proceeded to do just that.

The next ten days passed in a frenzy of work and a cloud of bliss.

Jerry got one of Maud's granddaughters to take over my shifts at the pub and I spent every waking minute writing *Throbbing Member*. That is, every minute that I wasn't spending making love with Hugh.

Lucy saved the Chancellor from the Minister's nefarious plottings to destroy his career and his life, by a clever trick involving a cleaner's uniform, a bottle of Plymouth Gin, and an iPod. Hugh and I lounged in bed on Sunday morning, arguing what was better, the cryptic crossword or the Sudoku, then getting distracted by the baby doing somersaults. Then getting distracted by each other.

Lucy cornered the Chancellor in a stationery cupboard, ripped off both their clothes, and at the climactic moment, confessed her feelings for him. Hugh and I had an oral sex competition, decided it was a tie, and decided we'd make it the best out of three. Or four. Or a dozen.

Lucy wallowed in the depths of despair after the Chancellor dumped her brutally, only to discover that he'd done it because he feared for her life. I wrote about a car chase, a thrilling brief encounter in a taxi, and a death-defying episode on the London Eye where it looked as if the Minister might triumph at last. And then I sneaked into Hugh's house while he was at work and greeted him with a silk blindfold and an assortment of feathers.

Writing a book, when it is going well, is like falling in love. Every piece seemed to fall together. There were considerably fewer orgies than my readers were used to, but Lucy and the Chancellor had this chemistry that swept me up so that I typed and typed and still couldn't get the words down quickly enough.

I even cried when I was writing the ending, something I'd never done before. Okay, so these days I cried at nappy advertisements, but I felt as if there were something special about how the Chancellor admitted his feelings for Lucy. I felt as if it were real.

I typed 'The End' twelve hours before my deadline. I did a lightning-fast edit, printed it off, and sent it to Bryce and my editor Duane before I could think twice, before I fell out of love with the story. And then Hugh made the biggest raspberry cheesecake I had ever seen and we brought it to the Mouse and Duck and everyone celebrated. Even the baby, who kicked like mad after I ate so much sugar.

I was incredibly happy.

And then I hit my third trimester, and things started getting tricky.

Six to Nine Months: Who's Your Daddy?

It didn't get tricky right away, though. With the novel done, I concentrated on cleaning.

Quite a bit of clutter accumulated in my office while I was writing frantically – notes, pens, the post I hadn't had time to open, and, for some reason, socks – and after I finished a book I always ritually cleared away. It was as if I were clearing my head space of the old book at the same time, ready for the next one. This time, when I'd finished clearing, I decided I needed to do a proper clean of the room of the sort I hadn't done since June had left. I took down the curtains and washed them, scrubbed skirting boards, shampooed the carpet. Hugh, who was a clean sort of bloke but who drew the line at ironing curtains, moved the furniture for me and then watched me with amazement.

'Is this what they call nesting?' he asked.

It probably was. Then again, it was something else, too. Every swipe of my rag was an attempt to swipe away some of the doubts I had about *Throbbing Member*.

I usually had these doubts after I sent off a manuscript. But *Throbbing* was different to any other manuscript I'd ever written, and so the doubts were even stronger. I kept on remembering things I'd put in it and cringing with doubt. Why'd I put in the karaoke-obsessed twin lobbyists? What was I thinking of giving the Chancellor a pet chicken?

And the biggest doubt of all: who on earth would want to read a sexy novel with a heroine who was riddled with faults, self-conscious and insecure, easily embarrassed and obsessively tidy?

That is, who would want to read a sexy novel with a heroine who was like me?

Bryce didn't ring. Neither did Duane. I knew they would both read it and confer before talking to me.

The fact that they hadn't rung me meant one of two things: either it was good enough and Duane was working so hard to get it straight to the copy-editor that he didn't have time to ring me or Bryce, or it was so bad that they were both taking a long time trying to figure out a way of informing me that my career was totally dead.

I wasn't going to ring them. No way. I was going to enjoy this limbo for as long as it lasted because, as the hours and the days passed, I was more and more certain that not only was this absolutely the worst book that *I* had ever written, but it was also the worst *book* that had ever been written, full stop.

The three days that passed felt like three months, particularly because I seemed to grow bigger by the day. When the phone rang I was on my hands and knees in my office cleaning the underside of the radiator, and it took me a while to stand up, grab on to the desk when I got dizzy, and then clump down the stairs to where I'd left my mobile.

'Estelle,' Bryce said as soon as I picked up. 'I've

just been talking with Duane. We cannot believe the rewrite you've done on *The Throbbing Member of Parliament*!'

Here it comes, I thought. 'Really?' I braced myself on the bookcase.

'It's astounding!'

Astounding good, or astounding bad? I couldn't ask. Instead I made an interested noise.

'And so different from your other novels! I think you've reached a totally different level with this one.'

'Level of what?' I blurted.

'Level of everything! The pacing, the plot, the characterisation – the Chancellor is quite something.'

I was beginning to think that I was being complimented, but I still needed convincing. 'You liked it, then?'

'Estelle! Duane and I love it! You have utterly raised your game. This is the book that's going to make your career, darling.'

I held the phone in both hands, tight to my face. 'You mean it's not rubbish?'

Bryce laughed as if I'd told a joke. I felt brave enough to push further, and said, 'But there isn't actually that much sex in it, for an erotic novel.'

'It doesn't matter. It's very sexy, very now. Quirky enough to be different, and mainstream enough to win you a much wider audience. You clever girl. I'll never look at Big Ben in the same way again.'

He didn't seem to be taking the piss. I sank into the nearest chair and started breathing again.

'But what's the best bit is the heroine. So realistic, darling, so sympathetic. And her relationship with the Chancellor is what makes this a great read. It's not only a rollicking adventure, it's a true-love story.'

Relief was breaking over me in waves. 'Oh, thank God,' I said, and then something struck me.

'Wait. Did you just say it was a love story?'

'Of course! The emotion is in every line, I loved it. That scene where Lucy tries to seduce the Chancellor and can't think of how! And I nearly cried at the ending. Now, I've been thinking about the possibilities for selling the rights for this one, and I think that –'

Bryce carried on talking, but I couldn't listen to him. Because the implications of what he'd just said were putting themselves together, like a jigsaw, in my head.

Lucy was me. And the Chancellor was Hugh. And if *Throbbing Member* was a love story . . .

'Estelle? Estelle! Are you still with me, darling? You've gone very quiet.'

'I'm still here,' I said, faintly.

My God. I must be in love with Hugh.

'So I'll pitch it to him at lunch next week, and we'll see where that takes us. What do you think of that?'

'Great,' I said. 'This is all great.'

This was all terrible.

I knew I *loved* Hugh, of course. I'd loved him for a long time. But being *in love* was different. It was gooshy and exclusive. It meant changing your entire life and nine times out of ten it didn't last.

'You sound awful, darling. Are you feeling well? Is it morning sickness or something?'

With some part of my brain, I wondered if Bryce had forgotten how pregnant I was, along with my real name. 'No, I'm fine.'

'You don't sound it. Listen, I'll ring you later and we'll talk. Well done, Estelle.'

He rang off and I sat, phone in hand. How had this happened? Why hadn't I noticed? Why would I do something so monumentally stupid?

Hugh walked in my front door without knocking. We were doing a lot of that lately; it was almost as if we were living together in two different houses.

As soon as I saw him, my heart leapt. Moreover, I realised that my heart had been leaping at the sight of him for some time now.

Bad news. I really was in love with him.

'It reeks of furniture polish in here,' he announced. 'And you are white as a sheet.'

He flung open the nearest window and came to sit beside me.

Not what I needed. I needed some distance from Hugh in order to come to terms with what was going on inside my head, heart and soul.

'I've got stuff to do,' I said, standing up. 'I haven't finished cleaning the radiator.'

'Right,' Hugh said, standing up. 'You are officially a crazy pregnant woman. You need fresh air more than you need clean radiators.'

'Okay, okay, I'll go for a walk.' I headed for the door. 'I'll see you later.'

Hugh, however, came right along with me. 'You don't need to come with me,' I said. 'I'm sure you're exhausted from work.'

'You can't be trusted,' he said. 'If you've been on your hands and knees cleaning radiators at seven months pregnant, who knows what you'll take it into your head to do while you're out on your own. Climb a tree or something, no doubt.' He fell into step beside me. 'Besides, it's a beautiful day.'

It was true. Even Reading was looking pretty good. Some of the houses on our street had window boxes full of spring flowers; the trees had a haze of young green leaf against the backdrop of the red brick Victorian terraces. I headed towards the lake at the University. There would probably be ducklings.

And damn it, it felt far too good to have Hugh walking beside me, even when we weren't talking about anything or even touching. Normally our silence would be comfortable. Today I was thinking too much not to fill it with conversation.

'Bryce and Duane liked my book,' I said.

'Brilliant!' Hugh grabbed me round my non-existent waist, lifted me up, and swung me in a circle. He set me down rather quickly at the end of it. 'Oof, maybe I'll wait a few months before I try that again.'

I searched my feelings. He'd just called me fat and I was still in love with him. Worse luck.

Relying on my emotions wasn't helping me much. Maybe if I figured out logically why I'd fallen in love with Hugh, I could work out a plan to stop it.

'I knew they'd love the book,' he said.

'How'd you know?' I asked. 'You haven't even read it.'

'I don't need to read it to know it's good. You're talented, and you were enjoying yourself so much writing it that it's bound to be good.'

The logical answer wasn't so difficult to come by. I sneaked a glance at his body as he walked beside me. The man gave me unconditional support and he had a great arse. I'd fallen in love in the past for far less compelling reasons.

'Did I ever tell you that you're partly to blame for my new job?' he asked me.

'I thought it was the macaroons in the dull meeting.'

'Partly. And partly because of you and your writing. Every day I was seeing you doing what you wanted to do, what you loved doing, and getting better and better at it, while I sat in a dull office working in I.T. Finally, I decided I'd had enough.'

'But I was ashamed about what I wrote. I never even told anybody but you about it till recently.'

He shrugged. 'I was proud of you.'

Agh! Was the man trying to make me fall more in love with him?

I had to talk about something else, quick. 'So I think I'm going to make my office into the nursery.'

'Where will you write?'

'Well, I'm thinking it's time I became less precious about that. I mean, I don't need a pristine place to write, do I? People write any old where. And the baby deserves a space of its own.'

'Are you just saying that or do you really mean it? I remember how annoyed you were when June was staying there.'

I thought about it. 'I really mean it. I'll get a laptop and sell the desktop. That way I can write on the kitchen table or on the couch while I'm rocking the baby to sleep.'

'How about you put your desktop in my spare room? It's not as if I use it for anything, I can move all the stuff out of there into the loft. If you get a baby monitor, you can write there and you'll only be a wall away from the baby when it's asleep.' He grinned. 'And we know how easy it is to hear through those walls.'

'Ross and Rachel did that with their baby in *Friends*,' I said, because showing my knowledge of television comedy was much safer than expressing what I was feeling at that moment.

'Or if you're not comfortable with the monitor, I can always hang out in your house while you work in mine,' he added.

The man was offering to give me a room in his house. That was nearly like living together. Maybe – and I stumbled over the pavement when the thought struck me – maybe Hugh was in love with me, too.

He had asked me to marry him, after all. Of course it wasn't exactly a romantic proposal, and he most likely hadn't meant it, but he had asked.

That counted for something, didn't it?

I didn't say much as we reached the university lake. Hugh told me about his day, making five hundred and sixty profiteroles for a wedding at the hotel, and we searched the water for exotic ducks. I listened extra carefully to his voice and what he said, and when he took my arm to help me around a mucky bit in the path, I analysed his touch, trying to work out if these were the words and actions of a man in love. But he sounded and felt exactly as usual, exactly as he always had.

We rounded the corner of the lake. Distracted by my thoughts, I didn't notice what was in front of us till Hugh grabbed my hand and stopped me walking. Two Mandarin ducks were standing in the muddy path, surrounded by fuzzy ducklings. The male, bright and tufted, stood guard while the female made broody sounds and snapped at the grass along with her children.

My hand drifted to my belly.

'Six of them,' Hugh said. 'They'll be busy.'

I thought of Hugh sitting on my couch, standing guard

while I wrote in his spare room. 'Do ducks mate for life, do you think?'

'I'm pretty sure that's swans. I think ducks do the thing where the male sneaks up on the female and has sex with her before she can notice.'

'Unlucky female.' We watched as the mother herded the ducklings into the shallow water among the reeds. They popped one by one into the lake and their parents waddled after, the whole family gliding away.

I made sure Hugh wasn't watching me and wiped away a tear.

This was utterly ridiculous. I was getting all romantic over ducks. Clearly I had to find out how Hugh felt before I went even more insane.

'I got another phone call today,' I said when we'd started walking again. 'From Gwen.'

'Oh yeah, from uni? What's she up to? Still serving divorce papers out in Henley?'

I hadn't actually heard from Gwen since Christmas, when she'd sent Hugh and me our usual joint card.

'She's got this dilemma,' I said. 'She's fallen in love, completely by mistake, mind you, with her best friend. She doesn't know what to do.'

I strolled along, holding my breath, waiting for his response.

We passed the log bench where, all those years ago, Hugh had made a pass at me and I'd laughed. Why had I laughed? Because the idea of kissing Hugh had actually been ridiculous, or because I'd known even then, deep down, that I had to do anything I could to avoid falling in love with him?

'Male or female?' Hugh asked.

'Huh?'

'Is her best friend male or female?'

'Um. Male. Why?'

Hugh kicked a clump of grass. 'No reason, I was just curious. Does her best friend love her back?'

'She's not sure. She's too scared to rock the boat.'

'What did you tell her to do?'

'What would you tell her to do, if you were me?' Inside my pockets, my hands were clenched tight. I couldn't look at him.

'I'd tell her to try her best to snap out of it. Falling in love with your best friend is a recipe for disaster.'

His voice was vehement, and my stomach sank.

'She should probably try to date someone else,' he added, 'get her mind off it.'

'That's what I told her to do,' I said.

32

If one of my confident, independent former heroines were falling in love with the guy she was having a red-hot affair with, she would probably break it off, on the premise that it would be much less painful to end the relationship sooner rather than later, when she'd had time to make her love him even more.

I was not that idiotic.

I was getting lots of the best sex I'd ever had and it was a pretty sure thing that after the baby came my sex life would be nil. Nappies and breastfeeding would be my primary focus for some time.

For another thing, I lived next door to Hugh and breaking it off with him – especially without a good reason – would be torture. It could kill the friendship, which was what I'd been trying so hard to avoid doing in the first place.

For a third (and most important) thing, I just did not want to. Why would you want to cut open your own chest, rip your heart out, and toss it casually into the street like so much rubbish?

So I pretended nothing had changed. I talked with Hugh

and I laughed with Hugh and I had meals with Hugh and I served Hugh drinks in the pub and I had the wildest sex I could manage with Hugh, and every moment of that time I did my very best not to reveal that Hugh was rapidly becoming more and more the love of my life. Even when he helped me wallpaper the nursery with stars and clouds. Even when he turned up with two teddy bears for the baby, saying he couldn't decide which one to buy so he bought them both. Even when he smiled at me and made my heart flip.

I thought about Hugh's advice to Gwen's fictional problem: try to date someone else to get your mind off your inappropriate emotions. That wasn't an option for me, especially as I was growing heavier with child by the day, but I did have one other man on my mind. Maybe it was time to think more about him.

This time when I rang and asked to meet her, Sophie Tennant told me to come to the cafe at the large Tesco outside the town centre. On the phone she mentioned something about surveillance on the Thames, which passed near to the supermarket, and when she turned up she was wearing jeans and wellies that were spattered with mud. I bought her a cup of tea and a scone and she gulped them both down as if she hadn't eaten in days.

'What have you been doing?' I asked, intensely curious, wondering if I could use it for a book.

'Can't tell you.' She rubbed her finger on the plate to get the last crumbs of scone. 'I've also nothing to report on your case. I've had no recognition on the drawing you and Andy produced. Actually, I tell a lie. Several people said initially that they recognised it, but when they thought more about it they realised they were thinking of George Michael.'

'He does look like him,' I said.

'The clues I thought I'd got from your description of the evening haven't panned out, not yet, anyway. I did discover one thing, which might give us a little more insight, but then again it widens the field considerably.'

'What's that?'

'On the evening of the eighteenth of September there was a serious disruption to rail services to and from Paddington. Several trains were cancelled and for a few hours there were no trains in either direction at all. This time coincides with when the subject turned up at your pub out of the blue.'

'So there's a chance he was a delayed rail passenger trying to kill some time,' I said.

'Well, I wouldn't have used the phrase 'killing time' myself, knowing what it was he ended up doing, but yes. We could well be looking for someone who's not local at all.'

'Someone from London?'

'Or any of the locations that the trains from Paddington via Reading serve – Swindon, Bristol, Swansea, or anywhere in between. Or anywhere with a connection from one of those places. You said he didn't have an accent, but that doesn't necessarily rule out other parts of the country.'

I thought of what I'd said to Hugh about Reading: that people were either stuck here or that they were passing through. I was stuck, and George was probably passing through. It was typical.

'Anyway, I'll keep looking,' Sophie said. 'I haven't exhausted every possibility yet, not quite. Sorry I don't have better news for you.'

She sat back in her plastic chair, stretched, and pushed back her hair, looking momentarily surprised when she found a bit of reed in it. Then she dropped the reed on her saucer and gave me one of her penetrating looks.

'Why did you ask to meet me when I could have easily given you all this over the phone?'

'I, uh, thought that was how it was done.'

'No, I told you I could give you an update over the phone, and you said you'd rather meet, remember? How come?'

'You know, when you start firing questions you're a little bit scary.'

She shrugged. 'You don't have to tell me anything.'

Of course, she meant exactly the opposite, and again I found I wanted to tell her.

'I'm in a new relationship, but I don't know how Hu— the man feels about me. I sort of feel like if you can't find the father of my child, then it's a sign that I should take a risk and tell this new man how I feel about him.'

Sophie's forehead wrinkled. 'So it sounds as if you don't actually want me to find the baby's father.'

'No, I do. He deserves to know, even if he doesn't want anything to do with it. And the baby deserves to know, too.'

'If I do find him, does it mean you're going to end this relationship you're currently in?'

'Maybe. I don't know. I'll think about that if it happens.'

She took some time to think about this, absently picking more bits of reed out of her hair.

'Eleanor, I always tell my clients not to hire me to find any information they don't really want to know. I think you fall into this category. Maybe you should pay me for my time so far and we should quit.'

'Sophie, I want the best for my baby. I have to find George, even if that means my current relationship doesn't work out.'

'Forgive me for saying, but how do you know that your current relationship wouldn't be the best thing for your baby?'

I thought about Hugh helping with the nursery, Hugh with two teddy bears in his arms.

Then I thought about Hugh two or three or ten years down the line, stuck with a woman whom he didn't love and a baby who wasn't his, all because he was chivalrous and kind and decent.

'I need to do my best to find George,' I said firmly.

'All right,' she said, standing up to leave, 'it's your life. Only make sure you prepare yourself for how you're going to feel if I do find the baby's father, and your relationship is over.'

H ugh wasn't in when I got home, though I knew his shift had finished two hours before. I tried to read a book and then took a bath, though every time I started to relax I heard some sort of noise from somewhere and started up, sure it was Hugh returning.

I fielded a phone call from Sheila. She didn't mention Richard the vicar, which was a relief, though the possibility did strike me that she wasn't mentioning him in the same way I wasn't mentioning the private detective.

Hugh still wasn't back by the time I was ready to go to work at the Mouse and Duck. I walked to the pub, chewing on my fingernail.

I wasn't worried about him being out. I knew Hugh well enough to know that although he got through more than his share of women, he wasn't a cheater. If there was any sort of relationship going he would always end it before starting something up with another woman.

However, even though I knew he wasn't off having wild sex with someone else (who would doubtlessly not be pregnant), his absence hammered home the fact that Hugh and I didn't have a proper relationship. There was no commitment, beyond our friendship. If he did meet someone else – if he had already – there was nothing stopping him from ending our arrangement.

I had secrets; maybe he did, too.

The pub was quiet, as usual. I greeted Martha and Maud, who were the only two regulars there. 'Have either of you seen Hugh?' I asked as casually as I could.

'Er,' said Maud, swirling her drink in her glass.

'No, love,' Martha said quickly. The two of them exchanged a look and then it was straight into the baby advice for me.

They were terrible liars. I smiled and assured them that yes, I'd put safety plugs in all the electrical sockets in the nursery, that the decorating was nearly all finished, thank you, that Hugh had put together a changing table only yesterday, and I had hung the curtains. Yes, I had been careful whilst on the stepladder. Yes, I was still planning to breastfeed. No, I hadn't started rubbing sandpaper on my nipples to toughen them up. I nodded and slipped away behind the bar before they started talking about engorgement and cabbage leaves again.

Why would they cover for Hugh? What was he up to? I wasn't sure whether any of the pub regulars knew about me and Hugh being lovers. He'd tried to lean over the bar and kiss me one Saturday night when he'd had a pint too many, and I'd pushed him away. It was going to be difficult enough to get our friendship on its prior footing if we broke up; I didn't need to be answering questions from all the punters, too.

Then again none of them had asked me who was the father of my child. Maybe they assumed it was Hugh since we were so close. Which made it even stranger that they would be covering for him.

I shook my head and picked up a plastic crate half full of empties, which was heavy enough for me and my belly. No matter how much I thought about it, it all boiled down to one thing: I was paranoid. And not because of Hugh; it was because our relationship was so ill-defined.

I couldn't live like this. I had to make the leap, one way or the other. I both hoped for and dreaded Sophie's report.

As I nudged open the door to the back alley with my hip I saw someone coming down the stairs that led to Jerry's flat. I recognised Hugh's shoes immediately; they had been under my bed that morning.

I waited till his face appeared and he could see me. He stopped dead. I saw that Jerry was behind him.

'Why do you two look so guilty?' I asked.

Hugh's guilty expression melted away beneath a smile. 'Do I look guilty?' He came down the rest of the steps and took the crate of empties from me. 'I'll put these out back and then I've got to get home and eat something. See you later, Jerry. El.'

I could have followed him, but I knew better. Hugh was too good at keeping secrets.

Jerry, on the other hand, was rubbish. 'Don't you carry them empties,' he said to me, but he couldn't quite muster the requisite sternness. He skulked past me, looking guilty as hell.

It took about an hour of unsubtle questions before I got it out of him.

'We want to give you a party here in the pub,' he admitted, and then downed the rest of his brandy in an attempt to cover up his embarrassment. 'A launch party, Hugh said it was called. For that book of yours.'

I blinked. 'Really?'

'Well, we figure you won't be doing any partying for a while after the baby. I didn't want to keep it a secret; it was Hugh who wanted it to be. I said a surprise party would probably make you go into labour or something.'

'You're most likely right,' I said, because I didn't want him to feel bad for dropping the secret, not after he'd been so thoughtful.

'Plus, you probably want to invite people yourself. All the exciting book-type people you probably know.'

Exciting book-type people. I pictured Bryce, hulking in a pink designer shirt and crocodile shoes, and Duane in his London suit, standing on the battered sticky carpet of the Mouse and Duck, drinking cava from half-pint glasses and pretending to snack on mini chicken kievs and pork scratchings.

And yet Jerry and Hugh had thought of it. I felt a wave of love for Hugh so strong that I had to swallow, hard.

There was a good deal of shame mixed up with that emotion, too. For years I'd treated Hugh as part of the furniture. And, while I was at it, what had I ever done to deserve the support Jerry was giving me? I'd grumbled about my job, nagged him to improve the pub, and dreamed about getting some other more exciting job.

'It's extremely kind of you, Jerry. I've never had a launch party before.'

He nodded, his face red. 'Well, you just keep the fifteenth of May free, and invite whoever you want, and leave the rest to me and Hugh. We'll do you proud.'

'I know you will. Thank you, Jerry.' I hugged him and he blushed harder, especially because Paul and Phil sent up a lecherous cheer from the other side of the pub.

*

'Still no news, I'm afraid,' Sophie Tennant said to me over the phone, her voice matter-of-fact as always.

I settled back in my chair with my hands cradling my stomach. The baby shifted and squirmed. At seven-and-a-half months pregnant I could identify the baby's legs and arms when they poked me.

'Sophie,' I said. 'Remember I said that if you found him, it would be a sign for me?'

'Yes, I remember that. I remember feeling particularly uncomfortable about it, to tell you the truth. But it's your life and your money.'

'Well, I've had another sign. If you haven't found George by the fifteenth of May, I want to call off the search.'

'All right. Why is that, if you don't mind me asking?'

I took a deep breath. I'd been thinking about this for days. I felt a squirming inside me where the baby's head was, as if he or she were nodding in agreement.

'I'm having a party that night – which you're invited to, by the way – and I've decided that's the night I have to bite the bullet and tell Hugh how I feel about him.'

'Mm,' she said. 'You're a brave woman. And, if you don't mind my saying, a little bit of a drama queen.'

'I'm a writer. Staging a scene comes with the territory.'

'Okay,' Sophie said. 'I'll do my best to find the subject before the fifteenth of May, and I'll write up my final report for that day. And I'll be at the party. I'm a private investigator, and nosiness comes with that territory.'

34

Hugh held me tight against him, my naked back to his naked front, and pressed a long kiss on my neck, damp with sweat. I had just about caught my breath, but my heartbeat was still raging.

'I don't know how much longer we'll be able to do this,' he murmured into my ear, stirring my hair. His hands wandered lazily over my body.

With the speed of light, my post-coital bliss transformed into post-coital anxiety.

It was about two hours till my launch party at the Mouse and Duck. Which meant there were roughly four hours before I poured Hugh another glass of champagne, took him by the hand, led him outside to the front of the pub, lit by streetlamps and the stars, and delivered my carefully rehearsed speech, telling him that I loved him and I wanted to make our relationship real and for him to be the father of my child.

That was, if Sophie didn't ring first to say she'd found George.

And if Hugh didn't jump the gun by breaking up with me.

'What do you mean?' I asked, trying to make myself sound satisfied and lazy instead of paranoid and crazy.

'I heard that sex can make a very pregnant woman go into labour,' he answered. He rubbed his palm briefly against my belly before sliding it up to cup around my breast, his fingers toying with my nipple. 'And if you get much bigger I'm not sure the two of us are both going to fit into this bed.'

Right. He was talking about mechanics rather than emotion. 'Quite honestly, now that we're in to thirty-seven weeks, I feel like going into labour wouldn't be such a bad thing,' I said. 'I'm sure nature makes you pregnant for nearly a year just so you can get so sick and tired of it that you're actually looking forward to labour pains.'

Hugh chuckled and gently manoeuvred me so that I was facing him. Not an easy task.

'Have you thought much about labour?' he said.

'A bit. Roisin and I are going to those classes. Last Wednesday I had to pretend to be a cervix.'

I was more preoccupied with risking my relationship with Hugh than with labour. I was, rightly or wrongly, confident that my baby was going to arrive healthy. But if Hugh and I went wrong, there was no epidural that could take that pain away.

'They say it's like forcing a bowling ball through a hole that's meant to fit a golf ball.'

I winced. 'Thank you so much for that analogy, Hugh.'

'You're welcome.' He nuzzled my neck again. 'Anyway, I figure you don't have to worry about that, because once you've had the Mighty Hugh, a bowling ball is nothing.'

'Don't flatter yourself, mate.'

The midwife leading the classes had talked about the importance of having a birth partner. It had been on the tip of my tongue to ask Hugh over the past weeks, but I'd refrained, for two reasons. One was that if Hugh said he loved me, he'd be with me in the delivery room as a matter of course, so asking him before I found out his feelings would be redundant. The other was that if Hugh didn't love me, and he'd committed himself to helping me deliver the baby, he would feel obligated to be there even if he didn't want to be. And I didn't want anything out of Hugh that he didn't want to give by himself.

It was another thing I'd know before tonight was over.

'It's not flattery if it's the truth,' Hugh said. 'I am exceptionally well-endowed. Everybody tells me so. Even that nurse back at the STD clinic, remember her? She said it was the finest one she'd ever come across.'

'Oh, I see,' I said. 'You're trying to tell me that you haven't been sleeping with everybody in sight for the past few years because you're an unrepentant sex maniac – but because you've been canvassing opinion about the size of your penis.'

I tried to keep it light, but a small hint of bitterness crept through. I disguised it with a smile.

Hugh, though, looked serious. 'Actually, Eleanor, the reason I slept with everyone in sight for years is—'

My mobile rang on the bedside table. I reached over and grabbed it before I could hear any more about Hugh's penis or his many lovers. In the split second before I picked it up I was certain it was Sophie ringing to tell me that she'd found George at the last minute, and my heart rolled over.

But it wasn't Sophie's number on the display. It was Bryce's.

'Estelle!'

His shriek was so loud that I held the phone away from

my ear for a moment. When it seemed he'd stopped, I spoke gingerly into it. 'Bryce? How are you? Are you still coming to my party tonight?'

'Yes! But there's some news that can't wait! I've sold the film rights to *Throbbing Member*, darling!'

'Oh my God. Really?' I clutched the phone. Beside me, Hugh sat up. 'I've sold the film rights to my book,' I told him, and then something occurred to me and I spoke into the phone. 'You haven't sold them to a porno company, have you?'

'No, I've sold them to Reuben Rogers! Remember, he won a Palme d'Or at Cannes two years ago for *The London Lads*? Very edgy, very funny, very now? He wants to try a romantic comedy that's different and he thinks *Throbbing Member* is perfect! Estelle, I told you this one was going to transform your career!'

'Wow,' I said. I grabbed hold of Hugh's hand and squeezed it, hard. 'You weren't wrong.'

Hugh was grinning all over the place.

'Reuben is dying to meet you and so he said he'd come along with me to your launch party tonight! I hope you have plenty of champagne lined up! Though I don't suppose you can drink it, can you?'

'I don't think I need to,' I said, dazed. I said goodbye, hung up the phone, and Hugh crushed me in a massive hug.

'A film!' he cried. 'I'm so proud of you, Eleanor.' He kissed me and grinned and kissed me again.

But do you love me? I was tempted to ask now, while we were celebrating, in the wake of the great news. It could make everything perfect.

Or it could ruin it all.

I played it safe. 'Hold on, let me go and get my tape measure.'

'Why?'

'I think we have enough time to put the Mighty Hugh to the test before we have to get dressed. I'd like to gather some objective evidence on whether that STD nurse was telling the truth.'

'This is the Mouse and Duck?'

I stood in the centre of the pub and turned slowly around. The fluorescent ceiling lights were turned off; instead, the place was lit by candles and strings of fairy lights. A fire blazed in the disused fireplace. In the dim light the walls looked warm, not dingy.

The bar was strewn with flower arrangements, filling the whole room with scent. I saw brand-new fluted glasses and an array of bottles that looked, from here, like real champagne.

And Norman, in his usual seat, was wearing a suit.

I turned to Jerry, who stood beside me. 'You did this?'

'We all did,' he muttered. 'Maud and Martha did the flowers and that, and us lads did the heavy moving.'

There had been some definite heavy moving. Many of the rickety tables and chairs were gone, replaced by a pair of sofas. One of them I recognised as the one from Jerry's flat upstairs, and the other was a long chocolate-brown leather one.

'You moved your sofa all the way down the street?' I asked Hugh, astounded. 'When did you do that?'

'This morning,' he said.

'Wow. And you still had energy for –' I stopped myself before I blurted out details of our sex life to all the regulars. '– The profiteroles?' I finished, spotting a huge pyramid of them on the bar beside the champagne.

'I've always got energy for profiteroles,' Hugh murmured in my ear, caressing my back in that secret intimate way that gave me delicious shivers.

'This place looks amazing,' I said. I hugged Jerry, Paul, Phil, Martha, Maud, even Norman, who politely refrained from grabbing my arse. When I got to Hugh I squeezed him extra tight and whispered to him.

'Thank you.'

'You're worth it.'

It felt as if my smile was actually shining bright, I was so full of happiness. Hugh's was hardly less so.

'I've got a surprise for you later,' I told him.

'I like surprises.'

I stepped away from him before our closeness got too obvious, or before I was tempted to snog him in front of everyone. In the corner was a table, polished till it was gleaming, and stacked with glossy copies of *The Throbbing Member of Parliament*. I went over to it and ran my fingers over the covers. Someone had been thoughtful enough to put a couple of pens on the table for signing the books.

I heard a pop of a champagne cork. Hugh pressed a glass of sparkling apple juice into my hand. 'Can't wait to read this one,' he said to me.

'Have you really read them all, or do you have them as decoration?'

'I've read them. Where do you think I've learned most of my tricks?' His wink warmed me up as I thought about his tricks.

'I've read a bit of it,' Jerry said from beside me, sipping his champagne. 'I mean, while the books were just sitting here. I'm not much of a one for books, but I liked this one. It was more like a film or something.'

'And I can't wait to find out what a filthy imagination you have,' Maud said, presenting me with a book to sign for her.

The guests began to arrive. Duane showed up with the rest of his editorial team (every single one of them a slim, leggy blonde in great shoes – I suspected Duane chose them on purpose). They exclaimed loudly over me, the pub, my bump, the book. Some more Mouse and Duck semi-regulars turned up, along with people I'd invited from the Reading newspapers and the local BBC radio station.

Roisin and Jimmy came in, and so did Gwen. I'd nearly not invited her because of that whole lie about her falling in love with her best friend. I was afraid Hugh would ask her about it and I would be found out. I'd agonised and agonised about how to warn Gwen about it without making myself sound like a psycho, till I came up with the simple solution of telling Hugh he wasn't supposed to know about it. After that I knew it wouldn't pass his lips. I watched Hugh greeting her with a bit of trepidation, anyway, but there was nothing untoward.

Sheila had come down from Upper Pepperton the night before, but I hadn't seen her yet. She'd insisted on staying in a hotel and said that as long as I was sure I didn't need help, she wouldn't dream about getting in my way while I was getting ready.

The minute she walked in the door I saw the real reason why she hadn't come to my house.

She was with Richard the vicar.

He wore a black suit and a tie with cartoon characters on it. Hugh was closer to the door than I was and he greeted Sheila with a kiss on the cheek. I watched her introduce him to Richard, and then I noticed that Richard was holding her hand.

That was why she hadn't mentioned him in her phone calls lately.

Sheila caught my eye and she blushed bright red from the collar of her dress upwards. In that blush I saw every single thing she and Richard had got up to in that hotel room together and I also saw that Mum was in love.

I went over to her and hugged her. She had on a new perfume.

'You look great,' she told me and I knew that she was lying; maternity clothes flattered no one, especially not someone eight months pregnant. I looked like a medicine ball in heels.

'Thanks,' I said anyway. 'I like your scarf.' I think it was supposed to be an evening wrap, but it looked more like a silvery version of what Tom Baker wore in *Doctor Who*.

'I made the baby a matinée jacket in the same yarn; it's in my bag.' She was still blushing furiously. 'You remember Richard.'

He held out his hand to me, and I noticed he did not look embarrassed at all. Just kind.

'Of course I remember you,' I said to him. 'I'm so glad you could come.' I hugged him. He had Sheila's perfume on his collar.

'I wouldn't have missed it for the world,' he said. 'I can't wait to read your book. Sheila is so proud of you.'

He exchanged glances with Sheila and I saw that he was in love with her, too. I suppose I recognised it because I was feeling the same way myself.

'I'm proud of Mum, too,' I said, and when she took my hand with her free one and squeezed it hard, I really was proud. 'I'll go get you a book and sign it specially,' I said to Richard.

Sheila followed me to the book table while Richard found glasses of champagne for them.

'Were you scared to tell me?' I asked her.

'Terrified,' she said.

'I hope you'll get married before you fall pregnant this time,' I said, and she giggled, and everything was all right.

'It's a wonderful party, love. I thought you said this place was a dump.'

I looked around again at the smiling people, the shining lights, my friends and family. 'I was wrong,' I said.

I wasn't drinking, but the vibe made me feel a little bit tipsy. There were lots of people laughing, the flickering lights and Hugh always somewhere in the range of my senses. Even when I couldn't see him I could feel him, like a pleasurable itch.

I didn't notice Sophie till I came across her in a corner of the room, wearing a slim black dress and sipping a glass of water. Evidently she was good at blending in.

'I've made up my mind,' I told her before she could say anything to me. 'I'm going to tell Hugh how I feel about him.'

Sophie followed my gaze across the room, to where Hugh was laughing while he talked with Sheila, Richard and Duane. He had his back to the editorial blondes. He was wearing a dark suit and a shirt with an open collar, his hair was rumpled in normal Hugh-style and he was so beautiful I wanted to run across the room and kiss him so hard we wouldn't be able to breathe.

'Love triumphs again,' she said dryly, and toasted me

with her glass of water. Her tone of voice was more cynical than romantic, but she added, 'You've chosen a good-looking one, anyway.'

'He's the best man I've ever met,' I told her. 'I can't believe it's taken me so long to realise it.'

'It's as well I couldn't find the father of your child,' Sophie said. 'Though I suspect this is a better outcome for you.'

'It really is.'

'Estelle!' Bryce's voice carried over the buzz of the party and the light jazz that replaced the jukebox's faded hits. I turned to see him looming over the guests. He air-kissed me on both cheeks and surrounded me with his cologne before he clasped both of my hands in his huge well-manicured paws and said, 'Darling! I am so thrilled! Let me introduce you to Reuben Rogers, who is making a film out of your fabulous book!'

He let go of one of my hands and gestured at the man who stood behind him, who had been obscured by his bulk. The man had an expensive suit, straight white teeth, and a goatee.

I stepped backwards on to Sophie's foot, ignoring her small yelp.

It was George.

35

'We've met,' he said.

I'd thought my memories of George had gone rather fuzzy, but as soon as I heard his voice I knew it was as I remembered it.

He held out his hand to me. 'It's good to see you again,' he said, 'although I thought your name was Eleanor.'

He was smiling, friendly, charming. He seemed not at all embarrassed by the situation. He also seemed to be doing an astoundingly good job at not glancing down at my swollen, pregnant belly.

I, on the other hand, couldn't say a word. I took his hand and shook it and although I hadn't thought I'd remembered his hands, I did as soon as we touched. I breathed in and smelled his aftershave and I remembered that, too. I even remembered being in my bedroom with him, inhaling his scent.

Though the memories were strong, they weren't as strong as any of my hundreds and thousands and millions of memories of being with Hugh.

I looked over at Hugh. He was staring straight back at

me. He had a glass of champagne in his hand and as I watched he slowly put it down.

'You've met already?' Bryce asked. His voice sounded even louder than usual and I realised it was because nearly everyone else had stopped talking.

'Yes,' George said. 'In this very pub, as a matter of fact. Although everything seems to have changed quite a bit since then.'

He was still pleasant, still casually friendly, but I could see him now registering something wrong in the room, glancing at my belly, wondering exactly how far gone I was.

Phil stood not far from us. 'Hey, you're the guy who owes Eleanor twenty quid,' he said, putting two and two together and making three.

Then he, too, glanced at my belly and I saw the calculation rapidly righting itself. 'Oh.'

'I need to talk to you,' I said to George-who-was-really-Reuben-the-producer-who-wanted-to-film-my-book.

'All right.'

The room was now totally silent except for light jazz. Jerry caught my eye and gestured towards the door up to his flat. I nodded and led George/Reuben behind the bar, to the stairs.

When I passed Hugh he had picked up his drink again and was staring at it as if the bubbles contained the secret of the universe. I willed him to look at me, so I could tell him without words that I hadn't wanted this to happen. But he didn't.

As we began climbing the stairs I heard Martha saying behind us, 'He doesn't look like George Michael.'

Jerry's living room seemed bare and comfortless without his couch, but he'd brought up quite a few of the chairs from the pub. I sat down on one and Reuben, who was by now looking distinctly worried, sat on another.

'Is the baby mine?' he asked right away.

I nodded.

I wasn't sure how I was expecting him to react, though I'd imagined this moment many, many times. He didn't get angry, as Hugh had been, and he certainly wasn't thrilled, as Sheila had been. He looked stricken and a little bit sad.

'I'm sorry,' he said. 'I didn't mean for that to happen.'

'No, me neither.' Though I put my hands over my bump, as if to shield the baby from any thought that he or she could ever have been a mistake.

'Were you going to tell me after the baby was born?'

'I didn't know how to get in touch with you,' I said. 'I didn't even know your name.'

Reuben blinked. 'Really? Didn't I tell you?'

He seemed genuinely surprised.

'I probably didn't ask,' I said.

'I guess we were both more interested in other things.' He shifted in his chair as guilt flitted over his face. 'I left early in the morning in a hurry to catch the first train to London. You were still asleep, and I only realised when I was halfway to Paddington that I hadn't left you my number. I should have rung you, but I didn't have your number either.' The guilt settled more deeply. 'Which is no excuse; I knew where you lived. I just thought – you made it so clear you only wanted a one-night stand.'

I couldn't remember whether I had or not, but I did remember my state of mind that evening, and it seemed at least likely.

'I got a lot more than I intended,' I said, and then

tightened my hands on my belly again. 'Not that I'm sorry. I want this baby.'

'Have you been planning to bring the baby up on your own?'

I thought about what I'd intended to ask Hugh tonight. Then I thought about him staring at his drink, avoiding my eyes. I bit my lip.

'Yes,' I said.

Reuben let out a long breath. For a while we sat and looked at each other. He had lines around his eyes I hadn't noticed when we'd first met.

'I really liked your book,' he said at last.

'Thank you.'

'I felt that it had a lot of emotional truth in it. I was actually quite touched.'

I nodded. Of course he wasn't to know where the emotional truth came from.

'I wasn't expecting this,' he said. 'I think we need to talk a lot more.'

'I think you're right.'

He frowned. I could see he was thinking hard. 'We'll work something out. I mean, I don't really know you, but I do like you, Estelle.'

'Eleanor. My agent calls me by my pen name.'

'He is a bit like that, isn't he?'

He smiled and I realised that I liked him, too. Mostly I liked how he wasn't trying to squirm out of what we'd done, but also I saw humour and intelligence there. It was partly what had attracted me in the first place, I supposed.

'You've got a party downstairs,' he reminded me.

Not only a party. A roomful of people who'd just found

out who the father of my child was, and who were probably discussing it thoroughly right now.

And Hugh.

I swallowed, but the lump in my throat didn't go away.

I gazed wistfully at the vodka optic as I passed it on my way back into the pub. Booze would be a welcome escape. Then again, considering what I'd done the last time I'd got drunk, it was a good thing I wasn't allowed any.

I'd expected silence when I came back downstairs, but I didn't get it. It was as if everyone knew that what I wanted most was for the party to continue as it had done before, as if my life hadn't turned itself totally upside down. People were talking and laughing, but not about me. I received a few glances but they were more of concern than of curiosity.

Sheila showed up at my side with Richard and another glass of sparkling juice. 'You need a drink,' she told me, and then she turned to Reuben, who was standing beside me. 'I'm Eleanor's mother,' she said, 'it's nice to meet you.'

'Reuben Rogers. Very nice to meet you, too.'

Well, if Reuben helps bring up our baby, at least it should have good manners, I thought. He didn't betray the slightest apprehension at being scrutinised by the mother of the woman he'd impregnated. And a vicar.

I craned my neck, but Hugh was nowhere in sight. 'Have you seen Hugh?' I asked Sheila.

'I think he had to nip out for a minute. So Reuben, what do you do?'

I excused myself from their conversation and threaded through the crowd. Not easy when you're both considerably bigger than usual and also the object of everyone's concealed interest. Martha looped her arm through mine and wanted to know about the film deal; Paul wanted to tell me that he'd read the first chapter of my book and he had never found politics so interesting; Phil wanted to apologise about shouting out about the twenty quid. I was stopped so many times that I began to suspect that the pub regulars were conspiring against me, trying to keep me from finding Hugh.

I was nearly at the door when Bryce pounced out of nowhere, quite a feat, considering his size. 'You are joking, Estelle,' he whispered, 'do you mean to tell me that Rueben Rogers is the *father*?'

I turned to him. 'It's Eleanor,' I said. 'My name is Eleanor.'

I was probably going to say something else, something sarcastic and unprofessional that could have cost me a very good agent, but before I could, long arms flung themselves around me from behind.

'El!' cried Hugh's voice, and my heart leapt and then dipped.

He sounded happy.

He turned me around to face him. There was a bright Hugh-smile on his face. 'You found George!'

'Yes,' I said, mystified. The last time I'd seen him he'd looked – well, I wasn't sure what he'd looked like, but it hadn't been happy. 'His name is Reuben Rogers. He's a film producer.'

He nodded. 'Was this the surprise you had for me?'

I thought of the speech I'd rehearsed. All the emotions I'd planned on revealing.

'Um,' I said.

'Let's go outside for a minute, you're looking a little pale.' He took my elbow and guided me out the door.

The night was balmy, lit by the stars and the orange streetlights. This was where I'd hoped to tell him I loved him.

'Hugh—' I began.

'What does he say?' he interrupted me. 'Does he want to know? If he doesn't want to know, tell me, because I'm happy to hit him. Unless of course that would scupper your film deal. I wouldn't want that to happen. Is he a nice guy?'

He was acting super-Hughlike, full of energy and words.

'He seems to be a nice guy,' I said.

'He doesn't look like how I expected him to. And he doesn't look anything like George Michael, you know. No wonder nobody could remember him.'

How could he be all cheerful about this?

'I think he looks like George Michael,' I said.

'Well, I've said it many times; you are a little bit mad. What does he say about the baby?'

'He says we'll work something out.'

He nodded rapidly. 'That's great. Excellent. That's what you wanted.'

'I'm not sure it is what I want.'

He took my hands in his. Just as he'd always done for as long as I could remember, whenever I needed a friend.

'El, remember how you felt when you found out that you didn't know who your father was. You've said it yourself, your baby deserves to know better.'

'Yes, but—'

'And look at me, look at how I grew up. I had a father and a mother who couldn't stand each other and who did their best to make sure I didn't feel as if I belonged anywhere. Your baby deserves better than that, too. Your baby needs two parents who love him. Or her.'

I stared at Hugh's expressive face and his dark bright eyes. I remembered every time he had put a protective hand over my belly.

'But what about us?' I asked.

For a moment I thought I saw something flicker in his eyes. Then he was all smiles again, all energy, all super-Hugh-like.

'Us was great,' he said. 'In fact, us was bloody amazing. But we'll always be friends, El. I'm not going to let anything in the world get in the way of that.'

He pulled me into his arms for a big hug.

I clung to him, my best friend who had broken my heart.

36

I stood at the floor-to-ceiling window, looking down at the bustling excitement of Chelsea. The baby squirmed inside me and I patted my stomach.

'We're not in Reading any more, Toto,' I said in a poor imitation of Judy Garland. I went back to my seat on Reuben's long, low black leather-and-chrome sofa, next to his long, low glass-and-chrome coffee table. I had my brand new laptop on the table, next to a marked-up copy of *Throbbing Member* and a stack of notes.

Reuben's Chelsea flat was modern, spacious, and spotless. It was the kind of place they used for interior shots in television shows featuring young and trendy creative people. He had original abstract art on the walls, shining hardwood floors, and the cleanest windows I had ever seen. Every few days, someone (though I never saw who) refreshed the flower arrangement that sat on a marble side table near the door.

It was, in short, the perfect pristine writing space, absolutely ideal for what I was supposed to be doing, which was adapting *Throbbing Member* into a screenplay.

I couldn't work at all.

At thirty-nine weeks pregnant, I could barely walk or type. My feet were swollen, my hands were swollen, and when I looked into the mirror I didn't recognise the round, dough-like person who looked back at me. The only things my pregnant body wanted me to do were to eat and to lie down, and rest up to give birth to this baby.

Pity I hardly had any appetite, and that I couldn't sleep.

With a grunt, I lifted my feet up on to the coffee table in an attempt to reduce the swelling. I knew I was kidding myself: being one week short of full term in my pregnancy was uncomfortable, but the real reason I couldn't do anything was because of Hugh. Or, rather, lack of Hugh.

How was I supposed to sleep at night in the vast bed in Reuben's spare bedroom? Hugh had made a lumpy pillow, he had angles and elbows and sometimes, deep in the night when he was really tired, he snored, but I had never slept so well as when I had been in his arms.

Reuben was nice about food. Reuben was nice about everything. He brought me elaborate sandwiches from the deli around the corner; he brought me delicate strawberry tarts from the patisserie down the street. He had even, with that wild look in his eye that men got when they were trying their best to deal patiently with hormonal women who looked as if they were about to explode, asked if maybe I fancied some pickles and ice cream.

I wanted the sloppy traces of cake batter from the bottom of Hugh's mixing bowl.

The baby kicked again, and began to hiccup. I smiled and rubbed the place where the baby's back pressed against my stomach. His or her hiccups were the strangest movement the baby made; they were, for me, the clearest evidence that though this baby was inside me, he or she was a separate being whom I was looking forward to meeting.

'I wish you'd hurry up and be born and give me something else to think about,' I said to my child.

Reuben came in from his study, clicking his mobile phone shut. 'I'm popping out for a meeting,' he said, 'but you can ring me if anything happens, okay? I can be back here in fifteen minutes.'

I nodded. 'I was telling this baby to get a move on.'

For a moment, the expression on Reuben's face was pure terror, but then he swiftly covered it up with one of his half-sardonic smiles. 'Don't tell it to come too fast, I just had these floors washed,' he said, and kissed me briefly on the cheek before he left.

Alone again, I let out another huge sigh. I couldn't blame Reuben for being freaked out. Anyone would be scared if they suddenly found out they were going to be a parent. I'd certainly been scared. Reuben needed time to get used to the idea, and he'd come around. There was no reason he couldn't be a perfectly good father.

If it was any indication, he was already doing his share financially. He'd put me on his private healthcare plan, found me an obstetrician and a paediatrician, and bought a sleek, minimalist cot and a trendy pram of the type you saw celebrities pushing. He'd suggested himself that I move in with him so that he could help take care of me in the last weeks of my pregnancy.

And since then we'd been dancing around each other. Polite, not too close. Doing our best to focus on today, rather than years down the line. There certainly hadn't been any repeat of our sexual escapades of nine months before, but then again, I was not exactly looking like a sex symbol at the moment.

We were making the best of it. We were giving each other a chance.

I was so lonely I couldn't stand it.

The doorbell rang. I heaved myself off the couch and waddled to the door. It was probably a delivery. In the first couple days I'd been in Chelsea, some of Reuben's friends had come round to visit, but when they'd encountered me and my belly they hadn't quite known what to say. These days, they rang Reuben first to make sure he was going to be home too, or they arranged to meet him elsewhere.

He'd ordered a digital baby monitor off the Internet; that was probably what was being delivered. Top-of-the-range model, to go with everything else in the sleek nursery.

I thought of the second-hand cot in Reading, the two teddy bears inside it, and swallowed before I opened the door.

June stood there; small, slim and tanned. The two duffel bags she'd had before were transformed into a matching set of luggage.

'Ellie!' she cried and hugged me. Then she stood back and surveyed me. 'My God, Hugh wasn't kidding. You're about to pop.'

Out of the thousand questions that could have rushed into my mind and out of my mouth at the moment, the one that chose to pass my lips was, 'You've talked with Hugh?'

'He told me where you were. Can I come in?'

I stood aside so she could fit past my belly. Aside from the tan, the luggage, and the lack of hangover, she was exactly the same as the last time I'd seen her, right before she'd disappeared. Beautiful. Assured. Sexy. A law unto herself.

And she'd spoken with Hugh more recently than I had.

She flung herself gracefully on to the low leather sofa and looked around. 'Nice place,' she said.

'Yes, it is.' I sat next to her, though it made me feel even more of a lump than usual. 'Where have you been?'

June shrugged and produced her pouch of tobacco from her teensy handbag. 'I went on holiday abroad for a while. I figured I could do with a change.'

'You must have been able to go somewhere very nice with your fifty thousand pounds.'

She laughed. 'Oh, you know about that? How?'

'Your ex-boyfriend broke into my house looking for you and he told me about it while he was threatening me with violence.'

'Oh, Ellie, I'm sorry.' She placed her hand on my arm for a moment and then went back to rolling her cigarette. 'I must have left my address book behind.'

I put my hands over my baby bump again. The mere idea of Jojo harming my baby made my entire being cringe with fear. I was June's child, and all I got was a 'sorry'?

'So how much of the fifty thousand do you have left?' I asked.

'Oh, that? It's been gone for ages. I've been working in Nice in a casino.' June looked around the flat again. 'You've really landed on your feet in this place. Hugh said something about the father being a film star?'

'A film producer.'

'Nice. Very nice. Good work.' She put her cigarette between her lips and rummaged in her handbag for her lighter.

'June, I'm pregnant and I don't want you to smoke near me.'

'Oh!' She took the cigarette from her lips, taken aback. 'Of course not. Where can I smoke?'

'Nowhere.' I folded my arms across my chest. 'What did you mean by "good work"?'

She put her unlit cigarette on the coffee table next to my laptop. 'I mean it was smart of you to pick someone with money to be the father of your child. Why stay in poxy old Reading if you can live in luxury?'

Anger propelled me off the couch faster than I would have thought possible. 'I don't believe I wanted to be like you,' I burst out.

'You wanted to be like me? Why?'

Her surprise wasn't the reaction I'd been expecting. I paused, but only for a moment. I was too angry to stop.

'You're the most selfish human being I know. You never did anything when I was growing up but swan in and out and give Sheila grief. You don't even know who my father is.'

'I told you, I don't have a maternal bone in my body.' She smiled.

'It's not something to brag about, June. Why did you have to tell me you're my mother?'

'Oh honey, it just slipped out, it just happened.'

'Sort of like how *I* just happened?'

'Yes. And that, apparently.' She gestured at my belly.

'At least I plan to stick around for this baby. It's going to know who its father is, and I'm going to care for it and love it.'

June only nodded. 'Anything else I've done wrong you'd like to tell me about?'

'How about leaving Reading without telling me where you were going?'

'Come on, Ellie, you've lived your whole life without me telling you where I was going. We're both adults with our own lives.'

'We are now. Not when I was a kid and you took off.'

June sighed. 'Yes. I'm a lousy mother. Let's move on from that, shall we?'

'Sure. Let's talk about how I was threatened by your psycho drug-dealing ex-boyfriend.'

'Ellie. Be reasonable, sweetness. I didn't tell him to come and threaten you. I never thought he'd—'

'That's what I keep telling you, you never think! You just take what you want! You palm off your baby on your parents, you lead your own little glamorous life, if you want to have sex with someone you go right ahead, don't even think about your own daughter and how Hugh is her best friend and he's—'

At that, tears flooded my eyes and closed my throat. I turned away from June, to the window, where I stared, unseeing, out at the street.

'Don't be ridiculous, doll,' June said behind me, in a voice so typical of her that I clenched my fists, knowing she hadn't understood a single word I'd said. 'I never—'

Someone pounded on the door. Grateful for the distraction from June, I hurried to the door, wiping my eyes on the hem of my maternity top, and unlocked it.

The door flew open, catching me on the shoulder and flinging me several feet backwards. My thigh banged against the marble flower table and I grabbed it to stop myself toppling over as six-foot-three of furious dreadlocked Jojo pushed me aside and strode into the flat.

'Darling!' June cried, her voice holding no trace of fear or surprise. She didn't even get up.

Jojo grabbed her by the front of her filmy dress and hauled her off the couch.

'Where the hell is my money, you bitch?' he growled, shaking her like a puppet. I could hear her teeth rattling.

'Calm down, Jojo,' she gasped between shakes. My leg burning with pain, I hobbled as fast as I could towards the telephone, on another table across the room.

Before I could reach it I heard a click. 'Don't ever think about using the phone,' Jojo said, and I looked over to see that he'd unflicked a large knife. He was holding it to the side of June's face. 'Not if you don't want your sister to get cut.'

'I'm her mother, actually,' June said, her big eyes gazing up at Jojo as if he were offering her a dozen roses.

'That's even better,' said Jojo; 'it means I can get rid of three generations of your scummy family at once if you don't tell me where my fucking money is.'

'It's gone. I spent it,' June said.

I could see Jojo's hands tightening on June and the knife, and I took a step closer.

'You spent it?' he growled dangerously.

'What can I say, I'm a high-maintenance girl, and things are expensive on the Côte d'Azur,' June said. 'I'll tell you what, though, sweetheart, those Frenchmen are incredibly well hung. Quite a welcome change for me after you.'

Jojo hardly let her finish her sentence. He tossed June to the floor. Her head made a sickening thump on the hardwood. He stepped forward and planted his foot in her stomach to pin her down as she lay there, her arms and legs flung wide, too stunned to struggle.

'Right, bitch, you just earned yourself a new face.'

My leg and shoulder were throbbing, my entire body was swollen and ungainly. I'd never moved so fast in my life. I launched myself forward, pulling back my right arm, dodged under his hand holding the knife, and let Jojo have it in the face.

My fist connected with his nose and I heard a crunch. Then I heard the knife clattering on the floor. I heard Jojo grunt in pain. And I heard two bumps as he fell to his knees.

In a single smooth movement, June brought one of her feet up and kicked the pointy toe of her boot straight into Jojo's crotch. His red face went white and he fell sideways on to the floor, one hand grabbing his groin, the other clamped around his nose, which was spouting blood on the spotless floor.

'Nice one, El,' June said, scrambling to her feet.

'You too.' I stepped back and shook my hand, which was aching from the impact. Jojo lay groaning. I picked up the knife from where he'd dropped it. 'What do we do with him?'

'Got any gaffer tape?'

'Maybe under the sink in the kitchen?'

June skittered off in her high heels and I stood, hefting the knife in my hand and watching Jojo writhe. From what I could see, his nose was a mess from being broken twice by two different Connor females.

She returned with a roll of silver tape and knelt beside Jojo, efficiently wrapping it around his ankles. He realised what was happening and tried to struggle, but June sent a well-placed knee into his bollocks again and he doubled over, gasping, as she taped his wrists together.

I was reminded of my heroine, Mel, in *Chained Melody*, and her talent for bondage.

'God, I really did make my heroines like you,' I said.

June looked up from her work. 'I don't do heroin,' she said vehemently. 'I only slept with this scumbag, I didn't sample any of his wares.'

'I didn't—' I thought that now was perhaps not the time to explain my career to June. 'I'll call the police.'

When I finished, June was perched on the couch, gazing down at the trussed and red-faced Jojo, who could do little but writhe and moan.

'You risked your life to save me,' she said.

'I couldn't let him hurt you.'

'Even when you were angry with me, when you were telling me how selfish I am. About how I spoiled your life. You could have run away and saved yourself and your baby. Instead you floored him with a right hook.' She smiled at me. 'Well done.'

'Thanks.' I sat down beside her and contemplated Jojo. 'You didn't really spoil my life.'

'I was a kid, Ellie. You're older now than I was and you can see things more sensibly but I was thirteen and I was desperately unhappy, dying to get out of that place. I could never breathe.' She sighed. 'I am selfish, I suppose. I've just always been on my own. I never wanted to settle down or be a good little girl. It never seemed like any fun.'

'Well, you can do something unselfish when the police come. You're going to tell them everything you know about Jojo so he gets put away and can't hurt any of us.'

'But sweetness, I don't—'

'You're going to do that, June.' My tone of voice brooked no complaint.

'All right.' She prodded him with her pointed toe. 'He deserves it, I guess.' She perked up. 'And the money I took isn't traceable.'

We sat there for a moment, watching Jojo bleed from his nose, waiting for the police.

'Was Peter my father?' I asked her.

She glanced at me. 'Who?'

'I found a note to somebody called Peter in your closet in Upper Pepperton, and you talked about me in it.'

An emotion crossed June's face. I couldn't tell which one it was, because I had never seen anything like it on her face before.

'No,' she said, and then her expression was back to careless, cheerful confidence. 'I told you, don't worry about who got me pregnant. I never think about it, and neither should you.'

'I just want to know who I am.'

'Believe me, doll, you know who you are.'

Jojo made a noise as if he were about to say something, but June crouched down so that she was face-to-face with him, and said sweetly, 'If you want some motivation to keep quiet, think about how you're going to breathe through that broken nose if I decide to gag you.'

She straightened up and rejoined me on the leather couch.

'Why did you want to be like me?' she asked me. 'You were Stanley's favourite. And Sheila's. They were ashamed of me.'

'You always seemed so free, and beautiful. You could do what you wanted and get away with it.'

'But you said what I wanted was selfish.'

'That's exactly why you're so free.'

'It's also why I'm alone,' she said.

We were quiet for another moment. I didn't feel angry at her any more. I felt sorry for her. Love hurt and made you worried and frightened. But it was better than the alternative.

'I didn't have sex with Hugh,' she said suddenly.

I looked away from Jojo and at her. 'What?'

'I wanted to. He's very tasty. We were hammered on whisky that night. He brought me home and we carried on drinking and I took my dress off and dropped it on the floor. He picked it up and gave it back to me.'

'You're joking.'

'No. He said –' June smiled, rather theatrically, the expression she got when she knew she was the centre of attention.

'He made me promise to keep it a secret,' she said. 'But I can't keep secrets, and besides, I don't want to. He said that he couldn't have sex with me because he was in love with you.'

I stared at her.

'But – that's not right. Hugh slept with lots of women. And he and I hadn't even—'

I stopped before I gave away the secrets of my love life.

'Oh, Ellie doll, he told me all about it. We were completely pissed. He said he'd been in love with you for seven years or something like that. Ever since he'd met you. And that all the other girls were a distraction.'

I couldn't say anything.

'All blondes, he said they were. And redheads. Never a brunette like you.' She reached over and tousled my hair. 'Or like me. I guess it was too much of a reminder for him. Let me tell you, I was horribly annoyed with you, darling. You ruined my fun without even knowing. No wonder I was tempted to get my own back.'

'That can't be right,' I said. 'Hugh can't be in love with me. Because—'

Because if Hugh was in love with me, if Hugh had been in love with me all along, he hadn't broken my heart.

I'd done that all by myself.

The doorbell rang. The police. June and I stood up at the same time to answer it, except when I stood, I was seized by a wave of pain across my belly and back that travelled up to my head and down to my feet, stealing my breath.

I clutched my stomach, which had gone rock hard, till the contraction passed. Then I straightened up and my brain started working again, realising where I was, who was with me, who wasn't with me, and that my baby had evidently heard me when I'd asked him or her to hurry up and be born.

'Oh, shit,' I said.

37

I had just about caught my breath and begun to look around me when another contraction came, which meant they were less than five minutes apart, which meant that the baby really was planning on being born soon. I held on to the back of the couch, bent over it, staring down at the cushions and trying to breathe through the tightness and pain.

I need to get to the phone, I thought. *To call Hugh.*

Except it wasn't Hugh I had to call. It was Reuben.

The contraction finished, leaving me doubled over the couch. Wanting Hugh. His big hands on my back, massaging. His calm voice in my ear. His excitement and his compassion.

His love, which I'd thrown back in his face by choosing Reuben.

I heard the click-click of June's high heels on the floor and the softer, heavier tread of someone with her, obviously a police officer.

'What's going on?' the police officer said, and I thought I must be going through some sort of labour-related madness because he sounded exactly like Hugh.

I straightened up and turned around.

It wasn't a police officer. It was Hugh.

Wonderful, beautiful Hugh, his hair rumpled, his shirt unironed, his hand clutching a copy of *The Throbbing Member of Parliament*.

I was so relieved to see him that my eyes filled with tears.

He ran to me. 'Eleanor, are you having contractions?'

I nodded and another one hit me and all I could do was stand and try my best to breathe.

'Steady, El,' Hugh said, putting his arms around me. 'Slow and easy, that's it, good girl. June, have you called an ambulance?'

'We're waiting for the police,' she said, and though I was staring at Hugh's shoulder, trying to breathe slowly and not to sob, I could tell that he had spotted Jojo on the floor.

He didn't let me go, but he did say, 'What the hell is that?'

'That's why we're waiting for the police,' June answered. There was another knock at the door. 'Oh, here they are now,' she trilled, and went off again.

The contraction passed. I relaxed my grip on Hugh's arms a little bit. But not much, because it felt too good to touch him.

'Why did you come?' I asked him.

'It's a bloody good thing I did, I don't fancy your chances of getting through labour successfully with only June and a bloke bound up in gaffer tape to help you.'

'But why did you come?'

'I finally read your book,' he said. 'I had to ask you what it meant.'

'The Chancellor—' I began, but then another contraction came and all I could do was hold on.

''Ello, 'ello, 'ello, what 'ave we 'ere?' I thought I heard a policeman say, but I couldn't swear to it because my spasming midsection was forcing all the blood into my head where it roared in my ears, so I thought I was probably making it up.

'We need to get to the hospital, she's in labour,' I did hear Hugh say. My contraction finished, I looked up and saw I had made up all the 'ello 'ello stuff because the policeman was a woman.

'And the man on the floor in gaffer tape?' she asked.

'He's a criminal,' I said, 'you need to arrest him.'

Jojo struggled and kicked and grunted.

'And,' June said, directing her words at Jojo, 'he's got a really small penis.'

'Listen, we need to get Eleanor to the hospital, *now*,' Hugh said.

The policewoman looked at me, and then looked at Jojo, and then she looked at Hugh and June. 'I'll call for back-up,' she said, and lifted her radio.

I missed what happened after that because another contraction came and all I could understand was Hugh holding me, smoothing my hair, and murmuring words of encouragement. I leaned into him and breathed through the pain, and when I opened my eyes again he was looking steadily at me. The same way as he'd looked at me for the past seven years. When we'd laughed, when we'd argued, when we'd made love.

'I heard that you're in love with me,' I said.

His grip tightened.

'What does your book mean, Eleanor?'

'What on earth is going on here?'

It was Reuben. I tore my gaze away from Hugh and saw

him striding into the room. A policeman followed him.

'She's having the baby,' Hugh told him.

'My ex tried to knife me,' June added.

'I've made a horrible mistake,' I said.

'Right,' cut in the policewoman, evidently used to dealing with crazy people, 'let's get this lady to hospital. I can take you, madam, and one other person, and the rest of you are going to have to stay and explain this man on the floor to PC Unwin. Are you the father?' she asked Hugh.

'I am,' Reuben said, stepping forward.

My body chose that moment to have another contraction but I used it as an excuse to cling on to Hugh as hard as I could. He rubbed my back and spoke soothingly in my ear and when I was done I didn't let him go.

'Reuben,' I gasped, 'I'm sorry. You've been brilliant about this whole baby thing but I've made a mistake.'

He frowned. 'What do you mean? Do you mean it's not mine after all?'

'Oh, it's yours. But it's just as much Hugh's. Hugh's been with me since the beginning. He's helped me and he's treated me as if I were carrying his child. And I've made up my mind.'

I took a deep breath, willing the next contraction not to start until I'd said what I needed to.

'You can see this baby as much as you want, and be as much of a father as you'd like to be. But I'm moving back to Reading as soon as I've had the baby. And I want Hugh with me when I give birth, because I want Hugh to be my child's daddy.'

Reuben had tried. He really had. But he couldn't hide the expression on his face at that moment, and it was pure relief.

'Eleanor,' Hugh said, and I turned to him.

'You're the Chancellor,' I told him, and then another contraction hit me, stronger than all the rest, and I screamed.

'Right, we're going now,' said the policewoman, and she took one of my arms across her shoulders and helped Hugh help me out of the flat and down the stairs.

'I'll bring your bag,' Reuben called after us. I glanced back and saw him standing in the doorway. June pushed past him and shouted.

'Good luck, sweetness! And remember, ask for all the drugs you can because it really bloody hurts!'

It wasn't till we were in the back of the police car, the blue lights flashing as we threaded through Chelsea traffic, that I could turn to Hugh.

'My book means I love you,' I said to him. 'I think I always have and I never knew it. I never knew you loved me, too.'

'That first day at university,' he said, his voice shaking but strong. 'You opened the door and that was it. I've loved you ever since, even though you've driven me crazy. I couldn't leave you. I couldn't say anything in case it meant I lost you. I've stood by and watched and I've waited and I've tried to settle for second best, but it was never enough. And when you told me you were pregnant, all I could think was that your child should have been mine.'

He pulled me into his arms so tightly I thought he would never let me go.

'It is yours,' I told him. 'We both are.'

The First Day

Epilogue

She was red and blue and wrinkled and I had never seen anything more beautiful.

The midwife wrapped her in a blanket, my daughter, and gave her to me. Her dark eyes opened and blinked at me.

'Hello,' I whispered to her.

Hugh, beside me, as always, pulled his chair closer. 'She looks like you,' he said, and reached out a gentle hand. The baby opened her fist and grasped his finger.

'Emily May,' I said.

'Emily May,' he repeated, and the name in his voice made it all seem more true. 'I'm pleased to meet you, Emily May.'

I watched him watching her. I knew the expression on his face because I'd seen it every day for the past seven years.

'For a writer, I'm spectacularly unobservant,' I said, and Hugh smiled at me.

'You got there in the end.'

You can buy any of these other **Little Black Dress** titles from your bookshop or *direct from the publisher*.

FREE P&P AND UK DELIVERY
(Overseas and Ireland £3.50 per book)

TO ORDER SIMPLY CALL THIS NUMBER

01235 400 414

or visit our website: www.headline.co.uk

Prices and availability subject to change without notice.

Please return/renew this item by the
last date shown to avoid a charge.
Books may also be renewed by phone
and Internet. May not be renewed if
required by another reader.

www.libraries.barnet.gov.uk